# MUSCLE MEMORY

## Also by William G. Tapply

# MUSCLE MEMORY

## A Brady Coyne Novel

### WILLIAM G. TAPPLY

St. Martin's Press
New York

Design by Nancy Resnick

Library of Congress Cataloging-in-Publication Data

Tapply, William G.
    Muscle memory: a Brady Coyne novel / by William G. Tapply. —1st   ed.
        p.   cm.
        ISBN 0-312-20563-5
        I. Title.
    PS3570.A568M87   1999                    99-22042
    813'.54—dc21                             CIP

First Edition: July 1999

10   9   8   7   6   5   4   3   2   1

To my students—past, present, and future—who always challenge and inspire me, and who help me to remember that there are more important things a person can do than make up stories.

# Acknowledgments

My thanks to Ken Quat, Dr. Jonathan Kolb, Dr. Randall Paulsen, Dr. Barbara Schildkrout, and Paul Keating, who generously contributed their professional expertise to various elements of this story; to Rick Boyer, who has been with me and Brady from the beginning; to Keith Kahla, whose insights and high editorial standards not only demanded my best but also showed me how; and to Vicki Stiefel, whose editorial readings of drafts of this book have been, I know, a labor of love.

# Muscle Memory

# PROLOGUE

A typical February Tuesday evening in Boston—hard, wind-driven snow in the air, slushy sidewalks underfoot. But it was cozy and dry at Skeeter's Infield, my favorite hangout down the alley in the financial district, halfway between my office in Copley Square and my empty apartment on Lewis Wharf on the Harbor.

Since Alex and I split back in September, I'd found myself stopping off at Skeeter's on my way home from work more regularly than was probably healthy.

I'd had one of Skeeter's famous burgers and a stack of onion rings, and now I was lingering over a Sam Adams draft watching a college basketball game on the big television over the bar. Mick Fallon had taken the stool next to me. Mick was a hulking middle-aged guy, a giant of a man who'd once played power forward for the Detroit Pistons, one of the many ex-athletes I'd run into a few times at Skeeter's. On the other side of me, two pretty thirty-something loan officers in business suits and short skirts—Molly and Joanne were their names—were sipping white

1

wine and yelling at the television. Molly was the lanky brunette, and Joanne was the stocky blonde.

Mick was leaning across in front of me explaining the pick-and-roll to the women, and I didn't notice when the two men in silk suits came in and took the stools down at the other end of the bar until Mick jabbed me in the ribs with his elbow, jerked his head in their direction, and whispered, "Watch out for those two."

Skeeter was standing behind the bar with his arms folded across his chest. Skeeter O'Reilly had been a reserve infielder for the Red Sox back in the early seventies. He was a tough little monkey who'd known how to take an inside pitch on the ass and steal a base, and he'd hung around baseball until he blew out his knee trying to break up a double play in the late innings of a meaningless September game that the Sox were losing by seven runs.

One of the guys in the silk suits was bending over the bar toward Skeeter. "Don't gimme this crap," he was saying. "Me and Paulie want a fuckin' beer." He looked to be in his late twenties. He had black hair and black eyes, black five o'clock shadow and a big black mustache, with a salmon-colored necktie and a matching show handkerchief in his breast pocket. His thick, corded neck and bulky shoulders suggested a narcissistic devotion to Nautilus machines. His companion—Paulie—could have been his twin, except he was clean-shaven and his necktie and handkerchief were turquoise.

Skeeter was shaking his head. "You better watch your language, Patsy," he said evenly. "Anyways, you ain't welcome here, and that's how it is and you know it. I don't want no trouble, and neither do you. So just get out, okay?"

"What?" said Patsy, jerking his thumb in our direction. "You only serve hookers and washed-up old jocks? We ain't good enough for this dump?"

Skeeter shrugged. "You better leave, both of you, before I call the cops."

Patsy glared at Skeeter for a minute. Skeeter stared right back at him. After a minute of that, Patsy glanced in our direction and grinned, as if he wanted to be sure that we were watching. Then he turned to Skeeter, nodded, and settled back on his barstool. "No need for cops," he said. "No hard feelings, huh?" He hooked his finger at Skeeter. "Come here," he said. "I wanna tell you something."

Skeeter shrugged. He unfolded his arms, wiped his hands on his rag, and leaned across the bar toward them.

Patsy smiled and patted Skeeter's cheek. Then suddenly his other hand shot out, clamped onto the front of Skeeter's shirt, and yanked the little guy off his feet so that he was half-sprawled on the bartop. Patsy shoved his face into Skeeter's. "Okay, you little fuck," he hissed. "Now you listen to me—"

Beside me I heard Mick growl "Sonofabitch," and the next thing I knew he was looming directly behind Patsy and Paulie. He grabbed each of them by the scruff of the neck, hauled them backwards off their barstools, and dragged them toward the door.

"Hey, Brady," said Mick. His voice was calm, but fury blazed in his eyes. "Gimme a hand here. Help me take out the trash."

I got up, went to the door, and opened it. Patsy and Paulie were both full-grown men, but Mick stood about six-seven and weighed close to two-eighty, and in his grasp they looked like a pair of plucked chickens being taken to slaughter by a big red-faced butcher. His huge paws nearly encircled their necks. They were gasping and flapping their arms in the helpless, doomed way a freshly caught trout flops his tail in the bottom of a canoe.

Mick flung them outside one at a time. First went Patsy, who landed on his feet, staggered across the narrow alley, and smashed against the brick wall. Paulie followed, skidding on his knees and then sprawling facedown on the hard, dirty old snowbank.

Patsy stood there rubbing his neck, sucking in deep breaths, and trying to look fierce. "You don't know who you're fuckin' with," he said.

"Yeah," said Mick. "Actually I do. A couple pieces a shit, that's what."

"Man," said Patsy, "you are dead fuckin' meat, pal."

Paulie slowly stood up, brushed off his pants, and turned to Mick. "You know who our boss is?"

"Sure," said Mick. "I'm not impressed."

"Big mistake, pal," said Paulie. "You'll be hearin' from our lawyer."

Mick grinned. "You know where to find me." He stepped inside, took two camel-hair topcoats off the coatrack, pretended to sniff them, then threw them out into the alley. "These must be yours," he said. "Same stink."

He slammed the door shut and returned to his barstool. I followed him.

Skeeter came over rubbing the back of his neck. "You shouldn'ta done that, Mick. You know who those guys are?"

Mick nodded. "Sure I know. Fuck 'em."

"Well, I don't know," said Molly, the brunette loan officer. "Who are they?

"Couple of Vinnie Russo's boys," said Mick.

"Wait a minute," she said. "You mean *the* Vinnie Russo? That godfather guy from the North End?"

"Yeah," said Mick. "Uncle Vinnie. Lives practically around the corner from here."

"God," she said. "He assassinates people."

"Not him personally," said Mick. "He has guys like Patsy and Paulie do it for him."

Molly turned to me. "I heard what that man said. You're a lawyer. Can those—those hoodlums really sue him?"

4

"Anybody can sue anybody," I said. "It's the American way."

"They'd be more likely to shoot him," said Skeeter.

Mick grinned. "I think Paulie's nice suit got ripped, and Patsy did bump his head against the wall. Wouldn't put it past 'em to strap on neck braces and take me to court." He looked at me with his eyebrows arched. "I don't have a lawyer."

"I couldn't represent you on this one," I said. "I'm a witness."

"So?"

I shrugged. "So it would be unethical."

Mick grinned. "Holy shit," he said. "A lawyer with ethics. You got a card?"

"Sure. But if you're worried about those two goons . . ."

Mick waved his hand. "You never know when you might need a lawyer with ethics, that's all."

I fished a business card from my wallet and handed it to him.

Molly clutched my arm and looked up at me. She had green eyes, I noticed. They crinkled when she smiled, as if she'd spent a lot of time outdoors. "Can I have one?" she said.

"You need a lawyer with ethics, too?"

She arched her eyebrows. "I might."

I gave her one of my cards. She looked at it, tucked it into her purse, then smiled up at me with her eyebrows arched . . .

And it wasn't until I was halfway home that I realized she'd expected *me* to ask for *her* business card.

I hadn't played those games for a long time.


I had showered and brushed my teeth, and when I opened the bathroom door I heard a woman's voice in my bedroom. My first—irrational—thought was that Alex had changed her mind, driven down from Maine, and snuck in while I was in the shower, that she'd decided she couldn't stand living without me after all, and it took me a minute to realize the voice was coming from the answering machine on the night table beside my bed.

"... asleep? Well, I didn't mean to wake you up. I was just thinking how I really need a lawyer." It was Molly, the pretty loan officer from Skeeter's. "Hey, Brady," she said, "pick up the phone. I've got a really good idea I want to run past you." She paused. "Come on. You're listening, aren't you?"

I sat on the bed, reached for the phone, hesitated, then pulled my hand back.

"Oh, well," she said after a moment. "At least maybe you'll call me sometime, huh?" She recited a phone number. "I was just thinking," she went on, "you might like a home-cooked meal. Believe it or not, I'm a pretty good cook. I heard you and Mick talking—I didn't mean to eavesdrop, but I couldn't help it—and I know you're divorced. Well, ta-da, me, too." She laughed quickly. "God, I feel like a jerk. I shouldn't have called. Stupid me. Oh, well. Too late now. So you've got my number. I'd love to hear from you. I really would. Every ethical lawyer needs a new client now and then, right?" She paused. "Wow. This is embarrassing. Call me? Please?"

She laughed again before she disconnected.

I liked Molly's laugh. It was low and throaty and intimate. I remembered the way her eyes crinkled when she smiled.

I watched the message light blink for a minute. Then I reached over and hit the erase button.

# ONE

❧ ──────────────────────────────── ❧

I had swiveled my office chair around so I could gaze out at a sun-drenched April morning. My window onto Copley Square looks east across the plaza to the dark-stoned, dour old Trinity Church, which crouches in the shadow of the sleek, glass-sided John Hancock Tower rising behind it. The old and the new Boston in counterpoint.

The view from my office window takes in a lot of concrete and steel and glass and enterprise. It barely qualifies as "outdoors," but on a pretty spring morning it's good enough to get me daydreaming about casting dry flies to rising trout, which is what I was doing when Julie buzzed me.

I rotated back to my desk and picked up the phone. "Yes, boss?" I said.

"There's a Michael Fallon on line two."

"What's he want?"

"He says he needs a lawyer. You're the lawyer around here. Why don't you ask him?"

"Good plan." I hit the blinking light on my telephone console and said, "Mick? How're you doing?"

7

"Not good," he said. "Not good at all. Actually, I am one miserable old jockstrap, Brady. I gotta talk to you, man."

"What's up?"

I heard him sigh. "It's Kaye. My wife. She's . . . well, she says she wants a divorce, and she tells me I better get myself a good lawyer, because she's got one, and . . ." He fell silent.

"Mick?" I said after a minute.

"Yeah, I'm here."

"I'll be happy to represent you," I said.

"The thing is," he said, "I don't want a fucking divorce. I don't want a lawyer. I just want my wife."

I glanced at my appointment calendar. "How about lunch? Say twelve-thirty?"

"You gotta help me fight it, man."

"Meet me at Skeeter's," I said. "We'll grab a booth and talk about it."


I left a little after noon for the familiar twenty-minute walk to Skeeter's. Newbury Street was swarming with lunchtime shoppers, and I was pleased to observe that the female secretaries and lawyers and college students had broken out their springtime outfits—short skirts, pastel blouses, flowered dresses. On the Common, the ancient beeches and stubborn old elms were leafing out, the pigeons were flocking, and even the bums on the benches who were feeding them seemed high-spirited. Ah, spring.

No matter how many time I saw Mick, I was always surprised at how big he was. The booth at Skeeter's seemed kindergarten-sized with Mick wedged into it. When he played for the Pistons back in the seventies, they'd listed him as six-nine, two-thirty in the program. Actually he was closer to six-seven, but the weight had been about right. He'd put on thirty or forty pounds since then.

I slid in across from him. He was hunched over with his forearms on the table. His catcher's-mitt hands dwarfed the mug of draft beer they were cradling. The beer was untouched.

He looked up. "Thanks for coming."

I held out my hand to him. "It's good to see you again, Mick."

He took my hand in his huge paw. "I know plenty of lawyers," he said, "but this . . ."

I nodded. I refuse to accept clients I don't like, but I liked Mick, considered him a friend. I haven't found that friendship gets in the way of serving my clients. "Tell me about it," I said.

At that point Skeeter sidled up to our booth. Skeeter, as usual, was wearing his old Red Sox cap. He was a little self-conscious about his bald head. He looked from Mick to me, nodded as if he could read Mick's mood, and instead of his usual friendly greeting, he simply said, "Lunch, fellas?"

"Just bring me some coffee, Skeets," I said. "We'll eat in a little while."

Skeeter nodded, glanced at Mick's full beer mug, and left.

I turned back to Mick. "So . . . ?"

"It's hard, man. It hurts bad."

"Of course it does."

"Will you help me?"

"Sure. We just—"

"We've got to bring her to her senses, Brady. I don't *want* a divorce. She can't really do this to me, can she?"

"I'm afraid she can, Mick. Here in Massachusetts, at least, if one party wants a divorce, and if it gets that far, the court makes the assumption that the marriage isn't working. The court aims to dissolve bad marriages fairly, not repair them. That's how the system works."

Mick stared at me for a minute, then dropped his chin onto his chest. "So what'm I gonna do?" he mumbled.

"I guess it depends," I said. "Why don't you start at the beginning."

9

He nodded. "We, um, separated a year ago January. Right after the holidays." He shook his head. "Some holidays."

"So you've been separated for—what, almost a year and a half now?"

"Not separated," he said. "Not legally. Just . . . not living together."

"I didn't know that," I said. "You always led me to believe you were happily married."

He flapped his hands. "It was easier to pretend, that's all."

I nodded. "Sure. Okay. It doesn't matter. Continue."

He talked down into the circle his big arms made on the table, staring into his untouched mug of beer. "It was Kaye's idea. I mean, I had no idea she . . ." He looked up at me. "She just said she needed some space for a while. Erin and Danny were both off to college, and it was just me and Kaye. I'd been kinda looking forward to it, you know? I mean, we have—had—a great family. We always had a good time. All four of us. So when she told me she wanted us to split, I didn't know what to think, Brady. I asked her if it was something I'd done, and she said no, that it was just her and she felt like she needed for us to be apart for a while. She needed space." Mick shook his head. "What the fuck is this space shit, anyway? I—"

He glanced up. Skeeter was standing beside me holding a mug of coffee.

"Thanks, Skeets," I said as he put it in front of me.

Mick watched Skeeter leave, then turned to me. "I didn't like it, Brady. It wasn't what I wanted. Hell, I just wanted my family. But what was I gonna do? She said she'd move out if I wanted, but I said no, I'd find someplace." He shook his head. "I figured it'd be a few weeks, she'd miss me, and I'd move back in and everything would be okay. So I found a shitty little furnished apartment near Union Square in Somerville, took my toothbrush and some clothes over there, and waited for her to figure it out."

"I didn't know any of this, Mick."

"I didn't want anybody to know. Like I said. It was easier to pretend. I guess the only person I was fooling was me." He lifted his mug, took a sip, put it down, and wiped his mouth on the back of his wrist. "You've never met Kaye."

"No," I said. "But I feel like I know her."

Mick smiled. "I'm always bragging on her, I know." He shook his head. "Anyway, after I moved out, we'd sometimes meet for lunch or supper, and it'd be like nothing was wrong. She'd chatter on about the kids or her bridge games or something in the neighborhood, telling her dumb jokes—flirting with me, for Christ sake—and I'm sitting there thinking, This is nuts. This is my wife, the woman I love, and we're not living together, and she's telling me about how Alma Crynock's fucking dog had puppies?" He waved his hand in the air. "The thing about Kaye, see, if she doesn't want to talk about something, there's no way you can make her talk about it. She hates to argue, and if there's something you don't agree on, she just keeps talking about something else until you give up. I've been married to her for twenty-two years, and I've learned to wait her out. Eventually she'll bring it up, whatever it is, and that means she's ready to talk about it. So I kept waiting for her to be ready to talk about the only thing that was on my mind, which was when I could go back home." He shrugged. "She never did. Then she called me last night."

"Saying she wanted a divorce," I said.

He nodded.

"Why"

"Huh?"

"Why'd she say she wanted a divorce?"

"She didn't."

"She gave you no reason?"

"No."

"There's always a reason, Mick."

He flapped his hands, shrugged, and shook his head.

11

"Her lawyer will be calling me, then?"

"Yeah, I guess so."

I took a sip of coffee, then lit a cigarette. "Mick," I said, "I've got to ask you some questions, okay?"

"I never cheated on her, if that's what you mean," he said. "I never hit her, I always supported her, I took care of the kids. Maybe she—she's got a boyfriend or something, I don't know." He shook his head. "Christ," he muttered, "that would kill me." He lifted his head and peered at me. "I haven't done anything wrong, Brady. I don't get it."

"Everybody's done something wrong," I said. "Look. Marriages wear out. People change. It happens, and it's nobody's fault. It happened to me. I loved my family, too, and I got divorced. Life goes on. If that's what this is, okay, we'll just have to deal with it. Kaye wants a divorce, and unless she changes her mind, that's what'll happen. Meanwhile, you've got some homework to do."

"Homework?"

I nodded. "If you and Kaye proceed with the divorce, there will be issues of alimony, child support, division of assets. So I need you to put together a complete listing of everything you and Kaye own, both together and separately. Bank accounts, investments, real estate, insurance, pension plans, cars, furniture, jewelry, paintings, heirlooms. Everything. Your old trophies. Her mink coat. And your debts, too. You've got kids in college, so I need to know what that's costing you. I'll have Julie mail you a worksheet."

Mick was looking at me. "Jesus," he said softly. "You make it sound so . . ." He shook his head. "This isn't about money, Brady."

"Actually, that's exactly what it's about," I said. "Her lawyer wants to talk to me because we'll have to work out a settlement. Your children are grown, so there are no custody issues. Money is the *only* thing it's about."

"You don't get it," he said. He looked up at me and smiled. "See, I don't care. She can have it all."

I shook my head. "I won't let that happen," I said. "My job is to watch out for you, even if you don't think you care. One, two, five years from now you'll care. That's when you'll be glad you hired yourself a good lawyer."

Mick took a sip of beer, which had to be warm by now. "All I care about is Kaye."

"Kaye's lawyer will take care of her," I said. "You didn't happen to get her lawyer's name, did you?"

He shrugged. "No. Why? Does it make any difference?"

I smiled. "It makes *all* the difference."


Three days later Mick called me. "I talked to Kaye," he said. "She asked for your name. Know what? I didn't want to tell her. I figured if I refused to tell her my lawyer's name, they couldn't do anything." He laughed quickly. "I know, I know. Dumb. Anyway, I told her. So I guess you'll be hearing from them."

"Okay," I said. "I hope you've been thinking about what you want out of this. Long-term marriages like yours, it'll be a fifty-fifty split of assets. But there are lots of different ways of dividing them. This is what her lawyer and I will be negotiating. If we can come up with a settlement that's acceptable to both you and Kaye, we can avoid a trial, and believe me, we want to avoid a trial if we can."

"A trial," murmured Mick. "Jesus."

"So I want to be able to present a proposal to them," I continued. "Let them react to it. Keep in mind, too, that assuming you've been the main source of income, you'll be paying child support until your kids are out of college. That's pretty much cut and dried. The state uses a formula based on your income and your assets and the kids' ages. There'll be the matter of alimony, which we will negotiate as part of the settlement. This

13

can be pretty easy and clean for you, Mick. That is how you want it, isn't it?"

"All I want is—"

"I know," I said. "You want your marriage. But it doesn't look like that's going to happen. Why not make it easy on everybody? Let your lawyers do their jobs and maybe you and Kaye can end up as friends, at least. Okay?"

"Friends, huh?" he muttered. He blew out a breath into the telephone. "Okay. Sure."

"Did you get her lawyer's name?" I said.

"Oh, yeah. It's, um, Cooper. Barbara Cooper."

"Oh, shit," I muttered before I could stop myself.

"What'd you say?" said Mick.

"Nothing, Mick."

"Do you know this Cooper broad?"

"By reputation only," I said.


Know your enemy. Good advice for generals and baseball managers and lawyers. All I really knew about Barbara Cooper was that she'd opened a one-woman law office in Lexington a couple of years earlier, that she was young and attractive and smart, and that she'd won some big divorce settlements for her female clients.

I'd heard other things about her, too, but I try not to place too much stock in second-hand reputations.

So after I hung up with Mick, I called a few of my friends to see what I could learn about Barbara Cooper. Some of them would say only that she was tough, relentless, and single-minded, which are not bad qualities for a lawyer.

Those who'd actually opposed her called her an unscrupulous bitch, a real ballbuster. The word around the divorce courts was that the proper pronunciation of "Barbara Cooper" was "Barracuda."

"I'm looking for a trial date in July," she said when she called me a week later. "That okay with you?"

In most divorce negotiations, scheduling a trial date did not mean the lawyers expected there would be an actual trial. Our aim would normally be to bring a settlement with us when we went to court that day, so that if we'd done our job well, Judge Elliot Kolb would ask a few perfunctory questions and then sign off on the agreement, and ninety days later it would become the divorce settlement by which the couple lived the rest of their lives.

But my sources had warned me that Barbara Cooper had no compunction about going to trial, that she didn't mind accruing hundreds of billable hours trying to negotiate a settlement, and when the dust finally cleared and you thought you had everything worked out, she'd refuse to settle.

"I've met with my client several times," I told her on the phone. "I'll fax a proposal over to you by the end of the week."

"For starters, my client wants the house," she said.

"That's certainly negotiable," I answered. In fact, Mick had told me he wanted Kaye to have the house, but I wasn't going to divulge that to Cooper. "My client was hoping your client would agree to counseling."

"Forget it," she said.

Over the next few weeks, I met with Mick several times. Barbara Cooper and I back-and-forthed proposals and counter proposals, and by the third week in May, it looked like we were closing in on an agreement.

So in spite of the warnings I'd received, I was not prepared for Cooper's phone call.

"I'm going to have to depose your client," she told me.

"Really?" I said.

"Really."

In divorce cases, a lawyer normally takes a deposition from her client's spouse only when she believes the spouse is lying or withholding relevant information. A deposition is a form of discovery that requires the deponent to answer all questions truthfully and fully at the risk of legal sanction, just as if he were in an actual courtroom. Responsible attorneys do not seek depositions on a whim. They are expensive and time-consuming and particularly for the deponent—in this case, Mick Fallon—stressful.

I'd been trying to remain open-minded, but I wasn't convinced that Barbara Cooper was a responsible attorney. If she was in fact a ball-buster, as I was beginning to think, she'd enjoy putting Mick on the hot seat.

I was hoping she might hint at what she was after—if anything—although I didn't expect it.

She didn't. "Can you have all the documents in my office by, say, next Tuesday?" she said. "I'll fax you a list of what we want."

"Better make it Friday," I said.

"No," she said. "I want all of it Tuesday. We'll take the deposition in my office the following Thursday—that's the twenty-eight—at ten o'clock. I hope that works for you."

"I'll have to check with my client," I said.


It emphatically did *not* work for Mick, and when I told him on the telephone, his reaction reminded me of his old basketball reputation as a hothead, a guy who clutched and grabbed and used his elbows liberally and got kicked out of games for fighting. The Mick Fallon I'd seen drag two reputed hitmen out of Skeeter's and throw them into the alley.

"What kind of bullshit is this?" he growled, and then I heard his fist—or maybe it was his head—crash against something.

"Calm down, Mick," I said. "They just want to be sure they have all the facts."

"You mean they think I'm lying. God damn it—"

16

"Take it easy, man. Calm down. Okay?"

He blew out a long breath. "She's just trying to bust my chops."

"Maybe so," I said. "Attorney Cooper—"

"I don't mean her," he said. "I mean Kaye."

"It doesn't matter," I said. "If you refuse to be deposed, we'll go straight to trial and she'll ask you the same questions in front of the judge."

"Fuck it," he said. "Let's go to trial, then."

"Bad idea, Mick. Listen. I think this is bullshit, too, and it pisses me off. But trust me, if we have the choice between a trial and a deposition, we take the deposition every time. That way, if anything pops up we didn't expect, at least we're prepared for it."

"What could pop up?"

"I don't know," I said. "You tell me."

"Nothing," he mumbled. "It's bullshit."

"You've told me everything?"

"Of course I have."

"Then let's get the damn deposition over with. Okay?"

He exhaled deeply. "Well, okay. So what do we do?"

"Attorney Cooper wants copies of all your tax returns for the past ten years, plus all your financial documents since you've been separated from Kaye. Tax returns, bank statements, canceled checks, deposit stubs, credit card and telephone bills. Everything."

"Then what?"

"Then we go to her office and she asks you questions."

"Questions about what?" he said.

"About anything."

"Jesus Christ," he growled. "Okay, so how does it work?"

"You bring in all those financial documents, and I'll copy them and ship them off to Attorney Cooper. Then we meet in her office and she'll ask you a bunch of questions. A shorthand

17

reporter who's also a notary public, an officer of the court, will be there to record it all."

"Will Kaye be there?"

"She might. She has the right to be there, but she can't participate."

"You'll be there, won't you?"

"Of course."

"So what'm I supposed to do?"

"It's easy, Mick. You just keep your cool and tell the truth."


Mick was pacing the sidewalk in front of his apartment building in Somerville when I pulled to the curb around nine-thirty on the morning of May 28. He was smoking a cigar and sipping from a Styrofoam Dunkin Donuts coffee cup.

He opened the passenger door of my BMW and folded himself into the front seat beside me. His knees pressed against the dashboard.

"Reach down between your legs," I told him. "You can push the seat back."

He did. "I'm a wreck," he said as I pulled onto the street.

"Relax," I said. "The only thing I want you to remember is to answer the questions directly. If it's a yes-or-no question, just say yes or no. Don't elaborate. If you don't know an answer, just say so."

"What's she going to ask me?"

"I don't know. Questions about money, I'd guess."

"I hate this shit," he mumbled.

He sat quietly besides me while I negotiated the clogged roads through Somerville and Cambridge, and it wasn't until I eased onto the westbound lane of Route 2 that he said, "Can I refuse to answer any of their questions?"

"Not really. The only time you shouldn't answer would be if you're asked for privileged information, or something that's actually incriminating. I'll be there to watch out for anything like that. But it's not like court. Generally speaking, anything goes at a deposition. That's because there's no judge at a deposition. Later, if we end up going to trial and attorney Cooper tries to bring dubious testimony from your deposition into evidence, I'll object to the question and let the judge rule on it."

"So I just answer everything," he said.

"Right. If a question is improperly formed, I'll object to that and let her rephrase it."

"What the fuck is she after?" he mumbled.

"I don't know," I said. "Maybe she's just busting your balls. We'll find out soon enough."

# Two

COMMONWEALTH OF MASSACHUSETTS

MIDDLESEX, S.S                    SUPERIOR COURT
                                 NO. 98D-1720-DV1


KATHERINE M. FALLON)
                plaintiff)
VS.
MICHAEL S. FALLON)
                defendant)


DEPOSITION OF MICHAEL S. FALLON, a witness called on behalf of the Plaintiff, taken pursuant to the applicable provisions of the Massachusetts Rules of Civil Procedure, before Ellen R. Samborski, Shorthand Reporter and Notary Public within and for the Commonwealth of Massachusetts, at the Offices of Barbara Arlene Cooper, 8 Muzzey Street, Lexington, Massachusetts 02173, on May 28, 1998, commencing at 10:15 A.M.

APPEARANCES:

ON BEHALF OF THE DEFENDANT:
BRADY L. COYNE, ESQ.
25 Huntington Avenue
Boston, Massachusetts 02126
617-442-5500

ON BEHALF OF THE PLAINTIFF:
BARBARA ARLENE COOPER, ESQ.
8 Muzzey Street
Lexington, Massachusetts 02173
781-863-9290

KRAMER & DAWKINS COURT REPORTING SERVICES
1229 COMMONWEALTH AVENUE
BOSTON, MASSACHUSETTS 02134
617-254-0089

Barbara Cooper's suite of offices occupied the first floor of a big converted colonial house on a tree-lined side street off Mass Ave., which is the main drag in Lexington center. I parked out back, and Mick and I entered into a reception area decorated with watercolor landscapes, potted ferns, braided rugs, and leather-covered furniture. Copies of *Audubon* and *Yankee* and *Today's Health* were scattered on the maple coffee table. I saw no ashtrays. Classical music—Schubert, if I wasn't mistaken—played softly over hidden speakers.

A cheerful, gray-haired secretary greeted us by name and offered us coffee, which we accepted. Mick and I sat on the sofa. Mick's knee was jiggling furiously.

I tapped his leg. "Relax, man."

"Sorry," he muttered. "I can't help it."

The secretary delivered our coffee in delicate bone-china cups. Mick and I sat there, sipping. His knee continued jerking up and down as if he was keeping time to a very fast piece of music. He kept clenching and unclenching his fists and glancing at his watch. "It's after ten," he said. "What the hell's going on?"

"I should've fed you a few Valiums," I said.

"Good stiff shot of Scotch'd be more like it."

A minute later an inside door opened and Barbara Cooper came out. She had her hand on the elbow of a petite blond woman. Kaye Fallon. I remembered her from photos Mick had shown me.

She stood no more than five-one or -two, and she had a solid, athletic body. She was as small and compact as Mick was big and sloppy. Her hair, which was pulled back in a ponytail and tied with a red silk scarf, hung nearly halfway down her back. Her narrow blue skirt stopped several inches above her knees, showing her shapely, rather muscular legs to good advantage. She had a nice tan and large, wide-spaced blue eyes. From a distance, Kaye Fallon could have passed for a bright-eyed college coed.

But when the two women approached us, I saw the crinkles at the corners of Kaye's eyes and the creases that bracketed her mouth like parentheses. They betrayed her age, which I guessed to be about forty-five, and made her face more interesting.

Barbara Cooper smiled quickly and held out her hand to me. "Mr. Coyne," she said. "The man behind the voice. Finally, we meet." She had olive skin, high cheekbones, and flashing dark, slightly uptilted eyes, and she wore her black hair short and straight. Medium height, curvy, and busty, an altogether sexy woman who carried herself with the confidence of someone who knew it, enjoyed it, and didn't mind using it.

I took her hand. "Hello, Ms. Cooper."

She stepped back. "Kaye Fallon, this is Mr. Coyne."

I nodded to her. "Mrs. Fallon. Nice to meet you."

Kaye looked up at me. "Hello." She had a soft, husky voice and a wonderfully warm, shy smile. She held out her hand, and I took it. "It's nice to meet you, Mr. Coyne," she said. "Michael speaks well of you."

"He speaks well of you, too," I said.

She glanced at Mick, then grinned and rolled her eyes at me. "You take good care of him," she said softly.

I introduced Barbara Cooper to Mick. He shook her hand and nodded mechanically, but he didn't take his eyes off Kaye, who was making a point of studying one of the watercolors on the wall behind his shoulder.

After an awkward pause, Mick said to Kaye, "Well, how's it going, honey?"

She glanced at him, then let her eyes slide away. "I'm fine, Michael."

"Talked to the kids lately?"

"Oh, sure." She smiled. "Just about every day. They're doing real well. We can be proud of them, Michael."

His eyes suddenly narrowed, and I saw his hands clenching each other. "Well, *I'm* not doing real well," he said. "Would you mind telling me what the hell—"

I grabbed his arm. "Come on, Mick."

He glanced at me, then shook his head. "Sorry," he grumbled.

I turned to Cooper. "Why don't we get started?"

She frowned at Mick for a moment, then nodded. "Sure. Come on."

We followed her into a conference room. The shorthand reporter was already set up. Cooper introduced her to the rest of us. Mick and I sat side by side at the rectangular table. She sat across from us, and the reporter was at the end. Kaye took a chair in the corner of the room, behind Cooper's left shoulder.

The reporter administered the oath to Mick.

MS. COOPER: In terms of stipulations, Mr. Coyne, I consider the standard ones are reserving objections to the time of the trial as well as motions to strike, except objections to form.

MR. COYNE: That's fine.

MS. COOPER: Privilege of course. I don't know—do you want your client to sign the deposition?

MR. COYNE: No.

MS. COOPER: You will waive the signing and filing?

MR. COYNE: Yes. Waive it.

MICHAEL S. FALLON, a witness called for examination by counsel for the plaintiff, being first duly sworn, was examined and testified as follows:

EXAMINATION BY MS. COOPER:

Q. Your name is?

A. Michael Fallon.

Q. Your full name, please.

A. Sorry. Michael Simon Fallon.

Q. I'm going to be asking you a series of questions today. If there is any question that you do not understand or that you wish repeated, please just say so. Okay? Is that understood?

A. Okay.

MR. COYNE: You have to say yes or no, Mick, because the stenographer has to take down yes or no. All right?

THE WITNESS: Got it. Yes, I mean.

Mick's knee was jiggling wildly under the table beside me, and his fists were clenched so tight that his knuckles were white. He kept glancing beyond Barbara Cooper to Kaye, who was sitting there with her fine legs crossed, her hands folded in her lap, and her head bowed as if the whole thing embarrassed her.

Q. Mr. Fallon, how long have you been unemployed?

A. What?

Q. I don't know how to rephrase the question for you. Can you please tell me when was the last time you held a job?

A. I don't know what you mean. I've always made money.

Q. I'm asking about the last time you earned an actual salary, went to work every day.

A. I guess the last time I got a regular paycheck, if that's what you mean, was when I was scouting full-time for the Pistons, and that ended in 1984. But it's not like I haven't been earning any money. I've supported my family.

Q. How have you supported your family? What's been your source of income?

A. Investments, mostly.

Q. Investments in what, specifically?

A. Look, she knows exactly what—

MR. COYNE: Please, Mick. Just answer the question.

THE WITNESS: They're just trying to harass me. There's no reason why—

MR. COYNE: I'd like a moment with my client.

(counsel confers with witness.)

I stood up, grabbed Mick's arm, and said, "Follow me."

I led him out of the conference room. His forearm felt like the business end of a Louisville Slugger where I held onto it. We stood in the corner of the reception room, and I looked up into his face. He was clenching his jaw, and his eyes blazed.

"We do not want this to go to trial," I said. "But if it does, and if you behave like this, the judge'll cite you for contempt and give everything to Kaye. Now listen to me. You've got to

26

keep it together. Attorney Cooper will not put up with any more of your childish bullshit. She'll terminate the deposition, and she'll refuse to negotiate a settlement, and then we'll have a trial where she'll ask you the same questions all over again in front of a judge. Do you understand?"

Mick nodded. "I'm sorry, but this is ridiculous, Brady. I mean, what is this unemployed bullshit? Kaye knows perfectly well where our money comes from. What the hell is she up to?"

"Attorney Cooper wants to know what will make a fair settlement," I said. "What's fair depends on your income, and what your income will be in the future, and without an actual salary to base it on, it's a little hard to figure."

"She's just busting my balls, man."

"Then we've got no problem. Answer the damn questions to the best of your knowledge, that's all. Keep your cool and let's get this over with."

"Kaye's playing with my head, Brady. She won't even look at me."

"Ignore Kaye. Concentrate on what Attorney Cooper is saying. Can you do that?"

"Okay." He nodded. "I'm sorry. I'll try."

"Hey," I said. "It's your divorce."

We went back into the conference room, and Mick, responding to Barbara Cooper's questions, described his various sources of income—a small pension from the NBA; residuals from a series of television commercials he'd done for a friend of his who owned a string of Ford dealerships; the chain of pizza houses in Brighton, Allston, Cambridge, and Brookline he held part ownership in; occasional appearances on an afternoon radio sports talk show; dividends from a variety of stocks; rent from the four-family house he owned in Acton; a stipend from the Pistons for part-time scouting. It averaged out to a little more than $75,000 gross for the past several years.

As Mick went through this, Cooper showed him copies of his

and Kaye's joint federal income tax returns, which were marked as exhibits one through eleven, and asked him to point to the line where each source of income was listed. He did this calmly and without once glancing toward Kaye, who continued to sit quietly in the corner staring down at her hands, which were folded in her lap.

Q. Now, Mr. Fallon, you have provided us today with a copy of your most recent tax return plus copies of your bank statements for the past sixteen months and of all your canceled checks for that period of time, the sixteen months that you and your wife have lived separately, is that right?

A. Yes.

Q. And for this past tax year, you and your wife filed separate tax returns?

A. Yes.

Q. Why was that?

A. Because she thought she'd get a big refund that way, and I guess she probably did. We weren't living together, and I was giving Kaye money for the kids and the house, and she was substitute teaching. It was her idea. My accountant said I was crazy, that being married and filing separately was the best way to get screwed, but I did it because Kaye wanted to. See, she could file as head of household, and with her income and not having to declare what I was giving her—

Q. Thank you, Mr. Fallon. You've answered the question.

A. Yeah, but see, the point is—

MR. COYNE: Just answer the questions, please.

THE WITNESS: That's what I was doing.

MR. COYNE: You were elaborating. Attorney Cooper will ask you to elaborate if that's what she wants. Do you understand?

THE WITNESS: Sure. Yes.

Q. Okay, now I call your attention to this document. Is this a copy of your last year's federal tax return?

A. Yes.

MS. COOPER: Let's mark this as Exhibit 12.

(Exhibit 12 marked for identification)

Q. Do you want a minute to review this document?

A. (Witness reviews document.)

Q. Mr. Fallon, you have had time to look at this document that's been marked as Exhibit 12?

A. Yes.

Q. This return was prepared by your accountant?

A. Yes. Ray Allen.

Q. Which you filed separately.

A. Right. Kaye and I filed separately last year. We've already been over that.

Q. And your accountant—Mr. Allen—prepared this return based on information you gave him, is that right?

A. Yes.

Q. And you reported a gross income of $71,772.

A. Right. Yes.

Q. Was that exhibit accurate when you signed it?

A. Well, sure. Yes, I mean.

Q. Is it still your opinion today that it was accurate—that it was accurate at the time you signed it?

MR. COYNE: Excuse me? Could you restate your question, please?

Q. Is it your opinion today, Mr. Fallon, that this exhibit was accurate at the time you signed it? Have you come into possession of any knowledge since March 16 of this year which would indicate to you that your tax return was not accurate?

A. I signed it and I wrote a check and mailed it off, and

I never thought about it again one way or the other. Why, do you think I—

MR. COYNE: Just answer the question.

THE WITNESS: What was the question?

MR. COYNE: Would you repeat the question?

Q. As far as you know, was your last year's tax return accurate?

A. As far as I know, yes.

Q. You didn't have any income that you failed to report?

A. Look, are you accusing me of cheating?

MR. COYNE: Okay. Time out.

(Counsel confers with witness.)

I steered Mick out of the conference room. We sat on the sofa in the reception area. I caught the eye of the secretary, who was seated behind her desk. She nodded, got up, and left the room.

Mick was leaning forward, gripping his thighs, shaking his head back and forth, and muttering, "I don't fucking believe this."

"Answer the question for me, Mick."

"What question?"

"Did you cheat on your income tax last year?"

"Jesus. You, too?"

"I'm not accusing you of anything, Mick. I just need to know."

"Of course I didn't cheat."

"If you did, you should refuse to answer the question on grounds of self-incrimination."

"Christ," he said. "I didn't cheat on my taxes, Brady."

"You gave your accountant all the figures he needed?"

"Sure. Ray's been doing our taxes for years. We've never had a problem."

"Okay." I put my arm around his shoulder. "You're doing fine, Mick. But you've got to keep cool. Answer the questions, and please resist the urge to elaborate or to express your feelings. Can you do that?"

"Yeah. I'm trying. It's just—it feels like I'm on the hot seat, you know?"

"Well, you are on the hot seat. But you should be used to that. You've been on the foul line at the end of a close game more than once."

He turned to me and smiled. "That was a helluva lot easier than this."

"You were a good free-throw shooter, Mick. I remember a playoff game in the Garden. They sent you to the line just as the clock ran out. The Celtics were up by a point, and you made both of them with thirteen-thousand hostile Boston fans screaming and stomping on the floor, me included. That old building was shaking, and Mick Fallon swished both of them to win the damn game."

"You were there?"

I nodded. "I was yelling as loud as anybody. I didn't see how anybody could be a calm as you were."

"It's not calmness, Brady. It's concentration. Free throws are all muscle memory. All you've got to do is focus on the front of the rim and block everything else out. Then you just let your muscle memory take over."

"Well, all I'm asking you to do today is concentrate. Forget Kaye and forget whatever implications you think might be behind Attorney Cooper's questions. Concentrate on what she's asking you, and then just answer it. If you can answer yes or no, that's what you should do. Just keep your eye on the front of the rim. Okay?"

"I'll try, man." He took in a deep breath and blew it out. "When this is over, you gotta buy me a beer."

"I'll buy you a six-pack, Mick."

———

Q. It was in January of last year, sixteen months ago, when you and your wife started living separately, is that right?

A. Yes.

Q. And you took your apartment in Somerville.

A. Yes.

Q. And did you at that time separate your finances?

A. I opened my own bank account.

Q. And you got your own credit card, is that right?

A. Yes. Kaye did, too.

Q. Whose idea was that?

MR. COYNE: Which idea?

Q. I'm sorry. Whose idea was it to separate your finances, Mr. Fallon?

A. Mine.

Q. Why did you want to do that?

A. Because Kaye is not very responsible with money. She never paid any attention to how much we had or how much was coming in. If she wanted something, she just bought it. So I figured if she had to worry about money a little bit, maybe she'd—she'd appreciate me.

Q. You were hoping to punish her because she asked you to move out?

A. Do I have to talk about this?

MR. COYNE: Answer the question, please.

A. I guess I was hoping she'd realize everything I did for her and want me to move back home.

Q. You gave your wife money while you were living apart?

A. Yes.

Q. How much?

A. I gave her twenty-five hundred a month.

Q. How did you arrive at that figure?

A. It's what I thought was fair.

Q. Did your wife agree to that figure?

A. It's what I gave her. I don't know if she agreed or not.

Q. She never asked for more or said she thought it was inadequate?

A. She might have. I don't really remember. It didn't matter. I was always the one who had to think about money. She had no idea what was fair. She has no concept of money.

Q. Do you recall any specific occasion when she told you she didn't have enough money?

A. I don't know.

MR. COYNE: Yes or no, Mick. Either you recall or you don't.

A. I don't recall any occasion, no.

Q. Did you think what you were giving her was adequate for her to meet her expenses?

A. If she was careful with her money and didn't buy everything she saw, it should have been plenty. She was teaching. She had income of her own, too.

Q. What did you do about your joint accounts and joint credit cards?

A. I canceled our credit cards. The joint bank account was the one she used. I took some money out of it and put it in my own account.

Q. When you canceled the credit cards, did your wife agree to that?

A. I don't know.

Q. Did you consult her about it?

A. No. I did it, and then I told her that her credit cards were no good, and if she wanted one, she better get one for herself.

Q. Okay, Mr. Fallon. Now I want to call your attention to some documents that you've provided for us. Will you look at these, please, and tell me if these are photocopies of your bank statements from the time when you and your wife separated and you established your separate accounts?

A. (Witness reviews documents.)

Q. You've had a chance to look over these papers. These are your personal bank statements for the months of February a year ago through April, last month?

A. Yes.

Q. And this account is the only bank account that you have, or have had, since you and your wife separated your finances?

A. Right. Yes.

Q. So all of your financial activities are reflected in these bank statements.

A. Is that a question?

Q. Yes. I'll restate. Are all of your personal financial activities since the time when you and your wife separated accounted for in this particular account, and are these the complete statements of that account?

A. That's worse than your other question. But, yes. The answer is yes.

MS. COOPER: I want to mark these as Exhibits 13 through 27 for the record.

(Exhibits 13 through 27 marked for identification.)

Q. Okay, now, Mr. Fallon. Here we have several pages of photocopies of canceled checks and others with photocopies of checks stubs. Are these what you provided for us today?

A. (Witness reviews documents.)

Q. Have you had a chance to look at these documents? And are they what you provided for us?

A. Umm, yes. That's what these are.

MS. COOPER: Let's mark these exhibits now. They

will be Exhibits 28 through 57. There are thirty pages of photocopies here.

(Exhibits 28 through 57 marked for identification.)

Q. Now, calling your attention to Exhibit 16, Mr. Fallon. Your bank statement from last May, a year ago. Would you read this line here, where I'm pointing?

A. That's a deposit for $8,500.

Q. What was your source of that money?

A. I don't remember.

Q. Would you examine the documents on which the check stubs were photocopied, please, and point out the stub for that $8,500 check you deposited.

A. (Witness examines exhibit.)

A. It's not here.

Q. How do you account for that?

A. I don't know. It might've been a check with no stub. You know, like somebody's personal check.

Q. Could that have been cash that you deposited?

A. I don't know. I guess so.

MR. COYNE: Yes or no.

A. Yes. It could have been cash.

Q. Where would you get $8,500 in cash?

A. It might have come from a lot of different places, in smaller amounts, and I just held onto it until it added up and then I deposited it.

Q. Is that what actually happened?

A. I don't remember. Like I said, it might've been a check with no stub.

Q. And who would have given you a check for that amount?

A. I don't know.

Q. From where might you have received cash or personal checks that would add up to $8,500?

35

A. I don't know. Some people owe me money. Maybe they paid me in cash or personal checks.

Q. Who owes you money?

A. Friends. Business acquaintances.

Q. Can you be specific as to names and amounts and the conditions of these loans you've made?

A. I don't recall. I help out my friends sometimes, that's all.

Q. Okay. Now let's look at Exhibit 19. What is this where I'm pointing?

Cooper questioned Mick about several other deposits he had made into his account within the past sixteen months. A couple of them had been made on consecutive days. All were substantial, but none exceeded $10,000. His responses were all the same—he couldn't remember where they came from, or whether they were cash or personal checks.

I knew that Cooper was thinking what I was thinking—that banks are obligated to report any cash deposit of $10,000.01 or more to the IRS, and that Mick appeared to have broken up larger amounts than that into separate, smaller deposits.

Q. These are fairly large amounts of money, Mr. Fallon—$8,500 and $6,000 and $7,500; $5,000; $9,500; $6,500—that's $43,000—not to remember where any of it came from. Are you sure you can't help me out here?

MR. COYNE: My client has answered your questions.

MS. COOPER: Yes. All right.

Q. Looking at Exhibit 15, now, Mr. Fallon. What is this here where I'm pointing?

A. (Witness reviews exhibit.)

A. It's a check I wrote, check number 43. It's for $10,000.

Q. Would you look through Exhibits 28 through 57 and find the photocopy of check number 43, please?

A. (Witness reviews exhibits.)

A. It's right here. Check 43.

Q. Who is this check made out to?

A. Cash. It's made out to cash.

Q. Do you remember what you did with this $10,000 in cash?

A. No. Maybe I owed somebody some money, or—

MR. COYNE: Just yes or no, Mick.

A. No. I don't remember.

And Barbara Cooper proceeded to question Mick about checks he had written to "cash." There were nine of them, all large. His answers in all cases were the same: "I don't remember."

Q. That's, let's see, that's $72,500 that you took in cash in the space of a few months, and you don't remember how you spent it. Is that your testimony?

A. Yes.

Q. Now, Mr. Fallon, calling your attention to Exhibit 12 again, which is a copy of your individual tax return for last year, would you please point out to me where on this return you have accounted for the income of $43,000 that you testified came to you as cash or personal checks and that you deposited into your bank account?

MR. COYNE: I want to go off the record for a minute.

(Counsel confers with witness.)

I steered Mick back out into the reception area. The secretary, who was talking on the telephone, looked up, gave us a quick smile, hung up the phone, and left the room.

"Sit down," I said to Mick.

He slumped on the sofa. I stood in front of him.

"Okay," I said, "now tell me. *Is* that forty-three grand accounted for on your tax return?"

He shook his head.

"Should it have been?"

"I don't know. I guess so."

"You testified you couldn't remember where it came from. Was that the truth?"

"No. I know where it came from."

"And the seventy-two-five you took in cash?"

"What the fuck is she trying to do to me?"

"Who?"

"Kaye, for Christ's sake. Don't you see what's going on?"

"I think I do," I said. "Now answer my question."

"About the seventy-two-five?"

"Right."

"Yeah, I know what I did with it."

"You paid off debts."

He nodded.

"What kind of debts, Mick?"

He looked up at me, then shrugged. "You know," he mumbled.

"Maybe I do," I said, "but I want you to explain it to me right now. And you better tell me the truth this time, or I'll fire you. You lied to me before. You said you didn't cheat on your taxes."

"You're pissed, huh?"

"I'm embarrassed, Mick."

He looked up at me, shrugged, then bent forward with his arms dangling between his legs.

"Gambling?" I said.

He nodded.

"You're supposed to report what you win gambling."

"I figured if I lost more than I won—"

"It doesn't work that way. You know that, don't you?"

Mick's eyes refused to meet mine. "Yeah, I guess I do. But, see, I figured—"

"Don't lie to your lawyer, Mick. Never again. Understand?"

"Okay," he said.

"Tell me about the gambling, Mick."

He let out a long breath. "When Kaye and I got married, she made me promise to quit. I tried, but . . ."

"But you can't help it, right?"

He nodded. "I've always gambled. I was lucky in college and in the pros. I mean, I never bet on my own games, and back then you could get away with it if you were careful. But Kaye knew. She hated it. So I promised her I'd quit."

"But you didn't quit."

"I really did try. But I—it's in my blood. I handled the money in the family, I did all my gambling with cash, I never lost too much more than I won, and I was able to cover it up from Kaye."

"Your accountant never questioned you?"

"Ray? Oh, he just used the figures I gave him. He never said anything."

"Do you realize what kind of trouble you could be in?"

He looked up at me. "I think about it all the time, man. Every time the phone rings or someone knocks on my door, I'm thinking, Uh-oh, the IRS. Here they come."

"And you're still gambling?"

"Oh, yeah. I need a big hit. I owe 'em big time. I'm in bad shape, man."

"Well," I said, "this explains why Attorney Cooper wanted to depose you."

"What, so she could get me arrested for tax evasion?"

"No. Because she's protecting her client's interests."

"Kaye doesn't know about the gambling."

"Well, Attorney Cooper has figured it out, Mick. Come on. We're going back in there."

"You mean, I've got to tell them about the gambling?"

"No."

---

MR. COYNE: I've advised my client not to answer that last question, or any other questions pertaining to his bank account or his tax return for last year.

MS. COOPER: What about questions pertaining to his income and expenditures for the period before he and my client separated?

MR. COYNE: No more questions on those subjects, either.

MS. COOPER: I don't have any further questions, then.

(Whereupon the deposition concluded at 12:45 P.M.)

# THREE

Mick and I were halfway across the parking lot to my car when a soft voice behind us said, "Michael?"

We both stopped and turned around. Kaye stood on the porch. She was holding her purse in both hands protectively in front of her chest, squinting in the bright sunshine.

"Hang on a minute," Mick mumbled to me.

He walked back and stood on the ground, looking up at Kaye. She came down a couple of steps until their heads were even. She reached out, put her hand on his shoulder, leaned toward him, said something into his ear. He shook his head and glanced back at me.

I went to my car, climbed behind the wheel, and lit a cigarette. I watched Mick and Kaye through the side window. It appeared that she was doing all the talking. She kept touching his shoulder and arm, speaking earnestly, ducking down to try to look into his face. He had lowered his chin and was staring down at his feet.

After a few minutes he looked up at her. She smiled and nodded, and he shook his head. Then she put both hands on his shoulders, leaned forward, and it looked as if she intended to kiss him. But Mick put up his forearm to ward her off, spun around, and started back to the car where I waited for him. His jaw was clenched, and so were his fists.

Kaye stood there on the porch for a minute, watching Mick. Then she shook her head, turned, and went back into the building.

Mick slid in beside me. I did not turn on the ignition. We sat there in the parking lot behind Barbara Cooper's office, both of us gazing out the windshield.

"You okay?" I said.

"Oh, sure," he said.

"None of my business . . ."

"Nothin'," he said. "Just bullshit. She didn't say anything."

I glanced sideways at him. His eyes were glittery.

"Be nice if you two can end up friends," I said.

"Wouldn't it, huh?"

"Look," I said. "If you want to talk about it . . ."

Mick shook his head. "She said the deposition wasn't her idea. It was that lawyer's idea, and she went along with it, and now she wished she hadn't. She said she'd always trusted me, that she didn't know I'd been gambling, but she wouldn't've wanted to find out that way. She said she was sorry, that she wanted me to be happy, that there was no reason we couldn't be friends." He snorted. "Can you believe it? All that crap in there, and I'm supposed to think she wants me to be fucking happy?"

"It's divorce, Mick. It's never happy."

"This ain't over with," he muttered.

"Huh?" I said. "What do you mean?"

He shook his head. "Nothing, man. Forget it."

"Leave it to the lawyers, Mick. You hear me?"

"Sure, I hear you." He hesitated. "Well, now what? What's gonna happen?"

"Now I'll help you find another lawyer."

42

His head snapped around, and he frowned at me. "What does that mean, another lawyer?"

"What the hell do you think it means?" I took a deep breath. "It means I quit. I'm done. I don't want to represent you. Dammit, Mick. You lied to me. You withheld important information from me. You set me up—you set both of us up—to be humiliated in there. You think I'm willing to put up with that?"

"But I need you, man," he said. "You can't do this to me."

"You don't think so?" I said. "Watch me."

"You're pretty mad, huh?"

I tried to glare fiercely at him, but he wore such a purely innocent, childlike expression of hurt and fear that after a minute, and in spite of myself, I smiled. "Christ, Mick. Yes, I'm mad."

"I thought everything was going okay."

"Before today it was. Look," I said, "when they wanted to depose you, you must've at least suspected what they were after."

"I didn't think Kaye knew about my . . ."

"*Problem* is the word. Big problem."

"Okay. My *problem*. I didn't think she knew."

"Well," I said, "maybe she didn't, but it was all right there in the stuff we turned over to them." I flicked the cigarette butt out the window. "All you had to do was tell me the truth." I sighed. "My fault, Mick. I should've scrutinized it myself instead of trusting you. All that money you didn't declare. It would've jumped out at me, just like it did at Attorney Cooper."

"By then I'd already lied to you," he said. "I didn't want to admit it. I—it was important to me, what you thought of me."

"Right now, you don't want to know what I think of you." I turned the key in the ignition, backed up, and pulled out of the parking lot. "I said I'd buy you a beer," I said. "And I, for one, am a man of my word."

"You said you'd buy me a six-pack."

"Don't push your luck, pal."

I headed back to Somerville. Mick slouched in the front seat beside me, jiggling his knee, clenching and unclenching his fists, and staring out the side window, and neither of us spoke until I turned off Mass Ave. in Porter Square, heading toward Mick's apartment in Somerville.

"The Union Square Bistro's got a bar downstairs," said Mick. "Good food, too, if you feel like eating. It's right around the corner from my place."

"Sounds fine," I said.

"You're not really gonna quit on me, are you?"

"I should."

He reached over and tapped my leg with his fist. "I knew I could count on you. So what happens next?"

"Damage control," I said.

Barbara Cooper waited until the following Tuesday before she called me. "I'll get right to the point," she said.

"I figured you would."

She cleared her throat. "You can understand how my client is feeling about now."

"And maybe you can imagine how my client is feeling."

"Yes, well, some of us end up with stronger cases than others." She cleared her throat. "My client does not feel confident that your client will be able to meet his obligations for child support and alimony."

"He's always managed to support his family," I said. "He has adequate income."

"He gambles. He loses a lot of money."

I didn't say anything.

"He's unreliable, he's unstable, and he's angry," she said. "My client's afraid of him."

"Oh, come off it. Mick might be a very large man, but he's still in love with his wife."

But I understood what she was talking about. In my experience, love and anger are so closely related that sometimes it's hard to tell which is which. And Mick had revealed his quick temper to Barbara Cooper.

"I doubt if the court would give your assessment of your client's temperament much credence," she said. "And you know Judge Kolb."

I did know Judge Elliot Kolb. He had a reputation as a wife's judge, and he hated domestic violence or abuse of any kind. He'd take one look at Mick Fallon, all six-foot-seven, 280 pounds of him, and then he'd see pretty little blue-eyed Kaye gazing demurely down into her lap, and Judge Kolb would give full credence to any hint that she might fear for her safety.

"So what exactly are you proposing?" I said.

"I'm taking this one to court, Mr. Coyne."

"Well, that's—"

"Understand one thing," she said.

"I'm listening."

"My client is feeling insecure, and she's genuinely fearful. She's not being vindictive."

"No," I said. "She's got you to handle that part for her."

I heard her chuckle. "See you in court, Counselor."

It was close to midnight on Monday. I had just crawled into bed and picked up my dog-eared copy of *Moby Dick*, which has been my bedtime reading off and on for years, when the phone rang. I grabbed it, figuring it was one of my two sons calling collect from another time zone. I hoped it wasn't bad news.

Or maybe it was Alex, calling from Maine. That would've been good news.

But it was none of them.

It was Lieutenant Roger Horowitz. Horowitz was a homicide

detective with the state police, and if he was calling me, it had to be bad news.

"Get dressed, Coyne," he growled. "We got a situation here."

"Situation?"

"I'm on my way to your place now. Meet me out front. I'll fill you in."

"Wait a minute—"

But Horowitz had hung up.

It didn't take much imagination to figure out that when a homicide cop had a "situation," it probably involved a homicide.

I hastily pulled on a pair of jeans, cotton shirt, socks, sneakers, windbreaker. I patted my pockets for cigarettes, keys, and wallet, then took the elevator down to the lobby.

When I stepped out the front door, a state police cruiser was waiting. An arm stuck out the window and waved me over.

I climbed into the back. Horowitz was in the passenger seat up front and a uniformed state trooper was behind the wheel.

"Hit it," said Horowitz to the driver.

Tires squealed, the siren wailed, and I slammed back against the seat.

I grabbed the back of Horowitz's seat and pulled myself forward. "So who murdered whom?" I said.

"It ain't that kind of situation," he said. "At least not yet it ain't. We got a hostage situation here, and the hostage happens to be a friend of yours."

"Yeah, well—"

"And the guy who's holding the hostage is one of your clients, okay? And he's asking for you."

"For Christ sake, Horowitz—"

"Mick Fallon is holding a steak knife at Skeeter O'Reilly's throat, all right? And he's saying that unless he can talk to you, he's gonna cut him. So here I'm giving you a chance to be a hero, do something useful for a change."

We swerved around one last corner and screeched to a stop

46

halfway up onto the sidewalk on State Street at the end of Skeeter's alley. Three or four cruisers had pulled in at odd angles, and they sat there with their doors hanging open, their lights flashing, and their radios blaring static. About a dozen city cops were holding a small crowd of people away from the mouth of the alley. The Channel 7 Mobile Unit was already there, and a red-headed female reporter I thought I recognized was talking to the camera that was perched on the shoulder of a tall, skinny guy wearing dreadlocks.

Horowitz was already out of the car. He yanked my door open. "Step lively," he said. "Time is money, Coyne."

I climbed out. "You better fill me in."

"Not much to fill in. We had a Boston detective track Fallon down to Skeeter's. He went inside, flashed his shield, said he needed to talk to him, and Fallon picked him up by the scruff of his neck, dragged him to the door, and threw him out into the alley. Then—"

"Wait a minute," I said. "This was *one* detective?"

Horowtiz nodded.

"And this one detective, he didn't have a partner with him?"

"The partner was outside in the car. Says he had a call. They figured this was a routine thing."

"Bad police work," I said.

"Agreed," said Horowitz. "But it don't change what Fallon did."

I nodded. "Okay. So then what happened?"

"So after he tossed that cop out of the door, your client went back in, cleared the place out, snagged a knife off one of the booths, and grabbed Skeeter. He's a big sonofabitch, huh?"

"Yes, he's very big," I said. "But what—?"

"We got him on the phone. He says he'll only talk to you."

Outside the front door, a pretty dark-eyed woman, early thirties, I guessed, was holding a cellular phone to her ear. When she saw Horowitz she said, "He's not talking."

47

"This is Coyne, Fallon's lawyer," he said to her. He looked at me. "Benny. Marcia Benetti. My partner."

She nodded to me and gave the phone to Horowitz, who handed it to me. "So talk to him, Coyne."

I frowned at Horowitz, then put the phone to my ear. "Mick?" I said. "It's Brady."

I heard what sounded like a sob. Then Mick said, "Oh, Jesus, man. I really fucked up this time, huh?"

"No problem, Mick. Is Skeeter okay?"

"Yeah, he's okay."

"Let me speak to him."

A moment later Skeeter said, "I'm okay, Mr. Coyne."

"You sure, Skeets?"

"Yeah, I—"

"Brady?" It was Mick. I guessed he'd grabbed the phone back from Skeeter.

"I'm right here, Mick. I'm coming in, okay?"

"I don't know. Shit, man. I don't know what to do."

"Don't do anything," I said. "Just stay right there. I'm going to put the phone down now, and then I'll be coming in the front door."

"Alone," said Mick. "If anyone's with you, I'll . . ."

"You better not hurt Skeeter. He's my friend, and I'll be really angry with you if you so much as scratch him."

"You better be alone. I trust you, man."

"Here I come. Don't hang up that phone."

I handed the phone to Horowitz. "Stay tuned," I said. I took a deep breath, pushed open the door, and stepped inside.

Mick and Skeeter were behind the bar. Mick was standing behind Skeeter and had one arm across the much smaller man's chest. His other hand was hanging down out of sight. I assumed that was the one that held the knife.

"Let Skeeter go, Mick," I said.

"I didn't hurt anybody. You know me, Brady. I don't want trouble."

"I know that. No harm done. Let's keep it that way."

"I just need to talk to you. Okay?"

"We can do that, sure." I approached the bar, lifted the hinged section, and held it up. "Go on outside, Skeets. Mick and I need to talk privately."

Mick did not let go of Skeeter. He lifted his hand. It held a steak knife with a serrated blade, and he pressed it against Skeeter's throat. Mick's eyes were red and glittery, and the hand that held the knife trembled. "Wait a minute," he said. "I gotta think."

"You've got me now," I said to him. "Just let Skeeter go, and you can hang onto me while we talk. All right?" I pointed at the phone on the bartop. "I'm going to tell them what's happening."

Mick shrugged.

I reached my hand slowly for the phone, keeping my eyes on Mick.

"Okay?" I said.

He nodded.

I picked it up. "Horowitz, you there?"

"I'm here."

"Skeeter's coming out. Mick's got his knife on my throat now, so don't do anything stupid, please."

"You gonna bring out Fallon?"

"Give us a few minutes."

"We ain't got all night, Coyne. If you aren't out of there in fifteen minutes, I'm calling in the SWAT team."

"No need for that." I put the phone down and arched my eyebrows at Mick.

He pulled his arm away from Skeeter, then patted him on the shoulder. "I'm real sorry, man. I never would've hurt you."

Skeeter looked up at him. "I never thought you would, Mick.

**49**

Hell, you probably got my joint on the news. Best publicity I ever had, huh?" He tugged at the beak of his Red Sox cap. "Any TV cameras out there, Mr. Coyne?"

I smiled. "I saw that nosy redhead from Channel 7. I'm sure she'll want to interview you."

Skeeter grinned, then turned to Mick. "Don't worry, Mick. I'll tell 'em how you and I go way back." He looked at me. "I ain't gonna press charges or anything, Mr. Coyne. Mick was just feeling pretty low, and maybe I gave him a couple beers too many, you know?"

"Thanks, Skeets. Now if you don't mind . . ."

"Sure. I'm outa here."

I picked up the phone. "Skeeter's coming out now," I said.

"Gotcha," said Horowitz.

I clicked the Off button on the phone. I didn't want Horowitz to overhear any privileged lawyer-client conversation.

Mick and I watched Skeeter leave. Then I turned to Mick. "Okay, my friend. Talk to me."

Mick came around from behind the bar. He dropped the knife on the bartop beside the phone, then sat on a stool. He put his elbows on the bar and lowered his face into his hands.

I sat beside him. "Tell me about it, Mick."

"You think I could mess up my life any worse?"

"Ah, come on. No harm was done. Skeeter won't press charges. Tell me what happened."

He lifted his head and looked at me. "I guess I—I just snapped, Brady. I've never been so damn depressed as I have since the other day. Kaye, refusing even to think about working it out, and then that crap about my gambling. I mean, it just feels like it's all falling apart and there's nothing I can do about it."

I put my arm around his shoulder. "I'm going to help you through it," I said. "There are things we can do, okay? We'll get you a divorce settlement, we'll get together with Ray Allen and file some amended tax returns, we'll straighten out this evening with the police. Everything's fixable. All right?"

He nodded. "I guess I had too many beers. When that guy said he wanted to talk to me . . ."

"That guy was a cop, Mick."

He let out a long breath. "I know, but . . ."

"Did he announce himself, show you his shield?"

"He just touched my arm, said he wanted to talk to me. If he had his badge out, I didn't see it." Mick shook his head. "I didn't know what I was doing, Brady. It's like it wasn't me. I just— something exploded in my head, you know? I hope I didn't hurt anybody."

"You didn't," I said, although I wasn't sure that was true. I lit a cigarette and put my arm around his shoulder. "I'm going to smoke this butt, and you're going to calm down, and then we're getting out of here. Okay?"

"You'll stay with me?"

"Of course I will."

When I finished my cigarette, I turned to Mick. "Before we leave, there's one thing I need to know."

"What's that?"

"Why did that cop want to talk to you?"

He shrugged. "I don't know, man. I didn't give him the chance to say. Like I said, I wasn't thinking. Guess I blew it, huh?"

"That you did." I touched his arm. "We'll straighten it out. Ready?"

He nodded.

I picked up the phone and hit Star 69. It rang once, and then Horowitz said, "Coyne?"

"We're coming out," I said. "For Christ sake, don't shoot me."

# FOUR

Horowitz's unmarked car was parked in the alley right outside the door. When Mick and I stepped outside, a uniformed state cop grabbed his arms and Marcia Benetti cuffed his wrists behind him.

Horowitz came around from the other side of the car. "Good work," he said to me.

"Take the cuffs off my client," I said. "You're not going to arrest him."

"Christ," said Horowitz. "He assaults a police officer, he holds a man hostage at knife point. That's not enough?"

"Skeeter won't press charges," I said, "and if anyone ever tried to put that cop on the stand, a first-year law student would chew him up and spit him out. So don't play games with me. Tell me what's really going on here."

Horowitz glared at me for a minute. Then he shrugged. He was a homicide cop. Homicide cops don't get involved in hostage situations. Not unless somebody gets killed. "I got some questions for your client."

"Well, fine," I said. "All you've got to do is ask. Uncuff him,

53

and we'll go into Skeeter's and sit down like civilized people. You can ask him your questions while you keep a couple of officers at the door so nobody interrupts us. How's that?"

Horowitz cocked his head and peered at me for a minute. He was a stocky guy with a perpetual five o'clock shadow, rimless glasses, thinning black hair, and old acne scars on his cheeks. When he smiled, which he did rarely and at unexpected times, he reminded me of Jack Nicholson.

He didn't smile this time. "I'll want to tape our conversation."

"That's fine," I said.

He nodded. "Okay." He jerked his head at Benetti. "Uncuff him."

She took the cuffs off Mick, and we trooped inside and sat at a booth, Mick and I on one side with Horowitz across from us. Marcia Benetti pulled a chair up to the end of the booth and put a tape recorder on the table.

Horowitz reached over and flicked it on. "It's June first—no, wait, it's turned into June second, and it's, um, one-twenty A.M. This is Massachusetts State Police Lieutenant Roger Horowitz, and with me are Michael Fallon and Brady Coyne, Mr. Fallon's attorney, along with Officer Marcia Benetti. We're at Skeeter's Infield in Boston." He looked at Mick. "Are you willing to answer some questions for me, Mr. Fallon?"

Mick looked at me, and I nodded. "Okay," he said.

"Good," said Horowitz. "So, Mr. Fallon. Can you tell us where you've been and what you've been doing for the past thirty-six hours?"

"Come on, Lieutenant," I said. "You know better."

Horowitz frowned at me, then shrugged. "Tell you what," he growled. "Suppose I rephrase the question?"

"Please," I said.

He looked at Mick. "Mr. Fallon," he said, "can you think of anyone who'd want to murder your wife?"

54

Somehow his question didn't surprise me. If Horowitz was involved, it probably meant somebody had been murdered, and ever since he'd called me at home, possibilities had been bouncing around in the back of my head. Kaye Fallon had been one of those possibilities.

Still, his words kicked me in the stomach.

Mick stared at Horowitz for a long time. Finally he whispered, "What the hell?"

Horowitz nodded.

"You're saying somebody . . . ?"

"She's been murdered, Mr. Fallon. I'm sorry."

Mick turned to me. "What's he trying to do?"

"He's telling you the truth, Mick. He's not a pleasant man, but he's a good cop. He doesn't play games. Not with something like this." I turned to Horowitz. "Is my client a suspect? Because if he is—"

"Not at this time," said Horowitz.

Mick had tilted back his head, and he was looking up at the ceiling. Both of his fists were drumming on the table in front of him. When he dropped his eyes, I saw that they were red and watery. He stared at me, and I knew what he wanted from me.

But I couldn't deny it. Kaye had been murdered. I held his eyes and shook my head.

Horowitz cleared his throat. "So, Mr. Fallon . . ."

"Give me a minute with my client, okay?" I said.

He nodded and slid out of the booth. Benetti clicked off the tape recorder, and the two of them went over and sat on stools at the bar.

I touched Mick's shoulder. "Don't lie to me this time."

He nodded. Tears had overflowed his eyes and wet his cheeks.

"You've got to tell me the truth," I said.

"I didn't kill her," he said, "if that's what you want to know."

I peered into his eyes, then nodded. "Okay. You got anything to hide?"

He shrugged.

"If you do, tell me now."

"No," he said. "Nothing you don't already know."

"You don't know anything about this?"

He shook his head.

"We better talk to the police, then, okay?"

"I'm not up for this, Brady. Jesus . . ."

"Somebody killed Kaye," I said. "Let's help them figure it out."

He looked up at me, then slowly nodded. "Sure. You're right."

I glanced over toward Horowitz, caught his eye, and jerked my chin at him. He and Benetti slid off their stools and came back to the booth.

After they'd sat down and got the tape recorder switched on, I said to Horowitz, "Tell us what happened."

He shrugged. "I'll tell you what I can." He leaned forward on his elbows and spoke in a low, matter-of-fact monotone, but now and then—at the oddest, least appropriate moments—he flashed his evil Nicholson grin. His eyes never left Mick's face the whole time.

Kaye Fallon's body, he told us, had been discovered by Gretchen Conley, a friend of hers, at about ten o'clock on Monday evening. Kaye was lying on her back on the living room floor of her contemporary home—the home she used to share with Mick—in the Moon Hill section of Lexington. Preliminary observation by the medical examiner on the scene indicated that she'd been first bludgeoned and then stabbed. She'd been dead for about twenty-four hours, meaning she'd been killed sometime Sunday evening. She was fully clothed. She was wearing a short-sleeved jersey, a plaid kilt, pantyhose, no shoes. The front of the jersey was dark reddish brown from the dried blood, matching the stain on the carpet. The kilt was bunched up around her waist, but her pantyhose had not been pulled down and it did not appear that she'd been sexually abused.

Kaye had a depressed skull fracture above and behind her right ear, Horowitz continued. She'd been stabbed several times in the torso, and her throat had been slashed. There were no defense wounds on her hands or arms. The ME guessed that the blow to the head, which came before the knife wounds, would've killed her, although all the bleeding indicated that her heart was still pumping when she'd been stabbed and cut.

From the location of the blow—and here Horowitz had touched the back of his head delicately with the tips of his fingers—the ME speculated that she'd been hit from behind. A vicious blow that dented and splintered her skull.

"He hit her when she turned her back on him," I said.

Horowitz nodded. "We figure they'd been in the living room—maybe sitting on the sofa, judging from where her body fell—and then she got up and turned to leave the room. She might've started for the kitchen where there's a phone when he hit her."

"Right side of the head, did you say?"

He nodded. "From behind, a right-handed blow."

"What'd he use?" I said.

"A brass sculpture. A replica of Rodin's *The Thinker*. Weighs five or six pounds."

Mick, who'd been staring down at the table the whole time, looked up. "Kaye gave that to me for my birthday a few years ago." He smiled quickly. "It was sort of a joke between us. Kaye used to tease me about, you know, going off half-cocked, not stopping to think. We kept it on the coffee table. Sort of to remind me to—to think before I did something."

"Mr. Fallon," said Horowitz, "are you right-handed?"

Mick turned to me.

"It's okay," I said.

"Yeah," said Mick. "When I played ball, I had a decent left hand, though."

"Did you find prints on that statue?" I said.

Horowitz shrugged. He didn't know—or wasn't saying. I figured if they'd pulled Mick's prints off that sculpture, they would've arrested him.

"What about the other weapon?" I said.

"Carving knife," said Horowitz. "It matched a set of cutlery on the kitchen counter."

I tried to imagine it. When Kaye gets up off the sofa and turns her back on him, the killer bashes her head with heavy sculpture. She falls to the floor, mortally wounded. Not good enough. He goes into the kitchen, finds a knife, comes back, stabs her, and then cuts her throat for good measure. What kind of rage drives somebody to do that?

I guessed they hadn't found Mick's prints on the knife, either.

I knew what Horowitz was thinking, of course. I'd have thought the same thing. Mick was angry and depressed over his divorce. If that wasn't enough, he owed big gambling debts, not to mention back taxes, and he faced possible criminal charges with the IRS.

Plus, of course, whenever a woman is murdered, her spouse is the first and most logical suspect.

Throwing the detective out of Skeeter's and then holding a knife at his friend's throat didn't exactly make Mick look innocent, either.

But Horowitz wasn't arresting him. He had told us Mick wasn't an official suspect, though I was positive Horowitz suspected him.

I could almost believe Mick would hit her. I'd seen how easily she could provoke him, and he had a quick temper. But I couldn't see him sustaining his anger long enough to go find a knife, come back, and do what he did. That just wasn't Mick.

"You know Gretchen Conley?" said Horowitz to Mick.

He nodded. "Kaye's best friend. Friend of mine, too. At least she was."

"What do you mean?"

Mick shrugged. "I haven't seen her since—since Kaye and I split. For all I know Gretchen doesn't like me anymore."

The two women had been college classmates, Mick said, and their friendship had deepened over the years. Now they were best friends and confidantes. Before Mick and Kaye separated, they used to go out to dinner or a movie with Gretchen Conley and her husband almost every week. When their kids were younger, the two families had taken vacations together.

Horowitz told us he'd interrogated Gretchen Conley at length. She and Kaye had agreed to meet at six-thirty on Monday evening for dinner at Aigo's, a little restaurant in Concord, the town where Gretchen lived. Getting together for dinner on Monday evenings had become a ritual for the two women ever since Mick had moved out over a year earlier.

When they'd talked on the phone the previous afternoon to confirm their dinner date for Monday, Kaye had seemed upset.

"Upset about me," said Mick.

Horowitz shrugged.

Gretchen had arrived at Aigo's at six-thirty. She went upstairs, took a table, had a glass of wine. When Kaye hadn't shown up by seven, Gretchen phoned her at home. There was no answer, so she assumed Kaye was on her way. She went back to their table, had a second glass of wine.

But by seven-thirty she was worried. Kaye was always on time, and if something had come up to make her late, she would've called the restaurant.

So Gretchen phoned again and still got no answer. She tried again at eight. Then she left the restaurant and went home. She was concerned, but she figured that Kaye had a lot on her mind and something had come up. Still, it was odd that she hadn't called. Gretchen kept phoning Kaye's house and getting no answer.

Finally, she drove to Kaye's home in Lexington, arriving a little after ten o'clock. She rang the bell several times, and when there was no response, she used her key and entered through the front door.

"The door was locked?" I said.

Horowitz nodded. "That's what Mrs. Conley said."

"And she had a key?"

"Yes. She said Mrs. Fallon had been away on vacation back in February. She'd given her friend a key so she could water the plants and feed the cat."

I looked at Mick. He nodded. "She'd do that," he said.

"Mrs. Conley pushed open the front door," Horowitz continued. "She called Mrs. Fallon's name, received no answer. She stepped into the foyer. She said she noticed that all the downstairs lights were on. Then she saw the blood."

I tried to imagine what it must have been like for Gretchen Conley. She saw the blood, then she saw the body. So much blood from such a small body. The carpet was soaked, spatters on the wall and some of the furniture, and Gretchen suddenly feeling dizzy, nauseated, thinking she was going to faint, leaning against the wall, then sliding to the floor, hugging her knees and taking deep breaths until her head cleared, and after a while, standing up and staggering down the hall into the kitchen, where she knew there was a telephone, holding her hand beside her face, trying not to look at Kaye's body, all that blood . . .

She dialed 911, Horowitz said, told them where she was and what she'd found, gave them her name, and agreed to stay there. Then she went out, sat on the front steps, and waited for the police.

"There was a half-filled glass of white zinfandel and an empty bottle of Pete's Wicked Ale on the coffee table," said Horowitz.

Mick, of course, was a beer drinker.

"Any prints on the bottle?" I said.

"We don't know yet."

The locked door meant whoever it was either had a key or Kaye had let him in. Him or her. It had to be someone she knew. She poured herself a glass of wine, fetched him a beer. They sat on the sofa.

"What else?" I said to Horowitz.

"That's it," he said. "That's all I can tell you."

"What about Gretchen Conley?" I said. "You know where she was Sunday night?"

He nodded. "Says she was out to dinner and a movie with her husband and another couple. We'll check it out, of course."

Mick sat beside me in the booth, his face wet, staring down at his hands, which were grappling with each other on the tabletop.

Horowitz was leaning back, peering at Mick. "So who'd want to kill your wife, Mr. Fallon?" he said. "Help me out here."

"I don't know." Mick turned to me. "It wasn't me, if that's what he's thinking. I didn't kill Kaye."

"If you did," said Horowitz, "it'll go a lot easier for you if you tell me now."

"I didn't fucking kill her."

"Can you tell me why you assaulted a police officer here tonight and then held Mr. O'Reilly at knifepoint?"

Mick shrugged. "I was just having a beer. I got a lot on my mind. I guess I—I don't know. Something snapped. I lost it."

"You've got a quick temper, Mr. Fallon?"

"That's enough," I said. "My client has already told you he didn't kill his wife."

Horowitz shrugged. "So where were you Sunday evening, Mr. Fallon?"

"My client will not answer that question at this time," I said.

"I wasn't there," said Mick. He turned to me. "I *wasn't*."

Horowitz grinned quickly at me. "Okay. So, Mr. Fallon. Give me a hand here, then, okay? Can you think of anybody who might have reason to murder your wife? Somebody who could've done this thing?"

Mick shook his head.

"Answer it for the tape, Mick," I said.

"No," he mumbled. "I can't think of anybody. But if I ever find them—"

I grabbed Mick's arm. He looked up at me, and I shook my head.

Horowitz frowned and exchanged a glance with Benetti. Then he turned back to Mick. "Boyfriend, maybe?" he persisted. "Ex-lover?"

"Christ, no."

"Maybe an enemy of yours, Mr. Fallon? Someone who wanted to get to you, send you a message. Revenge, maybe."

Mick shook his head. "I don't know." He turned to me. "Brady . . ."

"Go ahead," I said. "Tell him, Mick."

Mick told Horowitz how he gambled, owed a lot of money.

"Your wife didn't like that," said Horowitz.

"No. She hated it."

Horowitz nodded. "You were about to be divorced," he said. "You stood to get cleaned out."

Mick shrugged. "I didn't care."

"What about insurance? Was your wife insured?"

"Sure. We're both insured."

"Life insurance?"

Mick nodded.

"Each other's beneficiaries?"

"Look," said Mick, "I didn't kill her." He turned to me. "Brady, do we have to . . . ?"

"That's it for now," I told Horowitz. "My client is tired and upset. No more questions tonight."

Horowitz nodded. "Terminating the questioning at, um, two-oh-seven A.M." He nodded to Benetti, who clicked off the tape recorder. Then he fixed Mick with that annoying Nicholson grin. "Stick close to home, Mr. Fallon," he said. "We'll want to talk with you some more." He turned to me. "Got it?"

"I got it," I said.

Benetti whispered something to Horowitz, who nodded and turned to Mick. "You gotta do something, I'm afraid."

Mick shrugged. "Whatever."

"We need you to identify the body for us."

Mick turned to me and frowned. "This guy some kind of joker, or what?"

"No," I said. "It has to be done."

Mick gazed up at the ceiling for a minute. Then he said, "Yeah, okay. I want to see her."


Horowitz gave us a ride to the morgue where Mick did his duty. Then a state cop took us over to my apartment. We got in my car, and I drove Mick back to Somerville over the quiet city streets. There had been a spring shower while we'd been inside Skeeter's, and the roads glistened in my headlights. Mick didn't say anything, and neither did I, until we pulled up in front of his place.

Then I turned to him and said, "You okay?"

He snorted a quick laugh out of his nose. "Oh, sure."

"That had to be rough."

He shrugged. "I'm just kinda numb, man. It ain't making any sense to me. It ain't real." He turned his face away from me.

"Mick," I said after a minute, "I hope you've got a good alibi for last night."

He was staring out the side window. "He thinks I did it, doesn't he? That Horowitz?"

"You're a logical suspect. Give me an alibi and you won't be."

"I was home watching television."

"Anybody with you?"

"No. No one's ever with me."

"Talk to anyone on the phone?"

He turned to look at me. In the glow of the streetlight that filtered down through the leafy maples that lined the street, I saw that his face was wet. "Brady, I couldn't even tell you what I saw on TV. I was just thinking about Kaye, missing the hell out of her, remembering all the good times, all the things we did together, me and Kaye and the kids when they were little, just driving myself nuts. That's what I found myself doing tonight, too, and I couldn't take it anymore. Being alone like that. That's why I went to Skeeter's. Just to—to get away from myself."

"You've got to be prepared—"

"I know," he interrupted. He reached over and gripped my arm. "I'll tell you one thing," he said softly. "I didn't do it. But if I ever get my hands on who did . . ."

I nodded. "I know how you feel, Mick. We'll figure it out."

He smiled quickly. "No way you know how I feel."

# FIVE

B y the time Mick shambled into his apartment and I'd driven back to mine, the sky was starting to turn from black to purple. The sun would rise in an hour or so, and I hadn't been to sleep yet.

When I got upstairs, I shucked off my clothes and flopped down on my bed. I was exhausted, but too wired from all the adrenaline to sleep. So I lay there staring up at the ceiling, fragments of thoughts and hypotheses ricocheting around inside my skull, while the sky outside brightened and lit my bedroom and a bunch of sparrows began chirping out on my balcony.

Eventually I dozed off. When I woke up, it was nearly ten in the morning. I felt more tired than before I'd slept. I staggered out of bed, put on some coffee, and tried to call Mick. I let it ring about a dozen times before I gave up.

When I'd left him off at his place at around four in the morning, he'd been muttering and slurring his words, and it wasn't from booze.

I showered, climbed into my office clothes, and tried him again. Again, no answer.

I tried to imagine what it must be like, having your wife brutally murdered and being considered a suspect. Mick had been right: I had no idea. But I understood that it could make a man crazy.

"What's the point?" Mick had mumbled as we'd driven along the slick streets to his apartment in Somerville. "It's not enough that Kaye's gone, but I gotta tell my kids that their mother's been murdered and everybody thinks I did it? Fuck this."

So instead of heading for the office, I drove to Somerville and found a parking slot on Mick's street.

Some climbing pink roses were blossoming on the wrought-iron fence in front of the three-decker next door to Mick's. I stopped and bent over to take a whiff. When I straightened up, I heard a sudden buzzing noise directly behind me. I whirled around, then smiled. A ruby-throated hummingbird was hovering in midair, so close I could've reached out and touched him. He paused there—sizing me up, I thought, trying to decide whether I was friend or foe or flower—then darted away.

That hummingbird reminded me of kingfishers swooping along a riverbank, making their odd clattering sound in flight, and kingfishers reminded me of trout rivers.

At the Deerfield, my favorite trout stream this side of Montana, the trout would be sipping mayflies on a beautiful day in June, and I could be there by early afternoon.

I didn't want to think about Kaye Fallon's sprawled body, emptied of its lifeblood, smashed and sliced in the living room of her own home. I didn't want to consider the possibility that her husband—my client—had done that to her, and whether or not he actually had, that he was a suspect and it was my job to defend him. I just wanted to go fishing.

Not today.

A realtor's red-white-and-blue Apartment for Rent sign hung on the chain-link fence in front of the big square three-decker that Mick Fallon now called home.

Half a dozen aluminum trash cans were jammed into one corner of the porch. Two unpainted wooden rocking chairs sat facing each other in the other corner, and a row of plastic flower pots were lined up on the rail with brown plants drooping out of them.

Although I'd never been inside, I knew that Mick had the top floor flat, the cheapest and smallest in the rickety old tripledecker. I opened the front door, stepped into the tiny inside entryway, and hit the bell for apartment three. A minute later I heard heavy footsteps coming down the inside stairs.

The door opened, and a man I'd never seen before stepped into the entryway. "Please," he said, "will you people just leave him alone?"

He wore a gray summer-weight suit, pale green shirt, blue-and-green necktie. He was a couple of inches shorter than me, neither fat nor skinny, brown hair, brown eyes, neatly trimmed mustache, glasses. An utterly nondescript guy.

He was peering over my shoulder. "Where are the rest of them?" he said.

"The rest of who?"

He frowned at me. "Who are you?"

"Suppose we introduce ourselves," I said. "Then maybe we can start over again. I'm Brady Coyne."

He cocked his head, looked me up and down, then nodded. "You're his lawyer. Jesus, I'm sorry. I assumed—"

"What, that I was a reporter?"

He nodded. "They've been here all morning, swarming all over the sidewalk, creeping around out back, double-parking their vans on the street. Mick's up there crying his eyes out, and these—these *monsters* are banging on the door and yelling for him to come down and talk to them." He blew out a long breath, then held out his hand. "I really apologize. I'm Lyn Conley. Mick's best friend."

I shook his hand. "Good of you to be with him."

He shrugged. "I was up all night with my wife. I tried to call Mick early this morning, but he wasn't answering. I figured he could use some company, so I came right over. He's a mess." He smiled. "I guess you know that. You were with him last night."

"Conley," I said. "Gretchen . . . ?"

He nodded. "My wife, yes. She's the one who found Kaye's body."

"How is she doing?"

"Better. She's calmed down a little. Her mother's with her now. Look, Mr. Coyne, Kaye and Mick are—were—our best friends. Our families were very close. Kaye was—well, everybody loved Kaye. You met her?"

"Just once," I said. "Not under the most favorable conditions."

He nodded. "The deposition. Sure. Well, that's your loss. She was warm and funny and just a terrific person. I cannot imagine anyone wanting to do anything except hug her. And Mick?" He shook his head. "This is a terrible, terrible thing as it is. But the way they're playing this story on TV, it's as if Mick has been tried and convicted already. And that incident at the bar last night . . ."

"What's Mick told you?"

Conley shrugged. "He's a wreck. There's no way he killed her. You never saw a man who loved his wife like Mick."

"Well," I said, "I just came over to see how he was doing, maybe try to reassure him a little."

"I know he'll want to see you," said Conley. "Next time just ring and come on up. This door here doesn't lock."

I followed him up the narrow flight of stairs, which paused at a landing on the second floor, took a 180-degree turn, and climbed steeply to Mick's third-floor apartment. The entire stairway was lit by two bare sixty-watt bulbs, one in the ceiling at each landing.

The door at the top opened directly into the kitchen—cracked linoleum floor, open shelves above the sink, dirty white refrigerator, scarred wooden table in front of a sooty window that looked out onto a small weedy backyard and, beyond it, the back side of another three-decker. A door in the corner of the kitchen led out to a small porch. Soot—or just years of house dust—covered the windowsill, the top of the baseboard, the edges of the linoleum. Three rickety wooden chairs were pushed in against the table. Beer bottles and dirty glasses and dishes and pots and pans were piled in and beside the sink and on the table. It smelled of old cigar smoke, sweaty socks, stale beer.

"Mick's in the living room," said Conley. "Coffee?"

"Please," I said.

Conley picked up some beer bottles and dropped them in a trash basket that was already brimming over. "I keep telling him," he said. "He drinks too damn much. He doesn't watch out, he'll end up where I was."

I arched my eyebrows at him.

He nodded. "I've been dry for four years, seven months, and thirteen days. I came damn close to blowing everything."

"You think Mick's an alcoholic?"

"I see my old self in him." He shrugged. "He's not ready to face it. I don't know. Maybe this—" he waved his hand "—this tragedy will make him see the light."

"You don't think . . . ?"

"What, that Mick killed Kaye?" He shook his head. "No. Absolutely not." He found the electric coffee pot and began filling it at the sink. "He's in the other room. Coffee'll be ready in a minute."

Mick's living room was smaller than my bedroom. An old faded sofa, two ancient chairs, and a new big-screen console television made it feel cramped. A goldfish bowl sat on top of the TV, and a rather large blue fish hovered motionless in the water.

Aside from an insurance company calendar featuring an

Audubon bird print hanging behind the TV—it was still turned to May—there were no decorations in the room.

Mick was lying on the sofa staring up at the ceiling. The television was on but muted, tuned to an exercise show. A muscular young brunette in skimpy Spandex was leading a gang of senior citizens in a slow-motion aerobics class.

Mick lifted his head. "Hey," he said.

"How you doing, Mick?"

He let his head fall back. "You seen the TV this morning?"

"No." I sat in the wing chair. A spring poked at my left cheek through the upholstery.

"Well, you should. You're on it. You're a fucking hero, man. You saved poor Skeeter O'Reilly's life from a crazed, knife-weilding, wife-killing monster at an early-morning hostage-taking. They're already debating whether they should restore the death penalty specifically for me. They got some footage from outside Skeeter's—you arriving with Horowitz, going inside, us coming out, me getting cuffed. Somehow they even got some of the conversation Horowitz and I had on the damn telephone. How in hell did they do that? Horowitz give it to 'em?"

"Of course not," I said. "They're expert snoopers, that's all."

Mick shook his head. "And then they showed the crowd gathered outside our house—mine and Kaye's—in Lexington, with all the police cars there, lights flashing, the EMTs loading Kaye's body bag into the back of an ambulance. They interviewed some of my old neighbors, people I've known for twenty years, friends whose kids played with my kids, folks who we had neighborhood barbecues and yard sales with. Know what they're saying?"

"They're saying," I said, "that Mick Fallon was a loving husband and a good father and they never would've guessed he could do something like this."

Mick turned his head and smiled quickly. "Exactly. Like, well, he obviously did it, and we sure are surprised."

Lyn Conley came into the room. He handed me a mug of coffee, started to sit in the other chair, then straightened up. "Oh," he said. "Am I interrupting?"

I waved my hand. "Not at all."

"Lawyer-client conversation?"

"No. Friend-friend conversation." I took a sip of coffee, then lit a cigarette. "I'd like to talk to your wife," I said to Conley.

He frowned. "Why?"

"He thinks I'm gonna be arrested," said Mick.

I shrugged. "I want to be prepared, that's all." I turned to Conley. "Gretchen—Mrs. Conley—was Kaye's best friend, right?"

"Yes," said Conley. He glanced at Mick. "We were all best friends. The four of us. I don't know what kind of shape Gretch is in to talk to anybody, though."

"I imagine the police spent some time with her."

"Hours."

"The whole experience must've been horrific for her," I said. "But she's an important witness. I've got to interview her. I was hoping sometime today or this evening . . ."

He nodded. "I guess it's important. Why don't you come by around seven, seven-thirty. I'll give you directions."

He went back into the kitchen, and a minute later returned. He handed me a piece of notepaper. "It's not hard to find," he said. "I wrote our phone number there, too."

I folded the paper, jammed it into my jacket pocket, and fished one of my business cards from my wallet. "If you need to reach me," I said, handing it to him.

He nodded, then turned to Mick. "I gotta get to the office, my friend. Anything I can do?"

Mick shook his head. "Appreciate everything, man. Give my love to Gretchen. Tell her how bad I feel that she had to . . ."

"I will." Conley held out his hand to me. "Good to meet you, Brady. See you tonight."

We shook hands, and then he left.

I turned to Mick. "Get up. We've got things to do."

He lifted himself onto one elbow. "I don't feel like doing a damn thing, Brady."

"I want to get this place cleaned up, and I don't intend to do it by myself."

"Oh, fuck the place."

I took off my jacket and draped it over the back of the chair. I rolled up my cuffs as I headed for the kitchen. "Get your ass out here," I said. "This is a dump."

I started moving the dirty dishes from the table to the sink. A minute later Mick appeared in the doorway. "My wife's dead and you want to clean up the kitchen?"

"Yeah," I said. "Right now, that's exactly what I want to do."

He frowned at me, then shrugged. "You rather wash or dry?"

An hour later we had the dishes all washed and put away and a fresh pot of coffee brewing.

On our way back into the living room, Mick paused at the TV. He bent over and tapped the goldfish bowl with his fingernail. The blue fish tilted its face to the top of the water.

Mick turned to me. "Erin gave him to me when I moved in here. To keep me company, she said. My daughter."

I smiled.

"I call him Neely. Named him after Cam Neely. Helluva hockey player, Neely. I ran into him a couple times at Skeeter's. Would've had a great career, weren't for bad wheels."

"He had a pretty good career as it was," I said. "But I don't exactly get the connection. A blue fish and Cam Neely?"

Mick shrugged. "No connection. Good name for a fish, that's all." He picked up the little fish food shaker and sprinkled some onto the water. Neely began to gobble the flakes off the surface. He reminded me of a trout sipping mayfly spinners off a slow-moving stream.

Mick tapped the bowl again, smiled, then slouched into one of the chairs. I sat on the sofa.

He looked at me and spread his hands. "Okay, so the dump's cleaned up and the goldfish is fed. So what's the point?"

"The point," I said, "is that you've got to live your life. We can't do anything about what happened. It couldn't be more tragic, but it's done. I know you've got to mourn Kaye, and you should. But you've still got to eat and take care of yourself and get through the days."

"I really don't want to do anything," he said. "I just want to go to bed and stay there."

"Sure," I said. "It was a late night."

"I mean, like forever."

"What good would that do?"

"What harm?"

"Look, Mick," I said. "Somebody murdered Kaye. It wasn't you, okay, but it was somebody. Now aside from the fact that I'd just as soon you weren't convicted of it, I think both of us would like it best if the actual murderer was found. Don't you want that?"

He cocked his head and frowned at me as if that were a new idea. Then he nodded. "Well, sure. God damn right I do."

"Here's what I think, then," I said. "I know Horowitz. He's a good cop. One of the best, actually. But he's seen a helluva lot of homicides. To you, this is the worst thing that's ever happened. To Horowitz, it's just one more in a long string of tragedies that he's had to investigate. Want to know something?"

"What?"

"Probably three-quarters of the cases Horowitz investigates are domestics. Husbands and wives, boyfriends and girlfriends, ex-spouses, children. Now I know Horowitz is open-minded, fair, and thorough. He's not likely to cave in to political or media pressure. But—"

"But he's got me," said Mick.

I nodded. "Objectively, you're a great suspect, Mick. You've got no alibi for Sunday evening, you were in the process of getting divorced and probably cleaned out financially, you were upset with Kaye, and your behavior at Skeeter's last night was—well, it was bizarre, to say the least."

"So what're you saying?"

"I'm saying that Horowitz is human. The cops like to say, 'The commonest things most commonly happen.' When a wife is murdered—especially when the murder is obviously passionate—most commonly it's the husband who did it. They've got a good circumstantial case against you already. God knows what they'll find when they get their forensics and physical evidence and talk with witnesses. But you've got to be prepared for the possibility that they'll arrest you."

He shrugged. "It's a certainty, if you listen to the TV."

"If I'm going to help you," I said, "you've got to help me."

"What can I do?"

"Well," I said, "the question is simple. Who killed Kaye? Think about motive, means, and opportunity. Start with motive."

"Well, there's the bookies I owe. I guess they'd have a motive to whack me. But Kaye . . ."

"Besides them," I said.

He shook his head. "I don't know anybody . . ."

"Mick," I said, "*somebody* killed her. That's a fact. Whether they did it in a sudden rage, or whether they planned it out, we don't know."

"Nobody would want to hurt Kaye," he mumbled, and when he looked up at me, I saw that his eyes had begun to brim with tears.

"I'm sorry, Mick, but we know that's not true. Because somebody did kill her. Now listen to me. You can't afford to lie around here feeling sorry for yourself. I want you to focus on the fact that somebody murdered your wife."

74

He nodded.

"I don't want you to stop thinking about that, okay? Some bastard out there killed Kaye. You should be angry. I want you to feel it. Put that anger to work for you. Can you do that?"

"Yeah," he said. "I guess so." He shook his head. "I just can't think straight right now."

"That's all right. It's been a long night. But your job is to help me. Anything you can think of, tell me. Doesn't matter how unimportant it seems. Anybody she had an argument with, any old grudges, no matter how trivial they seem to you. Anybody and anything. And I also want you to think about every move you made on Sunday evening. The ME is placing her time of death sometime between eight P.M. and midnight on Sunday. He'll probably be able to narrow it down when he finishes . . ." I waved my hand in the air.

"The autopsy," said Mick. "Go ahead. Say it."

I nodded. "Anyway, the point is, if there's any way we can prove you were not in Lexington when Kaye died, you're home free."

"I didn't go near Lexington. I was here all night."

"I know. We just need some way to prove it. Maybe something will occur to you." I stood up and put my jacket on. "I've got to get to the office. I suggest you take a shower, pull down the shades, and get some sleep. Shut the ringer off your phone but turn your answering machine on. I'll check in with you later on. Okay?"

"Yes. Okay."

I held out my hand to him, and he took it. "I'll be in touch." I opened the door leading down the stairway.

"Hey, Brady?"

I turned.

He lifted his hand. "Thanks, bud."

# SIX

I could tell Julie was upset by the angle of her neck and the hunch of her shoulders and the way her fingernails clicked on the keyboard of her computer. Of course, the fact that she didn't look up and say "Good morning" when I walked into the office was also a clue.

I went over to her and kissed the top of her head. "Morning, boss," I said breezily.

She kept typing—faster, if that was possible.

"Any calls?" I said. I rummaged in the In box, thumbed through the morning's mail, wandered over to Mr. Coffee, poured myself a mugful. "Want some coffee?"

"Check the time," she mumbled.

"Huh?" I looked at my watch. It was nearly one o'clock in the afternoon. "Oh, okay. Good afternoon, then."

She stopped typing, swiveled around, and glared at me. "It's been a bloody zoo," she said.

"Sorry. I—"

"The damn phone's been ringing off the hook. You're quite the hero. Let's see." She picked up a notepad and squinted at it. "Marisa Matson from the *Globe*, Bob DiVari from the *Herald*, Channels Four, Five, Seven, and Sixty-eight—they're all looking for exclusive interviews. Oprah wants you this afternoon, and—"

"Oprah?"

She looked up at me from under her frown. "No. That was a joke."

"Well," I said, "I'm glad you're in a joking mood. As for me, I—"

"I am *not* in a joking mood," said Julie. "I am extremely annoyed, in case you couldn't tell. Mrs. Wadley flounced in at precisely her appointed time, and—"

"Oh, shit." I slapped my forehead. "Mrs. Wadley. I completely forgot."

Julie gave me that smile that could mean she loved and admired me, but that sometimes meant she didn't know how she put up with me and was seriously considering not doing it anymore. "You could've at least called, you know."

"I'm sorry," I said in my smallest, most sincerely apologetic voice. "No excuse."

"I covered for you, of course," she said. "I told her you'd been involved in a hostage situation last night, that it had been very harrowing, that you had left a message for her, and that it was my fault for not calling and rescheduling. She seemed pleased to have a hero for a lawyer." She let out a long sigh. "Yes, I'll have some coffee, thank you."

I poured a mug for Julie and brought it to her desk. "What'd you tell those media people?"

"I told them to go pound sand. In the nicest possible way, of course."

I smiled. "I can't talk to them. It concerns my client."

"Well, you know that, and I know that, and I think even they know that. It didn't faze them. But that's what I told them. I suspect they will not surrender that easily."

78

I patted her shoulder. "Well, hold the fort. It won't last long. Tomorrow it'll be yesterday's news." I turned for my office. "Hold all calls for a while, okay? I need to take a deep breath."

"You've got the Farnsworths at three, don't forget," she said.

"Oh, yeah. Their new will."

"Everything's on your desk ready to go." Julie started to look down at her keyboard, then her head jerked up. "Oh, wait."

"Yes?"

She hesitated, then smiled. "Nothing. Go ahead. Take your deep breath."

I pushed open the door into my office and let it shut behind me. I started for my desk, then stopped. Standing directly behind it, looking out the window, was a blond woman. Her back was to me—a slim, sleek, shapely back, wearing a pale green silky blouse and nicely tailored white slacks. I wondered why Julie had failed to tell me someone was waiting for me in my office.

"Hello?" I said.

She turned and smiled, and it felt as if I'd been punched in the solar plexus.

"Jesus," I whispered. "Sylvie."

"Hello, Brady."

I patted my chest. "I gotta sit down, honey. God. You're the last person I expected . . ."

I went around behind my desk. She held my chair for me and I slumped into it.

"You don't have a kiss for Sylvie?" she said softly.

She was standing directly behind me. Her fingers touched the back of my neck, and I could practically feel the heat radiating from that body that I'd known for nearly thirty years. I reached up behind me, steered her face down to mine, turned, and kissed her on the cheek.

Sylvie Szabo had been a freshman when I was a senior in high school. She was an extravagantly beautiful blonde even as a teenager, with a husky voice and a delicious accent and a penchant for hilarious verbal inventions that belied her intelligence and wit.

Sylvie had been a child—no more than a toddler—when her mother smuggled her out of Hungary during the 1956 revolution, but she had vivid memories of it. Explosions disturbed her dreams, even as an adult. I knew from personal experience that she sometimes kicked and thrashed and emitted strangled cries when she slept.

She'd been my first love—and lover—and I hers. She was fifteen, and I was eighteen, and back then I was positive that Sylvie and I would be together forever, although things hardly ever work out that way.

But we'd kept in touch through college, through my marriage, and afterwards. Sylvie had moved around. For a while after my divorce, she'd lived in Boston. We'd spent a lot of time together in those days. We loved each other in that special way that first lovers do, but with me and Sylvie, it was always like high school—fun and carefree and lusty.

Eventually we drifted away from each other. I'd gotten involved with Terri Fiori about the time Sylvie moved to New York to pursue her career as an illustrator of children's books.

That had been several years ago. Terri dumped me, and then Alex came along, and we eventually split, too. I hadn't heard from Sylvie in all that time.

Her fingers moved on my neck, touched my ears, began softly massaging my temples. "You're tense," she murmured.

"You always make me tense," I said.

She chuckled.

"I had no sleep last night," I said. "I'm tired and grouchy. I don't like surprises."

"Even me?"

"You're always a wonderful surprise, Sylvie. But I wish you'd called. I've got clients to see this afternoon, and afterwards I've got to meet with some people, and—"

She twirled my chair around so that I was facing her. She braced her hands on my shoulders and leaned down to me. "Poor Brady," she murmured. She bent closer until her lips touched mine. I looked into her smoky green, slightly tilted eyes. Freckles dusted the bridge of her nose. Her tongue flicked out, touched my lips. Then, abruptly, she straightened up. "You do look tired," she said. "We're getting old, aren't we?"

"You haven't changed," I said. "You still look like the laughing girl I saw in the corridor tiptoeing up to her locker wearing that little skirt and that tight sweater." I laid my head back on my chair. "Except your accent. Where'd your accent go?"

"Oh, Brad-ee." She smiled. "You always like Sylvie's sexy accent, yes?"

"That's more like it."

"I've been in New York," she said. "The accent, I guess it just went away. I didn't even notice."

"New York'll do that."

She combed the fingers of both hands through her hair. "I'll be in Boston for a couple of weeks."

"Great," I said. "Where are you staying?"

"The Ritz." She grinned. "I'm on expenses."

"Something good, sounds like."

She shrugged. "Maybe." She moved over to the sofa, kicked off her shoes, wedged herself into the corner, folded her legs under her, and smiled at me. "I couldn't be in Boston and not see my best old friend, could I?"

"You definitely couldn't do that," I said. I went over and sat beside her. "We'll have dinner sometime."

Sylvie cocked her head. "Sometime?"

"One day very soon. I promise."

She peered at me for a moment, then abruptly unfolded her legs, bent over, and slipped her shoes on. "I'm sorry," she said. "I'm keeping you from your work." She stood up, smoothed

81

her slacks against her thighs, then turned and frowned at me. "Did you get married when I wasn't looking?"

I shook my head. "No, honey. Close, though."

"Are you in love with somebody?"

I shrugged. "I don't think so."

She smiled. "A bad one, huh?"

"I blew it, Sylvie. It could have worked. But I sabotaged it."

"Do you want to tell Sylvie all about it?"

I looked up at her. "Yes." I nodded. "I'd really like to."

"Well," she said, "I'm at the Ritz."

She bent down, took my face in her hands, stared into my eyes for a moment, then kissed both of my cheeks and my mouth. Then she straightened up, turned, smiled quickly over her shoulder, and walked out of my office.


The Conleys lived in a big white hip-roofed colonial house on a winding, wooded country road near Nine Acre Corner in Concord. I never would've found it without the map Lyn Conley had drawn for me.

A gunmetal gray Lexus, a black Jeep Grand Cherokee, and a red Honda Accord, all new-looking and shiny, were parked side-by-side in the wide driveway in front of the attached three-car garage. A sprinkler rotated on the front lawn, going *tick-tick-tick* in the hush of the late suburban afternoon.

I parked on the road, got out, stomped on my cigarette butt, and went to the front porch. The inside door was open, and through the screen came the muffled *thump-thud* of rock music from some distant room inside.

I rang the bell, waited, and a minute later a face materialized on the other side of the screen. "Hello?"

She was short, on the pudgy side, fourteen or fifteen, I guessed. Her sand-colored hair was damp, and she was wearing a Michael Jordan basketball jersey and running shorts.

"I'm Brady Coyne," I told her. "I'm here to see Mrs. Con-ley."

"You that lawyer?"

"Yes."

"I'm Linda. Mom's upstairs. She might be asleep."

"I believe she's expecting me."

She shrugged, then turned and yelled into the house, "Hey, Daddy. That lawyer's here to see Mom." Then she disappeared.

A minute or two later Lyn Conley came to the door. "Brady," he said. "Come in, come in. Gretchen'll be down in a minute."

He pushed open the screen door and held it for me, and when I stepped inside he clapped my shoulder as if we were great old pals and steered me through the hallway and out onto the deck that hung off the back of the house. "Thought you could talk with Gretch out here, catch a little breeze. Mosquitoes won't be too bad for another hour or so. Beer or something?"

"Coke, if you've got it."

He nodded. "Have a seat. She'll be right with you."

The deck was furnished with a gas grill, a round table with a folded-up umbrella poking out of it, and half a dozen sturdy wooden outdoor chairs lined up along the railing. I sat in one of the chairs.

The Conleys' back lawn sloped down to a broad expanse of meadow, which gradually merged into marshland. The silvery ribbon of the Sudbury River glimmered in the distance. A pair of cardinals pecked at sunflower seeds in a feeder that hung from a big maple tree.

"Sir?"

I turned. A teenage boy—he looked sixteen or seventeen—was standing behind me holding a can of Coke and a tall plastic glass filled with ice cubes. He was about my height, but skinnier, of course. A silly blond mustache shadowed his upper lip. Otherwise he would've been a handsome kid.

I held out my hand. "Hi," I said. "I'm Brady Coyne."

He nodded and shook my hand. "I'm Ned. Here. Dad said you wanted a Coke." He handed it to me.

"This is great. Thanks."

He flopped into the chair beside me. "Boy, that's something, isn't it? What happened to Auntie Kaye?"

I nodded. "How's your mom doing?"

Ned rested his forearms on his knees and leaned toward me. "I don't know. She's been in the bedroom all day. I peeked in on her a couple times, but she was asleep. They gave her some sleeping pills or something."

"You know the Fallons pretty well?"

"Me? Oh, yeah. All my life. Their kids are a little older'n us, you know. Erin's like eighteen and Danny's about twenty. We're good friends. They're like us. Their family, I mean. Real close. My parents and Auntie Kaye and Uncle Mick still hang out. Well, they did, until they split." He shook his head and blew out a quick breath. "So dumb. Makes no sense, you know?"

"You mean, what happened to Kaye?"

"Well, jeez, yeah. That's unbelievable. Obviously. But what I meant was how adults think they've gotta choose up sides. It's like, okay, Dad can't be friends with Auntie Kaye anymore because that'd be disloyal to Uncle Mick, so Mom has to stick with Auntie Kaye. I mean, they all used to be really good friends. All of us did. Divorce really sucks." He looked at me. "Well, I guess murder sucks, too, huh? That why you're here?"

I nodded. "Mick is my client. I need to talk to your mother."

"Why?"

"I need to know what happened."

"It's pretty obvious, isn't it?"

"No," I said. "It's not obvious at all."

"How come they didn't arrest him?"

"Ned, I can't—"

He suddenly pulled his feet off the table and stood up. "Uncle Mick killed her, and the cops are dicking around, and you want

**84**

to get him off." He stood there, frowning down at me. "Right? He did it, right?"

I shook my head. "No, I don't think he did it."

"Who else, then? I saw on TV—"

"Neddie?" The soft voice came from behind me.

I turned. A woman—Gretchen Conley, I assumed—had stepped out onto the deck. She was a big woman, nearly as tall as Ned, fleshy and big-boned, with short brownish hair streaked with gray. She was wearing baggy jeans and a man's blue Oxford shirt with the sleeves rolled up above her elbows. Her face was puffy and her eyes were red—from crying, I assumed—but she gave me a little smile and nod.

Ned went over to her and put his arm protectively around her shoulder. "You don't have to talk to him," he said. "He's just some lawyer who's trying to keep a—a murderer out of jail. I told him you've been through enough already."

She looked up at him and patted his arm. "It's okay, sweetie. Really. I'm fine. Mr. Coyne needs to talk to me."

Ned frowned at her, then turned and glared at me. "Why don't you just leave her alone?"

"Ned, please," said Gretchen.

He shrugged. "Yeah, okay. I'm sorry. I didn't mean to upset you." He kissed her cheek, gave her a quick hug, and without another word he stalked back into the house.

Gretchen plopped into the chair beside me. "Teenagers," she mumbled. "I apologize for his rudeness."

"He seems like a good kid," I said. "He's upset, that's all. He's concerned about you."

She nodded. "He was very fond of Kaye. It's hard for him. For all of us."

Just then I heard a car starting up from the front of the house, the whine of an engine, the sudden squeal of rubber on asphalt.

Gretchen smiled and shook her head. "Well," she said, "I assume you want to talk with me about last night."

"I know you've gone over it all with the police," I said, "and I hate to have to put you through it again. But I'm Mick Fallon's lawyer—"

"It's all right," she said. "Please. Anything I can do that will help convict the monster who did this to Kaye . . ."

"Why don't you just tell me about Kaye."

Gretchen Conley and Kaye Fallon had been classmates and friends in college, and they'd settled in neighboring towns when they were married. Their families had gotten together regularly over the years, taken vacations together, grown into middle age together.

When Kaye and Mick split, Gretchen said, it was a shock to her and Lyn. It became awkward. She liked Mick, but she'd felt that Kaye needed support. So she and Kaye had started getting together, just the two of them. They met for dinner weekly. Mostly, Kaye talked about her confusion, how she still cared for Mick, but how he'd grown distant and inattentive, how the mystery and romance were all gone, and how she'd woken up one morning depressed to the point of suicide at the thought that she'd have to grow old married to Mick Fallon.

"Suicide?" I said.

Gretchen shrugged. "That was a figure of speech. Kaye was always a pretty upbeat person."

"So after they split," I said, "you didn't see Mick?"

"No. Lyn used to get together with him sometimes. He never came around here."

"And Lyn didn't keep his friendship with Kaye?"

She shook her head. "We wanted to keep them both as friends, but it felt as if we had to split them between us, take sides. Kinda silly, when you think about it."

"Was Kaye seeing anybody?" I said.

She gazed out over the meadow, shook her head, then shrugged. "Kaye was a very private person, even with me. There were some things we just didn't talk about."

86

"But she talked about her problems with Mick."

She cocked her head and smiled at me. "Those are things that women talk about, Mr. Coyne."

"So you don't know if Kaye had a boyfriend."

"No."

"Did it ever occur to you that she might?"

She shrugged. "It was none of my business. It was Kaye's business. If she'd wanted to talk about it, okay, I'd've been more than happy to listen. If she didn't . . ."

I nodded. "Did she ever indicate that she suspected Mick of cheating?"

"Well," she said with a smile, "it wouldn't really be cheating if they were separated, would it?"

"I guess it would depend on their agreement."

"As far as I know, they didn't have any agreement on that," she said. "Mick is a very jealous person. It wouldn't have been anything they could've discussed. Anyway, Kaye never said anything about Mick having a woman. He just wanted her back. At least, that's what she believed."

"Tell me about last night."

She told it to me pretty much the way Horowitz had. "I've never been so—so utterly shocked in my life," she said softly. "I was horrified. It was—it still is—an absolute nightmare. All that blood from such a little body." She shook her head. "Kaye was always so, so alive. It still doesn't quite seem real."

"You had a key to her house," I said.

She nodded. "She went away for school vacation week in February and asked me to feed her cat, water the plants."

"Did Kaye have a key to your house?"

"No. I never went away. Two kids, a busy husband . . ." She shrugged.

"Where did Kaye go in February?"

"Somewhere in Vermont, I think. It was sort of a spur-of-the-moment thing. She liked cross-country skiing."

"She went alone?"

Gretchen shrugged. "As far as I know."

"Did she talk about it?"

"Not much, actually. I gathered she didn't have that much fun."

"She didn't . . . ?"

"Meet someone?" Gretchen smiled quickly. "If she had, I doubt she would've told me."

"You know the police think Mick killed her," I said.

"It's logical, isn't it?"

"What do you think?"

She looked up at me. "Who else?"

"Mick says he didn't do it," I said. "If he didn't, somebody else did. You were Kaye's closest friend. Maybe she mentioned something to you."

"She was afraid of him," said Gretchen. "He was furious that she wanted to divorce him. He threatened her."

"Threatened her?"

"Yes. She told me that more than once he'd said he simply would not allow her to divorce him. After the deposition last week, he called her and screamed at her. Accused her of getting him in trouble, of trying to ruin him, said he wouldn't let it happen."

"You know Mick," I said. "Do you think he could do this thing?"

Gretchen stared out over the backyard. The shadows were growing long, and the sharply angled rays of the setting sun painted the meadow and marsh in rich glowing shades of orange. "Before the deposition," she said softly, "I'd've said no way. Mick loved Kaye more than any man I've ever known could love his wife, including my own husband. He adored her. But I think he believed she'd betrayed him, violated something sacred between them. And Mick always had a quick, awful temper. He's a huge man, you know." She looked up at me. "Lyn told me the same thing. That Mick just snapped after that deposition."

"Can you think of anybody else?" I said.

"Who'd want to murder Kaye?"

I nodded.

She smiled softly and shook her head. "No. She was a substitute teacher, Mr. Coyne. She played bridge, worked out at the health club, grew tomatoes, cried at old movies on cable, read Jane Austen novels. Mainly, she was a mother and a wife and a homemaker. She was sweet and funny and warm. Everybody loved her. You couldn't help it. People like Kaye Fallon don't get murdered."

I didn't say anything, and after a moment, Gretchen said, "I know, I know. They do and she did." She frowned. "Well, there was that boy . . ."

"What boy?"

"I don't know his name. Kaye taught at a regional high school out towards Worcester. She was what they call a permanent sub, which meant she worked every day wherever she was needed. She generally filled in for someone who was hospitalized or on maternity leave or something and going to be out for a long time. A couple years ago she filled in for a special ed teacher. One of those small classes full of misfits—what they euphemistically call 'special,' you know? Kids with emotional problems, A.D.D., dyslexia. Mostly she tutored them, helped them with stuff for their regular classes, made sure they got from here to there when they were supposed to. Anyway, I guess there was one boy who had quite a crush on her."

"What happened?"

Gretchen shrugged. "At first he'd come in after school when she was getting ready to leave, ask her for help. Then he'd walk her to her car, carry her stuff for her. He was older than the other students—eighteen or nineteen—history of truancy, had dropped out a couple times. I guess one time he tried to kiss her, and—"

"He tried to kiss her?"

"It was one of those times he walked her to her car. Kaye didn't take it very seriously, but when she told Mick about it, he threatened to go to the police if she didn't do something about it. So Kaye spoke to her principal, and he got that boy out of her class." Gretchen shrugged. "Kaye was awfully cute, and she was a very caring person. I can see why a boy might confuse her caring with—I don't know, with another kind of interest, I guess."

"Would Kaye flirt with a student?"

"Flirt?" She narrowed her eyes at me, then let them slide away. "Kaye was not a flirt. She was actually quite demure. But she was very attractive and warm. She could make you think you were the most interesting person in the world just by smiling at you. Kaye always got a lot attention from men. All her life. I don't think she was even aware of how men looked at her."

"So this boy might think—"

"Yes," she said. "That's possible."

"She never mentioned the boy's name?"

She frowned. "She might have. I don't remember. I'm sorry."

"Can you think of anybody else? Anybody at all?"

"Somebody who'd want to *kill* her?"

"We're not dealing with logic here, Gretchen," I said. "Just anybody she might've had some kind of conflict with. Somebody with a motive—no matter how twisted. Somebody who might've been angry with her."

Gretchen let her head fall back against the chair and gazed up into the darkening sky. "*I* used to get angry with her sometimes. But I loved her."

"So did Mick," I said.

"I can't think of anyone." She shook her head. "Just Mick, I guess."

# SEVEN

❖————————————————————————————❖

Around noontime the next day I went out to the reception area. Julie was on the phone. When she looked up at me, I arched my eyebrows at her, and she held up a finger.

A minute later she hung up. "So how's it feel, putting in a full morning at the office, actually accruing billable hours?"

"That's very funny." I give her a quick fake smile. "Listen. Would you see if you can get the principal of Dolley Madison Regional High School on the line for me?"

"Huh? Where's that?"

"Not sure, exactly. Somewhere out around Route 495, towards Worcester."

"So you can't call him yourself?"

"Sure I can. But in my experience, high school principals fancy themselves busy, important people, and they're more likely to take a call from someone who's at least equally busy and important. Busy, important people have their secretaries place calls for them. See?"

"Move over Machiavelli." Julie smiled. "So what'm I supposed to tell this principal?"

"Tell him Attorney Coyne must speak with him. Impress upon him the gravity of the matter, but say nothing about what the matter actually is. You're good at that."

"You got that right," she said. She grinned. "Gravity, huh? So what *is* the matter, actually?"

"It concerns the Mick Fallon thing."

Julie nodded. "Okay. That's certainly grave. I'll get right to it."

I refilled my coffee mug, went back into my office, swiveled my chair around so that I could gaze out the window and day-dream about trout streams and mayflies, and I'd barely gotten into it when my console buzzed. I rotated back to my desk and poked the flashing button.

"I've got Dr. Ronald Moyle on line two." said Julie. "The principal of Dolley Madison Regional High School his own self."

"Wow," I said. "The actual principal. Excellent."

I hit line two and said, "Mr. Moyle?"

"This is Dr. Moyle, yes."

"Excuse me. Sure. Look, um, Dr. Moyle. My name is Brady Coyne. I'm an attorney."

"Yes?"

"I need to talk with you."

"About what?"

"Oh, this can't be discussed over the phone, I'm afraid. I can be there at three, all right?"

"Three? When?"

"Today, of course."

He hesitated. "What'd you say your name was?"

"Coyne," I said. "Attorney Brady Coyne."

"Sounds familiar, but . . ."

"My name is in the paper now and then. So you can expect me at three. I'll need about an hour of your time."

"Oh, gee, I've got an appointment at three."

"How long will it last?"

"Half an hour at the most, but—"

"Three-thirty works for me. I'll see you then."

"Look," he said, "it would help if I knew—"

"I'll see you at three-thirty."

"Well, actually—"

"Unless you'd rather come to my office in Boston."

"No, no," he said. "Three-thirty's fine."

Dolley Madison Regional High School looked like a hospital—half a dozen joyless two-story interconnected rectangular concrete-and-brick structures with large opaque Plexiglas windows and a forest of chimneys and pipes and vents sticking out of the flat roofs. It was situated at the end of a long curving driveway off a wooded side road a little south of Route 2 and west of 495 on the town line between Loomis and Harlow. I'd found it by stopping at a Cumberland Farms on the outskirts of Leominster for directions.

I parked at a Visitors Only sign in the turnaround near what seemed to be the main entrance, although it was unmarked. I was right on time—three-thirty on the nose—and the place seemed deserted. A large sweep of lush green playing fields off to the right—a baseball diamond, a track, and two soccer fields—were empty. So was the big fenced-in parking area on the other side of the structure. No gaily chatting high school kids were wandering into or out of Dolley Madison Regional.

I figured classes had ended at two or two-fifteen. By now, all the kids were off to their afternoon jobs, or riding around in their cars, or scoring some dope, or getting laid, or whatever it is high school kids do on a sunny afternoon in early June when the birds are singing and summer vacation is only a couple of weeks away. Hanging around the campus was apparently not a popular after-school activity at Dolley Madison Regional.

I sat there in my car with the windows rolled down and smoked a cigarette, determined to walk into Principal Moyle's office late enough to make him sweat a little. I had nothing whatsoever against the man beyond the fact that he insisted on being called "Doctor." By my way of thinking, if you sliced into people's abdomens to remove malignant tumors or fitted their shattered tibias back together or delivered their babies, you had a right to be addressed as "Doctor," and that title should be distinguished from the one they conferred upon the earnest folks who'd passed classes in Educational Psychology and Modern Multimedia Techniques and Advanced Secondary Administration at the B.U. School of Ed.

I waited until quarter of four to go inside. I followed the Main Office sign to an open area barricaded by a chest-high counter. Behind the counter was a cluster of desks, and beyond the desks were three closed doors. A secretary sat at one of the desks. She appeared to be somewhere in her forties, with short permed brown hair and bright orange lipstick. She was frowning at a computer screen through half-moon glasses and rhythmically poking her chin with the eraser end of a pencil.

I cleared my throat. "Excuse me?"

She turned, pulled her glasses down to the tip of her nose, and squinted up at me. "Yes?"

"My name is Brady Coyne," I said. "I have an appointment with Mr. Moyle."

"*Doctor* Moyle," she said. She glanced up at the clock on the wall, then scowled at me as if I had shown her a note containing a patently trumped-up excuse for being tardy to gym class. "Well, I'll see if he's ready for you." She got up, went to one of the closed doors, tapped on the glass window, then opened it carefully and leaned her head inside. I heard the murmur of voices. Then she stepped aside and held the door wide open. "Come in, please. Dr. Moyle can see you now."

I went around the counter, wended my way among the desks, and slipped past the secretary, who continued to hold onto the door as if it might otherwise get away. "Thanks," I said to her.

"Quite all right, sir," she said with a little sigh, implying that it actually had been a major ordeal for her.

Ronald Moyle stood up from behind his desk, smiled, and said, "Mr. Coyne. Hello." He leaned over his desk and held out his hand. I took it. His grip was manly enough, and he maintained excellent eye contact throughout, which I figured he'd been taught in his second-year graduate seminar on Public Relations and Crisis Management.

He was younger and more rugged than I'd expected. He wore chino pants and a checked shirt with the sleeves rolled halfway up his forearms, no jacket or necktie. Somewhere in his late thirties, I guessed. Shorter than me, but broad-shouldered and slim-waisted and fit. Sandy hair just beginning to form a widow's peak over his forehead, dark intelligent eyes, long crooked nose, hesitant smile.

A silver-framed portrait of himself along with a severe-looking dark-haired woman and two chubby grammar school girls sat on his desk. Behind it hung two diplomas. The doctorate was from Harvard. Okay, not B.U.

He came around from behind his desk and waved at a pair of leather chairs. "Let's sit," he said.

We sat—under a framed reproduction of an oil painting of Dolley Madison, if I wasn't mistaken. She was stitching together an American flag. "Mr. Moyle," I began. "Excuse me. Doctor."

He smiled quickly. "Ron," he said. "Please. And I have a pretty good idea why you're here. Mrs. Fallon, right?"

I nodded. "I'm her husband's attorney."

"I know. I did a little checking." He shook his head. "This is a terrible, shocking thing. Our students are very upset. Well, all of us are, of course. Kaye was very popular. We've had a moment

95

of silence in her memory every morning this week in homeroom. Some of the kids are talking about starting up a scholarship in her name."

I smiled and nodded.

"I know she'd been through a lot lately," he continued. "Separating from her husband, the divorce pending. She found fulfillment here at Madison, Mr. Coyne. Our little community was like a family for her, I believe. Kaye was just a wonderful person. Warm, patient, caring. Everybody loved her. She was a good teacher, very dedicated, very versatile. I could assign her to anything and feel confident that she'd actually teach something. Most subs, you know, the best you can hope for is that they take accurate attendance and keep the kids in their seats." He waved the back of his hand at me. "Well, I don't guess you wanted to see me about Kaye's professional qualifications."

"Actually," I said, "I'm trying to figure out who murdered her." I noticed a square glass ashtray on the corner of his desk. "Okay if I smoke?"

He grinned. "Madison is a strictly a no-smoking campus, Mr. Coyne. But I'll tell you a secret. Late in the afternoon, when everyone is gone except me, I sometimes pull the blinds, lock the door, and puff on a cigar. I hope no one ever sees me, of course. But if they did, I guess I wouldn't mind being an object lesson in independent thinking. Hell, I'm the damn principal, and I am frankly appalled at the extremes to which political correctness has gone. We've got three pages of guidelines in the student handbook, and it's even infiltrated the curriculum. There are community watchdog committees, for heaven's sake. I must get a dozen complaints a month about some poor history teacher who hasn't given equal billing to the Native American or the African American or the Greek American heroes and heroines who made this country great, or about some veteran Brit Lit teacher who spends more time on Shakespeare than on female poets." He smiled. "Why do you think they named this school after a president's wife? Sometimes I just want to smoke a cigar, you know? It makes me feel like an autonomous human being. Go ahead. Smoke if you want."

I lit a cigarette and held out my pack to Moyle.

He waved it away. "I thought Kaye Fallon was murdered by her husband."

"He hasn't been arrested for it," I said.

"Innocent until proven guilty, huh?"

I nodded. "Something like that. I happen to think he *is* innocent, and—"

"And you're trying to figure out who really did it," he said. "So how can I help you?"

"To be precise," I said, "I'm trying to round up ammunition for the defense, anticipating the possibility that Mr. Fallon could be arrested."

Moyle frowned. "I don't believe I ever even met the man. I don't think anybody here at Madison did. Kaye lived in Lexington, you know, which is a whole different world from our little blue-collar communities out here. She drove in every day, did her job, and left."

"But she was well known here."

"Oh, sure."

"Popular, I think you said."

He nodded. "I said she was loved."

"By the faculty as well as the students?"

"Well, Kaye wasn't much for socializing in the faculty lounge during free periods, and I'm not sure she had any close friends among her colleagues. But I'm positive she had no enemies, if that's what you mean."

"To tell you the truth," I said, "I don't know if that is what I mean. I'm just trying to track down people who knew Kaye." If I'd wanted to tell him the actual truth, I would've asked about the boy Gretchen Conley had mentioned, the boy who'd tried to kiss her. But I wanted to see if Ronald Moyle would volunteer that himself.

He stared up at the ceiling for a minute. "Well," he said, "I guess I knew her better than anybody. She wasn't in any one department. As a sub, she circulated to wherever I needed her. Most mornings she reported right here to me, and I sent her off. I hired her to substitute for one of our math teachers, oh, seven or eight years ago, I guess it was, and then three years ago I offered her the position of permanent sub."

"What's a permanent sub?" I said.

Moyle waved a hand in the air. "You come in every day and you cover anything that needs to be covered. Most days, you're on duty every single period. It's a lousy job, actually, but you'd have thought I'd told Kaye she won the Publisher's Clearinghouse Sweepstakes. She started down at the bottom of the salary schedule, but it gave her a regular paycheck." He smiled. "When she told me she was getting a divorce, she seemed very grateful to have a secure source of income."

"Did she express that to you directly?" I said.

He cocked his head at me. "Well, yes, actually. She came to me sometime this past winter and point-blank asked if her job was secure. I told her I intended to put her name in for tenure. She seemed very pleased. I inferred she did not feel confident that her husband would be able to support her." Moyle arched his eyebrows at me, asking for confirmation.

I did not bite. "Was there anybody on the faculty who she was friendly with, had a relationship with?"

"I can't think of anybody. Like I said, she didn't socialize much. A substitute teacher doesn't get much opportunity for socializing."

"How about you?" I said. "Would you say you had a relationship with her?"

"Relationship?"

"Would you say you were friends?"

"I'm not sure what you're getting at," he said. "I was her principal."

"But she confided in you about her marriage, her pending divorce, her financial insecurity."

"Well, yes. In the context of her job. I don't see—"

"I'm not accusing you of anything," I said quickly.

"If you're asking me if she ever mentioned anyone who might want to murder her," he said, "the answer is no. Not her husband, certainly no one here on the staff. Not anyone. If you're asking me if I myself had any reason to—to harm her, the answer is emphatically no." He cocked his head at me. "Were you asking me that?"

I waved my hand. "Of course not." I smiled reassuringly. "What about students?"

"Students?"

"Yes." I nodded. "Students."

"Who might have reason to . . . ?"

"Yes."

He frowned. "I can't . . . Well, there was one boy." He shook his head. "No, that's absurd."

"Maybe not," I said.

"It was a year and a half ago," he said slowly. "In the fall. Not too long before Kaye separated from her husband, as I recall. This boy apparently had quite a crush on her. Lingered after school, walked her to her car. That sort of thing. Finally Kaye told me about it. She said her husband was concerned."

"And what happened?"

"She was covering for one our special ed teachers who'd taken a maternity leave. I needed her to handle that class for the entire term. So I transferred the boy out."

"And that was the end of it?"

He shrugged. "I believe so."

"Did the boy actually do anything? Threaten Kaye?"

"Not as far as I know. She was quite fond of him, actually, very apologetic that she had to speak to me about it."

"And what about the boy? How'd he react when you switched him?"

"I don't remember any unusual reaction." Moyle combed his fingers through his hair. "Will Powers was his name. Actually, he dropped out of school shortly after that."

"Do you ever see him?"

"Last I knew, he was working the pit at the Jiffy Lube." He turned to face me. "Look, Mr. Coyne. Will Powers has a learning disorder. He's quite bright, but he doesn't process information in the normal way." He laughed quickly. "Sorry. 'Process information.' Jargon. What I mean to say is, the boy reads at about the fourth-grade level, okay? But he's not unstable or emotionally disturbed or antisocial. He's a pretty good kid who probably only connected with one teacher in his entire educational experience. He was held back a couple times in elementary school, ended up with younger kids as peers. A bit alienated, some minor acting-out behavior, but not really what you'd call a troublemaker. We have a lot of kids like Will. Sometimes we get somewhere with them and sometimes, I'm afraid, we fail. Will might've graduated and gone on to college if he'd had Kaye Fallon working with him. But . . ."

"Did Kaye tell you Will tried to kiss her?"

"Huh? Kiss her? God, no. She said nothing like that."

Moyle shook his head. "Where'd you hear that?"

I waved my hand. "Secondhand information, Ron. What we lawyers call hearsay. Maybe it's just a rumor."

"Well, I never heard that rumor, but even if it's true, it doesn't mean—"

"No," I said quickly. "It doesn't mean a thing. Still, I'd like to talk to Will Powers. So how do I get to this Jiffy Lube?"

When I pulled out of the school's driveway, I found myself at a figurative as well as a literal crossroads. Take a right and I'd be on Route 2 in ten minutes, heading west to the Swift River. A fly rod, a pair of waders, a fishing vest crammed with boxes of flies, and other essential gear always rode in the trunk of my BMW with me, and I had at least three hours of daylight left. In June, little sulphur-colored mayflies hatch on the Swift about the time the sun leaves the water, and the trout come to the surface to eat them. I could be there in an hour.

Turn left, bear right at the first set of lights, take another right, and I'd come to the Jiffy Lube where Will Powers changed motor oil for a living.

The choice should have been easy. I didn't fish nearly enough, whereas lately I'd had my fill of discussing other people's problems.

I took the left anyway.

I parked out front and went into the little Jiffy Lube waiting room. A television set was tuned to an afternoon talk show. A woman holding a sleeping infant on her shoulder sat in one of the plastic chairs reading a *Newsweek* magazine one-handed.

A big middle-aged guy in a dark blue shirt with *Frank* stitched over his pocket stood behind the counter. When I approached him, he leaned his elbows on the counter and grinned.

"How ya doin'?" he said. "Oil change today? Just pull your vehicle around to the second bay and we'll drive her in."

"Actually," I said, "I was looking for Will Powers."

"Yeah, well he's on the clock right now." Frank glanced at his watch. "He's got a break coming in about ten minutes, if you wanna wait."

I nodded. "I'll do that. Guess I'll let you change my oil while I'm waiting."

Frank nodded. "Park in front of Bay Two, leave the keys in it. I'll tell Will you're here." He frowned at me. "Who should I tell him?"

"He won't know my name. Friend of a friend. Tell him I'll be outside having a cigarette."

Frank shrugged. "Good enough."

I went outside, pulled my car in front of the middle bay, got out, went around to the sunny side of the concrete structure, and lit a cigarette. I smoked and leaned against the wall of the Jiffy Lube with my eyes closed, savoring the warm rays of the afternoon sunshine on my face.

"You lookin' for me?"

I snapped open my eyes and turned. He had black hair and black eyes and a black smudge on his chin, a wiry, quick-looking, handsome young guy in starched blue Jiffy Lube coveralls. He wore a baseball cap turned backwards and a hoop in his left ear, and he was wiping his hands on a dirty rag. *Will* was stitched over his left breast pocket.

"Are you Will Powers?"

He nodded. "Frank said something about a mutual friend?"

I held out my hand. "I'm Brady Coyne."

He make a point of slowly wiping each finger of his right hand with his rag. Then he took mine and gripped it quickly. "So who's our friend?"

"Kaye Fallon."

He frowned. "I heard she died."

"That's right. She was murdered Sunday night."

"Unbelievable, huh?"

"I heard you and she were friends."

"Where'd you hear that?"

I shrugged. "Actually," I said, "I had the impression that you and she were . . ." I let it hang there.

Will frowned. "Were what?"

I flapped my hands. "Close."

"Close? Fuck, man. What're you trying to say?"

"That's what I want to know," I said.

"How am I supposed to know what you're trying to say?"

He fumbled in his pocket, took out a pack of cigarettes, and lit one with a disposable plastic lighter. "Look," he said, exhaling a long plume of smoke, "I was in her class for a while, that's all. Hell, it wasn't even her class. She was a sub, you know? And then Moyle switched me to another class. And then I quit for good. I hardly knew Mrs. Fallon. Mostly I skipped her class anyway. I been in special classes all my life, and there was never anything special about any of them except you didn't have to do any work."

"How old are you?" I said.

"Nineteen."

"You're a man, then."

"Oh, yeah. I work forty hours a week, spend another forty trying to get the grease out of my hair. I sleep in my father's house, eat the food my mother cooks for me, and pay them room and board. I've got my own car, I registered for the draft, I could've voted last fall if I wanted to, and I even have sex once in a while. If that makes me a man, I'm a man. So what?"

"So you're old enough to answer some questions for me like a man, before the police do."

"Police, huh?" He smiled. "You trying to scare me?"

"No." I sighed. "No, I'm really not. I just want to talk to you about Kaye Fallon."

"I don't mind talking about her," he said. "Except there isn't much to say."

"Did you ever try to kiss her?"

He looked up at the sky and smiled. "Where'd you hear that?"

"Did you?"

He turned to me. "Don't be ridiculous. Why would I do that?"

"Because she was pretty? Because she was nice to you? Because you had wet dreams about her? How the hell should I know?"

"I never tried to kiss her, for Christ's sake. I hardly talked to

103

her." He dropped his half-smoked cigarette on the ground and stomped on it, then looked up at me. "You know, you really got it backwards."

"What do you mean?"

"Mrs. Fallon didn't exactly try to kiss me. But she kept trying to get me to come in after school for extra help, kept saying we should go somewhere, have coffee, talk about things, get to know each other." He took a deep breath. "Listen. When I was in her classroom trying to plow through some book or write something, she'd come up behind me, put her hand on the back of my neck, bend down so her face was practically touching mine and her boob was pressing against my shoulder, and ask some stupid question in this whispery voice, like it was real personal. She wore sexy perfume and these short little skirts, and she liked to sit on the edge of her desk and cross her legs. Sometimes when I'd be in there trying to read something, I'd look up and she'd be staring right at me." He shook his head. "It was way spooky, man. I mean, she was old enough to be my mother, you know?"

"But she was sexy and young-looking. And she liked you."

"Oh, it wasn't just me. She was all touchy-feely with everybody."

"How'd you feel when you got transferred out of her class?"

"Relieved, actually."

"So why'd you quit school?"

"What's that got to do with anything?"

"Did you ever try to see her again?"

"Who? Kaye?"

"Were you on a first-name basis with her?"

He flapped his hand. "That was her name. She called me Will. I didn't call her anything, actually."

"So did you—?"

"What, try to see her again? No. I quit school and got this shitty job, is what I did." He frowned at me. "Who the hell *are* you, anyway?"

"I'm Mick Fallon's lawyer."

"Mick?" He frowned, then nodded. "Ah. Her husband. The guy who did it. And you're trying to pin it on somebody else."

"Not really," I said, although he actually wasn't that far off. "I'm just talking to as many people as I can, people who knew her, to see if I can figure out what really happened that night."

"Well, if you're asking me who killed her, the answer is I don't have any idea. You probably ought to talk to Moyle."

"The principal? Why?"

He waved the back of his hand at me dismissively, then grinned.

"Are you saying . . . ?"

"I'm not saying anything," he said. "Talk to him."

"Do you remember where you were Sunday night?"

He looked at me sideways. "The night she was killed? Sure. I remember exactly."

"Where?"

"The same place I've been every Sunday night since May. Playing left field for the Jiffy Lube softball team, then eating hot dogs and pounding down a few Buds at Frank's house with the team. Ask Frank if you don't believe me."

"Oh, I'll ask him," I said. "And if you were me, what would you ask Dr. Moyle?"

"Do I have to spell it out for you?"

I nodded. "Maybe you better."

He held up both hands, palms facing me, and smiled. "Not me, mister. I'm a shitty speller."

"Look," I said. "If you know something . . ."

He laughed quickly. "Hey, I'm just a dumb high school drop-out. I don't know a damn thing. You can ask anybody." He glanced at his watch. "I gotta get back to the pit." He waved his hand quickly, turned, and disappeared around the side of the building.

# EIGHT

———◆———

I followed Will Powers around to the front, went into the waiting room, and approached the counter. "My car ready?" I said to Frank.

"You're the BMW?"

"Yes.

He shuffled some papers. "Here we go. How do you want to pay?"

I handed him my Visa card. "Will tells me you guys have a softball team."

He glanced up at me and grinned. "Oh, yeah. Slow pitch. You know, for us old wannabe jocks. We ain't much good, but we have fun."

"You're winning a few games, I hope."

He shrugged. "We pulled one out the other night."

"That was Sunday?"

"Right. Nineteen–seventeen." He grinned. "Pitcher's duel."

"Is Will any good?"

"Oh, hell, yes. Bats leadoff for us. Runs like a damn deer."

"So what time was your game over the other night?"

"Around six. Then we all trooped over to my house, grilled some burgers and dogs, had a few frosties like we always do. Tell you the truth, for most of us the game's more like an excuse to get together, you know?"

"It sounds like fun," I said.

Frank handed me a computer printout that listed all the parts of my car they'd looked at. "Sign right here," he said, jabbing a greasy finger at a line on the bottom.

I signed it and pushed it back to him. "Did Will go to your place after the game?"

"Sure. He always does."

"What time did he leave?"

"Will?" He rubbed his cheek. "Why? You checkin' up on him?"

"You might say that," I said.

Frank ripped the edges off the computer sheet and handed me a copy. "Come back in three months or three thousand miles, you get a discount. We'll send you a reminder in the mail." Frank picked up a clipboard and began flipping through the papers that were clamped onto it.

I took the sheet, folded it, and stuck it in my jacket pocket. "You didn't answer my question."

He continued to riffle through his papers. "Seems like you're trying to nail ole Will for something," he said, "and I don't want any part of that. Who the hell are you, anyway?"

"I'm a lawyer," I said, "and I'm not trying to nail anybody for anything. But I'd like to know how long he was at your house on Sunday, and if you won't tell me, you should expect the police to come asking."

He looked up at me with his eyebrows arched, then smiled and nodded. "I figure there's probably a right and a wrong answer to that question, huh?"

"Yes," I said. "The truth."

"Well," he said, "the truth is, I didn't really notice. I guess

108

everyone was about cleared out of there by ten-thirty, eleven o'clock. Will might've left earlier than that, I don't know." He narrowed his eyes. "That the right answer?"

"If it's the truth, I guess it is."

"So no cops are gonna come asking more questions?"

"I can't promise you that."

I thanked Frank and went out to my car, which they'd left out back. I slid behind the wheel and lit a cigarette. It was a few minutes after six. I might still get in an hour or so of fishing if I headed for the Swift River.

I wasn't seriously tempted. Fishing, for me, is a way to escape pressure. I want to lose all sense of time when I'm at a trout river. Sometimes I just lie on the bank, cradle my head in my hands, and study the clouds until my eyelids fall shut. Sometimes I like to sit on a boulder in the middle of the stream, watch the insects flutter over the water, try to spot the gray shadow of a trout lurking in the currents. I enjoy seeing kingfishers and swallows swoop over the water, hawks riding the thermals overhead. And when I locate a trout I'd like to catch, I want to feel that I've got all the time in the world to study his habits, divine his weaknesses, cast to him, change flies, shift my position, cast again.

I love fishing, I've finally figured out, because more than anything, it gives me the illusion of being a kid again, when time was a limitless resource that I could squander with a guilt-free conscience. One hurried hour on the Swift River, regardless of how hungry the trout might be, would not give me what I wanted.

So I pulled away from the Jiffy Lube and pointed my freshly oiled BMW at the city.


I got back to my apartment a little after seven. I shucked off my lawyer pinstripes, pulled on a pair of jeans and a T-shirt, and poured a couple fingers of Rebel Yell over a glass of ice cubes. I took my drink and my portable phone out onto the balcony, tilted back in one of the aluminum lawn chairs, and propped my heels up on the rail.

The Boston Harbor is a poor substitute for the Swift River, and the steel balcony that hangs off the side of my apartment building is no streamside boulder. But the tankers and ferries and pleasure craft that leave white wakes behind them look trout-sized from six stories up, and gulls and terns wheel over the water and cruise on air currents just like freshwater birds. It's water, and I never tire of watching it.

Mick's answering machine picked up, and when I told him I wanted to talk to him, he said, "Hey. I'm here."

"So how're you doing?" I said.

"Oh, boy," he sighed. "Erin and Danny both called. Danny's working at a hotel on Block Island and said he'd be home as soon as he could. Erin was driving out to San Francisco with a couple friends. She's heading for the airport in Boise, and she'll be here when she can get here. Danny heard it on the damn news, Brady. Erin called him from a pay phone just to say hello, and he told her. I've been trying to call both of them, but Erin hadn't arrived yet, and I guess Danny never got my messages. Jesus, what a mess. Imagine, hearing your mother's been murdered on the fucking news."

"How're they taking it?"

"Oh, they're pretty shook up. Christ, who isn't? But they don't think I did it. That's a plus, I guess." He hesitated. "They both asked about a funeral. I didn't know what to tell them."

"The police will have to release Kaye's body," I said.

I heard him sigh. "I don't know if I can do this."

"Do what, Mick?"

"Be all the things I'm supposed to be here. Father to two kids whose mother was murdered. Murder suspect. Hell, I'm having enough problems being the husband of a murdered wife."

110

"You've got friends," I said.

"Yeah. You've been great. So's Lyn. He dropped in again today, stayed for an hour. We just sat here watching TV. I couldn't think of a damn thing to say to him, and I guess he felt the same way. But it was better than being alone. Gretchen called, too." He snorted quickly. "She thinks I did it."

"Did she say that?"

"Oh, hell, no. She was sweet as pie. But I could tell. God knows what Kaye's been telling her about me."

"I'll be talking with Lieutenant Horowitz," I said. "I'll ask him about making funeral arrangements." I paused. "Mick, I wondered if you knew anything about some boy, a student who Kaye had removed from her class."

"Sure. What about him?"

"Can you remember exactly what Kaye told you about him?"

"He had a crush on her. Followed her around. Walked her to her car one afternoon, opened the door for her, and when she started to get in, he grabbed her and tried to kiss her. She pushed him away. When she came home, she was very shook up. I told her to get the kid the hell out of her class or I'd go to that school and deal with him myself."

"She said he'd tried to kiss her?"

"Yeah. That's what I just told you. Why?"

"He denies it, and the principal of the school hadn't heard anything about it."

"Well, of course he denies it. Maybe Kaye never mentioned it to the principal, I don't know." He paused. "You talked to them, huh?"

"Yes," I said.

"Old Perry Mason."

"That's me."

"Gonna track down the killer, huh?"

"Sure. You bet."

"You don't think this kid . . . ?"

"I don't know. What do you think?"

"All I can tell you for sure," he said, "is that it wasn't me." He was quiet for a minute. "Brady?" he finally said.

"Yeah?"

"What'm I gonna do?"

"About what?"

"My kids. What the hell am I supposed to say to them?"

"Tell them you love them. Hug them tight."

"But everybody thinks I killed her."

"Not everybody," I said. "I don't. And Erin and Danny don't, either."

"If they did," said Mick, "I'd shoot myself."

"Please," I said. "Don't do that."

After I hung up with Mick, I went into the kitchen and made myself a ham-and-cheese on rye, slathered with Grey Poupon. I took my sandwich back out onto my balcony and devoured it while the sky grew dark over the water and the stars started popping out.

I finished my sandwich, then tried Horowitz at State Police headquarters on Route 9 in Framingham. The receptionist told me he was off duty, and I declined to leave a message.

A couple of years ago, when I was involved in a case he was working on, Horowitz gave me a secret phone number. It rang the cell phone he carried in his pocket so I could reach him no matter where he was—at his desk, in his car, out on his boat, or in the bathroom. He'd warned me never to use it except in an emergency.

So I dialed it.

He answered on the second ring. "Who's this?" Not a warm and friendly greeting.

"Coyne."

"You know where I am?"

"Gee, no. Where?"

"Fenway fucking Park."

"What's the score?"

"It's on TV, Coyne, and you didn't need to call me to get the score." He paused. "So what's up? This better be good."

"Just a quick question," I said. "Has the ME pinned down the time of Kaye Fallon's death?"

"Eight to midnight Sunday. Why?"

"You might want to check on the whereabouts of a guy named Will Powers. He works at a Jiffy Lube out in Loomis. He's got no alibi for the latter part of the evening, and he might have a motive."

"Yeah?"

"Yeah." I told Horowitz about my visit to Dolley Madison Regional and my interviews with Ron Moyle and Will Powers.

"Okay," said Horowitz when I'd finished. He paused, and I heard the sounds of thirty-thousand people yelling.

"What happened?" I said

"Nomar just hit one into the triangle. Stand-up triple. You about done with me here? My beer's getting flat."

"When're they going to release Kaye's body?"

"No idea."

"You gonna arrest Mick?"

"You'll be the first to know," he said. "How's that?" He sighed. "Look. I appreciate your sleuthing, Coyne, and we can talk about the damn case, all right? But I'm sitting here in Section Twelve with a hot dog in one hand and a paper cup full of warm beer in the other and this goddamn phone squeezed against my ear, and Nomar's standing on third base with one out, and I been spending sixteen hours a day at the job, and right now all I wanna do is see if one of these bums can hit the ball far enough into the outfield so Nomar can make it home. Call me tomorrow."

"Well, okay. I'll—"

But he'd disconnected.

I put my phone on my lap and lit a cigarette. A bank of clouds obscured the line between sky and water toward the east, and a damp breeze had begun to blow up off the water, carrying with it the rich mingled low-tide aroma of seaweed, diesel fuel, mud, and salt. The dolorous dong of the bell-buoy out at the mouth of the harbor echoed in the damp night air.

I got up, went inside, pulled on a sweatshirt, then returned to my balcony. Information gave me the phone number for Ronald Moyle out in Harlow. I thought it was either brave or foolhardy for the high school principal to have a listed phone number, but I was grateful for it.

A woman answered—the severe-looking dark-haired wife in the portrait on Moyle's desk, I assumed—and told me cheerfully that Ron was out back and she'd be very happy to fetch him for me if I'd give her my name, which I did.

A minute later, he said, "Mr. Coyne?"

"Hi, Ron. Sorry to bother you at home."

"That's okay. What's up? Did you track down Will Powers?"

"Yes. Had a good talk with him. You were right."

"How so?"

"He seems like a pretty good kid. Too bad you couldn't hang onto him."

"I agree. I hate it when kids drop out."

"He says he didn't stalk Kaye Fallon, never tried to kiss her."

"Did I say he did?"

"You removed him from her class."

"I did. Based on what Kaye told me."

"Was Kaye an hysteric?"

"I certainly never thought so."

"Did she flirt with her students?"

"Is that what Will said?"

"I'm just trying to read between the lines, Ron."

"Well, I never observed anything like that."

"Did she flirt with you?"

"Huh? That's ridiculous." He paused. "She was very friendly and approachable, of course," he said slowly. "Good teachers

**114**

generally are. And she was certainly attractive. Always dressed well, paid attention to her makeup. But she was quite proper with everybody. Certainly with me."

"This afternoon you mentioned putting her name in for tenure."

"Right. I did."

"Did she get it?"

"Actually, no."

"Why not?"

"The usual reason, Mr. Coyne. Budget. The school committee didn't think it would be fiscally sound to grant tenure to a permanent substitute. In fact, they eliminated the position."

"What do you mean?"

"Kaye was without a job. Well, I could still use her as a regular sub, of course. On the usual per diem. Which I hoped to do."

"When did all this happen?"

"Just a couple weeks ago. I'd talked them into reconsidering, but they wouldn't change their minds."

"What did Kaye say when you told her?"

Moyle hesitated. "Actually, I never did tell her."

"She didn't know?"

"I suspect she heard it through the grapevine. I put it off, to tell you the truth. I hate to give people bad news. I think she was counting on that security. With her divorce and all. Anyway, I finally sent her a message in class, asked her to see me after school. She didn't show up."

"When was that?"

"Last week. Tuesday or Wednesday."

"Just a few days before she died," I said.

He sighed. "Yes."

"Why didn't you tell me any of this when we talked this afternoon?"

"I don't know. You didn't ask. It didn't seem relevant. Is it?"

"What?"

"Is it relevant?"

"I don't know," I said. "But if you can think of any reason why it might be, you should tell me."

"Well, I can't." He cleared his throat. "What are you thinking?"

"I'm just trying to understand Kaye, her life, people who knew her, that's all."

"But you drove all the way from Boston to see me in my office, then you turn around and call me at home . . ."

"Will Powers implied that you might've been, um, close to Kaye."

"Close?" He was silent for a moment. "That's quite an accusation to make of a principal."

"I didn't mean it as an accusation, Ron."

"Well," he said, and he made his voice low as if he didn't want to be overheard, "I had no personal relationship with Mrs. Fallon whatsoever. I would be delighted if you'd check up with anyone you can think of to verify that. And I've got to tell you, I resent it. You've got no right—"

"I said it wasn't an accusation," I said quickly.

"Look, Mr. Coyne. My daughters are here with their pajamas on. I always read to them at bedtime."

"That's nice. I envy you."

"If I think of anything, I'll let you know."

"Yes," I said. "You should."

By the time I hung up with Ron Moyle, a fine mist had begun to fall. I took the phone inside, sat at the table, lit a cigarette, and watched the fog and mist move over the water.

Then I dialed the Ritz and asked to be connected to Sylvie's room.

After a dozen rings, the switchboard operator, a woman with a faint Smokey Mountain twang, said, "Ms. Szabo does not appear to be answering, sir. Shall I keep ringing?"

"No," I said. "I guess she's not there."

"May I take a message?"

"No, that's all right. You don't know when she's expected in, do you?"

"I'm afraid not, sir."

I disconnected, put the phone on the table, and let out a long breath. I couldn't figure out whether I was disappointed or relieved.

# NINE

Sometime a little before noon the next morning, Julie buzzed me. "Attorney Cooper's on line one," she said.

"Got it," I said. I punched the button on my console and said, "Brady Coyne."

"Hi, Brady," she said. "It's Barbara. Barbara Cooper."

"How can I help you, Ms. Cooper?" Damned if I was going to fall into the first-name, buddy-buddy trap she was laying for me. The last time I'd talked with Barbara Cooper, she'd informed me that she intended to castrate Mick—figuratively, of course—in divorce court.

"You can't help me," she said. "I thought I might help you." She paused, and when I didn't say anything, she continued, "The state's attorney has subpoenaed the Fallon deposition. I thought you should know."

"Yes," I said. "Thank you."

"They also interrogated me at length. I cooperated fully."

"Sure," I said. "No reason not to."

"They wanted to know everything Mrs. Fallon had told me about her marriage, her husband, his finances, plus my observations of your client. Client privilege, it seems to me, does not apply here."

"Your client being dead."

"Right."

"Well," I said, "I have no problem with that. We're all after the same thing. My client is innocent."

"Of course he is," she said, and if she intended to be sarcastic, I didn't detect it in her tone. "Anyway," she said, "I just wanted—"

"To get it off your conscience," I said.

She chuckled. "You're a hard case, Brady. No, my conscience is not involved in this. Call it professional courtesy. I didn't have to call you."

"You're right," I said. "I appreciate it."

"If you were sincerely appreciative," she said, "you'd offer to buy me a drink sometime."

"Why?" I said. "What do you want?"

"Want?" I heard her sigh. "Believe it or not, I don't want a damn thing, except maybe a relaxing drink."

"I'll call you sometime," I said.

"You ought to," she said. "You probably think I'm some kind of ball-buster, but I can be pretty good company when I'm away from the office."

I didn't tell her that "ball-buster" was precisely what I thought she was. If Barbara Cooper wanted to have a drink with me, I assumed it was because she had an agenda.


Sometime in the afternoon I called Mick. Nothing had changed. He hadn't heard from Danny or Erin again, and he was still going batshit. I decided not to tell him that the state's attorney seemed to be putting together a case against him. No sense in upsetting him any more.

I left the office on foot around six-thirty, feeling quite virtuous at the dent I'd made in my paperwork. I stopped off for a burger and beer at Skeeter's, where I watched the first three innings of the Red Sox game, and got home around nine.

After I changed out of my lawyer clothes, I took the phone out to the balcony, lit a cigarette, watched a ferry chug across the harbor, and called the Ritz.

"I decided you weren't going to call me," Sylvie said when they connected me to her room.

"Of course I was going to call you. I tried last night, but you weren't there."

"Well," she said softly, "I'm here now. Where are you?"

"I just got home. Long day."

"Do you still walk to the office?"

"Usually, yes."

"You walk right past the Ritz, and you don't even stop to see if Sylvie's here waiting for you?"

"It would've been an inspired idea," I said. "Guess I've been pretty preoccupied lately."

"Ah, yes. That terrible murder that Brady must solve."

"I'm not trying to solve it, honey. I'm just trying to help my client."

"Brady is always such a helpful person."

"That sounded almost sarcastic, Sylvie. Has New York City turned you into a cynic?"

"Maybe it has," she said. "Or maybe I just thought you'd be happier to see me."

"You caught me at a bad time, but I *was* happy to see you. I do want to see you again, when I'm more relaxed. What about dinner tomorrow night. Say six-thirty?"

"I'll be waiting in the bar."

The phone woke me up a little before seven the next morning.

"Horowitz," he growled when I picked it up.

"Christ," I yawned. "Don't you ever sleep?"

"Hardly ever," he said. "Waste of time."

"So what's up?"

"Thought you might want to bring your client around this morning."

"I've got a lot of clients."

"You know the one I'm interested in."

"Why would I want to do that?"

"Listen," he said. "I'm doing you a courtesy here, okay?"

"You planning on arresting Mick?"

"I didn't say that. So you gonna bring him in, or do I send a fleet of squad cars over to his place with their sirens wailing and their flashers going?"

"Oh, I'll bring him over," I said. "I guess I'm just a bit speechless here at your unprecedented and uncharacteristic concern for his feelings, that's all. 'Courtesy' is a word I don't normally associate with you."

"Me, neither. Rather you didn't say anything about it." Horowitz chuckled. "Figure Fallon won't talk to us without you holding his hand anyway, might as well get the two of you here at the same time, save my boys a trip in the bargain."

"You going to tell me what this is about?"

"When you get here," he said. "Shoot for nine o'clock. Much later, there'll be sirens. I'll be at the Leverett Circle barracks."

I hesitated. "This for routine questioning?"

"Don't push me, Coyne. No questioning is routine. You know that."

"Does that mean you've got some new information?"

"Just bring your client here. And don't try to give me any lectures about discovery. I know the law as well as you do."

Horowitz hung up on me the way he usually did—without saying good-bye. I fetched a mug of coffee, brought it into the bathroom, and sipped it between showering and shaving and getting dressed.

Then I poured a refill and called Mick. When his machine answered, I told him to pick up, and when he didn't, I told his tape that he should get his ass out of bed and put some clothes on, because I'd be there in an hour. I didn't say why. No sense making him anxious.

I pulled up in front of Mick's three-decker in Somerville a little bit after eight. The Apartment for Rent sign still hung on the chain-link fence, and the trash barrels and wooden rocking chairs and dead flowers still decorated the rickety front porch.

I went into the cramped entryway and rang Mick's bell. A little square grate above the button indicated that Mick could speak to me through an intercom. I waited for a minute, then rang the bell again. He didn't answer.

Well, my phone call hadn't roused him from bed, and I guessed the doorbell wasn't doing the job, either. When I'd been there on Tuesday, Lyn Conley had said the door didn't lock. I tried the knob. He was right. So I climbed the two flights of dark, steep stairs up to Mick's apartment and knocked on the door that opened into his kitchen.

I paused, listened, knocked again, then called, "Hey, Mick. Wake up."

When he didn't answer or come to the door, terrible thoughts began to ricochet through my head. I pictured Mick's enormous, white, bloated body crammed into a bathtub full of red water. Mick hanging from a rafter, his face swollen and blue. Mick lying in his bed, an empty jar of sleeping pills and an empty bottle of Jack Daniel's on the table beside him. Mick sprawled in his leather armchair, a big smear of blood and brains on the wall behind him and a nine-millimeter automatic on the floor beside him.

He'd been holed up in this dreary place since Tuesday morning with only his tortured thoughts and his blue goldfish for company, dreading the moment when he'd have to face his children, imagining the accusation he might see in their eyes.

I tried the doorknob. It turned in my hand. I pushed the door open and stepped into Mick's kitchen.

Beer cans, booze bottles, plastic glasses, and coffee mugs filled the sink and littered the table, but I saw no dirty saucepans or plates or opened soup cans or half-eaten sandwiches in the two-day accumulation since we'd cleaned it up together. It looked like Mick had been drinking plenty, but had eaten nothing.

One of the wooden chairs had tipped over. I picked it up and pushed it back to the table. The door out onto his little porch was ajar. I pulled it shut. "Hey, Mick," I called. "Rise and shine."

I noticed the telephone and answering machine on the counter beside the stove. The red light on the machine was blinking slowly and steadily, indicating just one message. That was probably mine from an hour ago. Either Mick had been erasing his messages, or he'd been answering the phone before the machine picked up. Or maybe no one except me had called him.

I spoke his name again, and when he didn't answer, I headed into the living room.

The first thing I noticed was the overturned wing chair and the sofa, shoved at an odd angle against the wall. Then I saw the big wet splotch on the threadbare fake-oriental carpet in front of the television. Big shards and slices of glass were scattered over the puddle, and in the middle of the shattered bowl lay the corpse of Mick's blue goldfish. Neely, he'd called it, after the hockey player. His daughter had given it to him to keep him company. Neely's mouth was open, and his scales and his boggled lidless eyes were dull.

I muttered, "Oh, shit," and picked my way around the broken goldfish bowl to Mick's bedroom. The door was wide open.

Mick's bed was empty and the covers were thrown back, as if he had just gotten up. Something on the pillow caught my eye. A big brownish red splotch stained the pillow and the sheet. It

124

had to be blood. It looked as if it had seeped deep into the mattress. I gingerly touched it with my fingertip. It was dry and stiff.

I yelled for Mick again, although I didn't expect him to answer.

Neither he nor his dead body was in the bathroom, or in either of the two small closets, or out on the little back porch off the kitchen. I noticed that a narrow wooden stairway without rails led down to the porch off the second floor. A fire escape, I guessed. I wondered if it would hold Mick's weight.

I hurried down to the second-floor landing, banged on the door, and yelled, "Open up! It's an emergency!"

When no one answered, I remembered the Apartment for Rent sign. This had to be the empty one.

I took the stairs down to the first floor two at at time, then pounded the heel of my fist against the door to the first-floor apartment.

It opened almost instantly, and a short bald man wearing a sleeveless undershirt, baggy black pants, and bedroom slippers was glaring at me. "Hey, what's a-matter with you? You want me to call the cops, mister?"

"Yes, as a matter of fact, I do," I said. "Something's happened to Mick on the third floor."

"Whaddya mean?"

"I need to use your phone."

He cocked his head and peered at me through his round, rimless glasses. Then he shrugged. "Sure, right. Come on in."

He led me through a short hallway into a living room that was considerably larger than Mick's. Like Mick's, it was dominated by a big console television, which was tuned to a news program. The room was crammed with dark old furniture, and it smelled of burned bacon and raw garlic.

He pointed at an old-fashioned rotary telephone on a table beside the sofa, then turned the sound off the television.

I sat down and dialed the state police barracks at Leverett

Circle. When the receptionist answered, I said, "I need to talk to Lieutenant Horowitz. This is Attorney Brady Coyne. It's about an appointment I have with him."

A minute later, Horowitz said, "What's up?"

"You better get over here," I said. "Mick's gone, and there's blood."

"Okay," he said, instantly all business. "Where are you?"

"First-floor apartment." I gave him Mick's address, then arched my eyebrows at the bald man, who was standing in the middle of the room staring at me. "What's your name, sir?"

"Mancini," he said. "Anthony Mancini. This is my house."

"I'm with Mr. Mancini," I told Horowitz. "He's the landlord." I looked on the phone and gave him Mancini's telephone number.

"Both of you, sit tight," said Horowitz. "Don't touch anything or let anybody in. The Somerville cops'll be there in a couple minutes to secure it. I'll be right along. Okay?"

"Okay," I said.

When I hung up, Anthony Mancini said, "What's going on?"

"My name is Coyne," I said. "I'm Mick Fallon's lawyer. He's gone, and it looks like something might've happened to him."

"Whaddya mean, happened to him?"

"He's gone. There's blood on his bed. The furniture is tipped over. His door was unlocked."

Mancini crossed himself. "Holy mother of God," he murmured. "You think . . . ?"

"I don't know what to think," I said. "Have you heard or noticed anything?"

He shrugged. "Empty apartment between us. I hear nothing that goes on up on the third floor."

"Nobody coming up or down the stairs during the night?"

He held out his hands, palms up. "I sleep sound. I snore. My wife, she used to say the whole house rattled when I slept. She's been gone six years now."

"I'm sorry," I said automatically.

"Yeah, well she ain't dead, if that's what you mean. Gone, understand? Living with her sister in Revere."

I nodded. "So how well do you know Mick?"

He shrugged. "Nice guy, Mick. Quiet. Good tenant. Minds his own business, pays his rent on time. Big strong fella. He always helps me lug the trash barrels out to the sidewalk on Tuesdays."

"Have you talked with him at all this week?"

"Since . . . ?"

"Yes," I said. "Since his wife was murdered."

"The other night," said Mancini. "Not last night. Night before last. Wednesday. I took a bowl of macaroni and some garlic bread up to him. He said thank you, he'd already eaten. I asked if there's anything I could do. He just shook his head. Sad man. I feel bad for poor Mick. Terrible thing, what happened to his wife."

"Has he had any visitors in the past couple of days?"

"That one fella, in the suit and mustache, he dropped in a few times."

"Lyn Conley?" I said.

Mancini shrugged. "Don't know his name. Drives a nice car. Sorta gray? A whatchacallit . . ."

"Lexus?"

He nodded. "That's it. He was here yesterday, around suppertime. That was the last time I saw him. Stayed maybe an hour." Anthony Mancini scraped the palm of his hand over his whiskery cheek. "There were all those TV people, you know. That was Tuesday, huh? You were here."

"You don't miss much, then, Mr. Mancini?"

"I'm here all day long. Window looks right out on the porch. I hear anything, I take a peek. I saw you come in a little while ago."

"So what about last night?"

He shook his head. "I always go to bed at ten. Then I see nothing, hear nothing." He shrugged. "You want some coffee?"

"If it's already made, sure."

"Milk?"

"Black, please."

He left the room. I looked around. Over the television hung a large full-color painting of Jesus on the cross. His blood was bright crimson, much brighter than the dull brownish splotch on Mick's sheets. A bunch of palms was stuck behind the painting.

The bookcase beside the TV was crammed with paperbacks. From where I sat, it looked like they were mostly westerns and mysteries, with a few romance novels scattered among them.

Mancini came back carrying two heavy ceramic mugs. He handed me one, then took the chair across from me. "So what's gonna happen?" he said.

"The police will be here. They'll secure the area. They'll probably want to talk with you."

"They gonna take me down to the station again?"

"I don't know," I said.

He smiled. "Wouldn't mind. Little excitement, you know?"

"Did they take you to the station before?"

He nodded. "Day after Mick's wife was killed. They were asking me about Sunday night. If I'd seen Mick."

"What did you tell them?"

He cocked his head. "Am I supposed to tell you?"

"Yes. I'm Mick's lawyer."

"Well," he said, "I told them the truth. I didn't know whether Mick was home or not. He was here during the afternoon, but he coulda gone out when I was in the kitchen or the bathroom or something. Or after I went to bed." Mancini shrugged. "I wish I could help Mick out."

"Telling the truth is always best." I stood up. "I think I'll wait out on the porch. I need some fresh air."

"I'll join you."

I shook my head. "You should stick near the phone. The police might need to contact us."

He nodded solemnly. "Gotcha."

I went out and sat on the front steps, sipping Anthony Mancini's thick, bitter coffee. A minute later, a Somerville police cruiser squealed up and double-parked in front. Two uniformed cops got out and approached me. "Who are you, sir?" said one of them, a young red-haired guy with a David Letterman gap between his front teeth.

"I made the phone call," I said. "Brady Coyne. I'm Mick Fallon's lawyer."

"Okay," he said. "Anyone inside?"

"Just Mr. Mancini, the landlord. He lives on the first floor. I told him to stay right there."

"Sure. We know Tony." He turned to his partner. "Take the back. I got out here."

The other cop disappeared around the side of the house. The redhead stood on the front path with his back to me, surveying the neighborhood. "They don't tell us nothing," he said without turning to me. "Just come, secure the place, wait for the staties."

I didn't say anything.

"Must be something big, state cops takin' jurisdiction."

I lit a cigarette.

The cop looked over his shoulder at me. "So what's going on?"

I shrugged. "I don't know."

"Tony in some kind of trouble?"

"I don't think so."

He turned back to watch the street. "Fuckin' staties," he mumbled.

I had just finished my cigarette when a blue Ford Taurus, unmarked except for the portable blue flasher on the roof, pulled up in front. Horowitz got out of the passenger side, walked past the Somerville patrolman without acknowledging him, and stood in front of me. "Where?" he said.

"Third floor."

"You touch anything?"

I shut my eyes for a minute. "One of the kitchen chairs had tipped over. I picked it up and shoved it up to the table. The door out onto the porch was unlatched, and I shut it. I picked up the pillow and touched the bloodstain on the sheet. The molding around the door to the bedroom. Um, the doorknobs to the two closets and the bathroom and both sides of the doorknob into and out of the kitchen. That's it, I think."

Marcia Benetti, Horowitz's partner, strolled up to us. "Should we wait for the others?" she said to Horowitz, ignoring me.

"Yeah. You go on in there and baby-sit the guy in the first-floor apartment."

Benetti brushed past me and into the house.

Horowitz sat beside me. "Tell me everything you saw."

He had his notebook out. I reconstructed everything as well as I could from the time I'd arrived here.

"The rug," he said. "It was still wet?"

I nodded.

"But the blood was dry."

"Yes."

Just then two other unmarked vehicles, both with blinking blue flashers on the roofs, pulled in behind Horowitz's Taurus. He got up and went to the sidewalk to greet them. They talked for a few minutes, then all of them except Horowitz trooped past me and into the house. "You sit tight," he said to me. "I'm gonna have to talk to you again soon's we get a good look up there."

"How long?"

"As long as it takes, Coyne. Don't push me."

I shrugged, and Horowitz went inside.

I'd been sitting there for about half an hour when I became

aware of loud voices out on the sidewalk. I looked up and saw the Somerville cop holding Lyn Conley by his shoulders. Conley's face was red, and so was the back of the cop's neck.

I got up and went to them. "Hey, Lyn," I said.

He blinked at me. "What the hell is going on, Brady? Did Mick—"

"He's gone missing," I said.

Conley stepped back from the cop, scowled at him, tugged on the lapels of his suit jacket, then smiled quickly at me. "Thank God," he said. "I was worried that—wait a minute. What do you mean, missing?"

"I can't say anything else, Lyn."

"But what the hell—?"

"He's not home," I said. "I think you better wait with me. I'm sure the police will want to talk to you."

He rolled his shoulders. "I don't get it. What do the police care if Mick's not home?" He narrowed his eyes at me. "Something's happened to him, hasn't it?"

"Looks like it," I said.

# TEN

The Somerville cop put his hand on Lyn Conley's shoulder. "I gotta keep you two separated," he said. "That big-shot detective'll have my ass if I let you guys compare stories."

Lyn pushed the cop's hand away. "I don't have any damn story," he said. "I'm here to visit my friend."

"Listen, pal," said the cop. "You wanna obstruct justice—"

"I want to know what happened to Mick."

"Just do what I say," said the cop. "And don't touch me again."

"Wait," I said to the cop. "We're just upset, both of us. My friend here doesn't mean anything."

The cop glared at Lyn for a minute, then turned to me. "Okay. That's good. I don't want trouble any more than you do. So why'n't you go back and sit on the steps where I can see you. And you—" he turned to Lyn"—you can take a seat in the back of my cruiser, there. How'd that be?"

"That's fine," I said quickly. I nodded at Lyn.

He frowned at me, gave his head a little shake, then turned and ducked into the backseat of the Somerville cruiser.

I went back and sat on the front steps. Ten or fifteen minutes later, Horowitz came out. He walked past me to where the Somerville cop was standing guard on the sidewalk, and the two of them conferred for a minute. Horowitz glanced at Lyn Conley, patted the cop on the shoulder, then leaned down and said something to Lyn.

A minute later he came back and sat beside me. "Let's talk about Fallon's enemies," he said.

I turned to him. "You think . . . ?"

He shrugged. "I don't know what to think. Looks like there was a helluva row up there."

"Was there blood anywhere else?"

Horowitz nodded. "A few spots on the living room rug and kitchen floor. Like a trail to the rear exit off the kitchen."

"If somebody killed him . . ."

"Why'd they bother taking his body?"

"You think Mick could still be alive?" I said.

"I think it's possible."

"Kidnapped or something," I said. "They had to hurt him. Disable him. Mick's a big guy. Unlikely to go along willingly." I nodded. "Sure," I said. "I see what you're thinking."

"I doubt if you see what I'm thinking, Coyne."

"Well, how do you figure it?"

"Kinda premature to be figuring it," he said. "What we got is some blood, a trashed apartment, a fire escape off the back of the house, a missing three-hundred pound man, one potential witness who claims he was sleeping, and Fallon's car still parked on the street. The only actual corpse belongs to a fucking fish."

"Mick's daughter gave him that fish," I said. "He called it Neely."

Horowitz frowned. "Neely?"

"After the Bruins player."

"Oh, yeah. The right winger. So the man loved his fish, huh?"

"Well," I said, "he sure loved his kids."

Horowitz stared at the ground for a minute, then turned to me. "I need to know who Fallon's enemies are."

I nodded. "You've got to understand that I don't know that much about him. He's only been my client for a few weeks, and before that, he was just a guy I ran into a few times at Skeeter's. He lied to me about several things. I do know he was a gambler. He owed money. In pretty deep, I think. And there were those two hoods at Skeeter's."

"Russo's boys. I know all about that."

I nodded. "Anyway, that was way back in February. Also, of course, there might be someone who thought he killed his wife and didn't like it. Or," I said, "the same person who killed her could've come after him."

"Some kind of grudge against both of them?"

I shrugged.

"What's his problem?" he jerked his chin toward the cruiser where Lyn Conley was sitting in the backseat. "That's the guy whose wife found Mrs. Fallon's body. What's he doing here?"

"He and Mick were old friends. He's been visiting every day since Kaye got killed. Sort of looking out for him, I guess."

Horowitz chewed his lip. "Look," he said after a minute, "I know you're his lawyer, and I know what you can and can't tell me. But I'm gonna tell you something."

"You were planning to arrest Mick this morning," I said. "Right?"

He nodded.

"You've been gathering evidence against him. You subpoenaed the deposition, interviewed Barbara Cooper." I arched my eyebrows.

Horowitz nodded. "And we found a witness."

"What kind of witness?"

"Solid eyewitness. Saw Fallon that night in Lexington."

"At Kaye's? The night she—?"

"Yep. Sunday night around eleven."

"This witness reliable?"

"Neighbor across the street. Retired banker, for Christ's sake. Sober, conservative. You know the type. Perfect witness. Recognized Fallon, of course. Fallon had lived there for a long time. Hard to confuse Mick Fallon with anybody else."

I blew out a breath. Mick had sworn to me he'd been in his apartment all night on Sunday. Assuming the witness was telling the truth, Mick had lied to me again. "This witness," I said to Horowitz, "he's sure of the day and the time?"

"I'll tell you his name," he said, "because I'm obligated to. I don't have to tell you anything else, and I ain't gonna."

"I'll interview him myself."

"Of course you will. Mitchell Selvy's his name."

"And he lives across the street from the Fallons' house?"

Horowitz nodded.

"Thank you." I stood up and arched my back. "Can I go?"

"Sure. Go."

"What happens next?"

"Me, I'm gonna go talk some more with that Conley guy in the cruiser, then head back to the office, catch up on my messages, think about lunch. You probably oughta go to your office, compose a will or something." He gave me his cynical Jack Nicholson grin. "Cops'll do their job, Coyne. You'll do yours."

"What about Mick?" I said.

"Oh, we'll find him. Let's hope it's not in a Dumpster behind some strip joint in Revere."

I nodded to Horowitz and started down the path toward the street.

"Hang on," he said.

I turned. "What?"

"Let's keep this out of the newspapers for now, huh?"

"I don't have a problem with that," I said.

I got to the office a little before eleven. Julie looked up from her computer and said, "You could've called, you know."

"Actually, I couldn't," I said. "Or I would've." I filled her in on the morning's adventures.

"So is Mr. Fallon—?"

"I don't know," I said.

Julie stared at me for a minute. Then she shook her head, sighed, and picked up a memo pad. "Mr. McDevitt called. Something about fishing." She looked up at me and smiled quickly. "Bet you won't forget to call him."

"No, indeed," I said.

I poured myself a mug of coffee, took it into my office, and called Charlie McDevitt at his office in the Federal Building where he prosecuted cases for the Justice Department. I exchanged gossip with Shirley, Charlie's secretary, about my two boys and her countless grandchildren, and then she put me through to him.

"Did you hear about that behavioral laboratory out in Mill Valley, California, that started using lawyers instead of white rats for their experiments?" he said without preliminary.

"This is why you called?"

"Some of those experiments were getting screwed up because the technicians were feeling sorry for the rats," said Charlie. "Besides, there were some things that rats refused to do. They figured lawyers would solve all their problems. Plus, of course, lawyers are more abundant than rats."

I was glad Charlie couldn't see me smiling.

"The lawyers didn't work out, though," he said. "They had to go back to using rats."

I waited for a minute, then said, "Okay. How come they had to go back to using rats?"

"With lawyers," he said, "they weren't able to extrapolate their results to human beings."

"Well," I said, "I know what you mean. Fact is, I've been feeling a lot like a stupid white rat in a maze lately."

"The Mick Fallon thing?"

"Yep."

"That's the reason I called."

"Steer me out of the maze."

"Yes. Trout, Coyne. And the gurgle of clean running water, and the soft June breeze whispering through the hemlocks. Cedar waxwings flitting in the aspens, mayflies and caddisflies clouding over the water, good manly conversation, none of it about business or finance or world affairs."

"Manly conversation," I said. "The Red Sox. Beer. Women."

"That sort of thing. Exactly."

"The Deerfield or the Farmington?"

"Deerfield okay with you? Been daydreaming about it all week."

"Tomorrow or Sunday?"

"Sunday. Meet me at the old HoJo's by the rotary in Concord at, say, nine?"

"It's an Italian restaurant now."

"Oh, good point. Another treasured New England tradition down the tubes. Well, screw it. Let's meet there anyway."

"Nine o'clock," I said. "Even if it's raining."

"Especially if it's raining," said Charlie.

I like to work late on Friday afternoons. It gives me a good rationalization for not lugging a briefcase home for the weekend. So I tried to put Mick Fallon out of my mind and spent the rest of the day scrutinizing contracts and divorce decrees and wills, touching base with a few clients on the telephone, setting up appointments and dickering settlements with fellow lawyers, sketching out the draft of an article I was supposed to write for the *Yale Law Review*, and in general depriving my conscience of any good reason to distract me from a Sunday of trout fishing.

Julie blew me a good-bye kiss precisely at five.

The next time I glanced at my watch, it was nearly seven-thirty.

Then I remembered.

Sylvie.

Shit.

I'd told her I'd meet her at the Ritz bar at six-thirty.

I turned off my computer and Mr. Coffee and the lights, turned on the office answering machine, and got the hell out of there.

I double-timed it down Newbury Street, slipped into the side door of the Ritz-Carleton, strode across the lobby, and stopped at the top of the two steps that descended into the bar.

The June sun still shone brightly outside, but the elegant Ritz barroom, with its dark woodwork, leather furniture, and glittering crystal, lay subdued and dim and conspiratorial. The nooks and crannies and thick carpeting and high ceiling muffled the voices, the clink of silver against glass, the occasional burst of laughter. It looked as if every table was occupied. A pinstriped businessman with gray at his temples leaned over his manhattan to confer with a thin blonde who, I'd've bet my favorite fly rod, was not his wife. Five swarthy Middle-Eastern investor types wearing light-colored silk suits were crowded around a table for two, jabbering loudly in foreign tongues. A middle-aged couple from someplace like Cedar Rapids, Iowa, were sipping wine and frowning at a menu. A fortyish rock star guy with a ponytail and two earrings grinned possessively at the three virtually identical raven-haired groupies seated with him. More pinstripes, more blondes. More middle-aged tourists from Cedar Rapids.

The Ritz bar on a Friday evening.

I spotted Sylvie sitting alone at a table by the window. Her chin rested in her hand, and her head was turned away from me. I guessed she hadn't seen me. She was gazing out across Arlington Street toward the Public Gardens.

I weaved among the tables and took the chair across from her. "Hi, sexy," I said.

She turned her head slowly. When she looked at me, she was not smiling.

I reached across the table and took her hand. "Sorry I'm late. I should've called. You must've thought . . ."

She squeezed my hand. "Oh, I knew you'd come," she said. "I'm not upset with you."

"Something's the matter," I said. "When you don't smile at me, I know something's wrong."

"I don't want to talk about it now." She gave me a quick, unconvincing smile. "Right now, I just want a martini."

I arched my eyebrows. "A *martini?*" Sylvie, I knew, liked domestic beer and jug wine, and when she ordered an actual drink, it was generally a Bloody Mary or one of those sweet rum concoctions that Chinese restaurants specialize in, the kind that comes with a paper parasol sticking out of it.

She shrugged. "I like martinis." She turned her head and gazed out the window onto Arlington Street.

As if he had heard Sylvie utter the word "martini," a waiter appeared at our table. "Perhaps Miss Szabo is ready to order now?" he said.

He was a short, sixtyish man, with slicked-down iron gray hair combed straight back, black eyes, and an accent similar to Sylvie's except thicker.

She turned and smiled up at him. "Vodka martini, please, Philip. Extra olives, don't forget."

Philip nodded as if Sylvie had made a particularly intelligent decision, then turned to me. "And the gentleman?"

"Bourbon old-fashioned," I said.

He gave a little shrug that implied my decision was significantly less intelligent than Sylvie's, although it might've simply meant that I was significantly less attractive than Sylvie.

"Oh," I said, "and bring me a telephone, please."

"A telephone," said Philip. "Very good."

After he left, Sylvie frowned. "Business?"

I smiled. "No, honey. Pleasure."

A minute later a busboy brought a portable phone to the table. I called Locke-Ober's, insisted on speaking to my friend Rocco, the maître d', and asked him to hold a table for two in what they still called the Men's Bar for me. Sylvie had always liked Locke-Ober's, and she especially enjoyed invading the old Men's Bar which, until sometime in the 1970s, no woman had ever entered.

When I hung up, she was smiling at me. "Brady remembers," she said.

"Brady," I said, "remembers a lot of things."

Like how when we were teenagers, Sylvie and I used to hike through the woods to Granny Pond on a golden summer's afternoon. I brought the spinning rods and army blanket, and Sylvie smuggled in a six-pack of beer that she'd filched from her mother's live-in boyfriend, a French-Canadian construction worker named Oliver, and how we fished, drank beer, caught frogs and crayfish, spied on herons and muskrats, swam nude, made love on the blanket, and dozed naked while the sun dried our bodies. I remembered how Sylvie always beat me at pool, and how hopelessly awkward she was at bowling, and how she taught me to do the twist, which we practiced in the basement of the little house her mother shared with Oliver until I finally lost my inhibitions and allowed the music to jerk my body around. . . .

Philip delivered our drinks. I picked up my squat, cut-glass tumbler and held it across the table. "To old friends," I said.

Sylvie clinked my old-fashioned with her martini. "Yes. To good old friends."

We sipped our drinks and stared out the window.

After a few minutes, Sylvie said, "You seem sad today."

I smiled at her. "No, honey. Not sad, exactly. One of my

clients—a friend of mine, really—was—well, he might've been killed last night. Murdered, I mean. They didn't actually find his body, but . . ."

She reached across the table and covered my hand with both of hers. "Oh, Brady."

I tried to smile. "I was also remembering Granny Pond. It seems like that was other people, not us."

"It would be fun to go back to Granny Pond," she said. "Bring beer, catch some of those pretty yellow perch, go skinny-dipping."

"Last I heard," I said, "they'd cut a road into the woods and built a big housing development all the way around the pond. They trucked in a lot of sand and made an actual beach where we used to swim, and they installed water filters and hired life-guards, and they test the quality of the water every week in the summertime. They have what they call common land with mulched paths through the woods there now, and tennis courts and swimming pools and a live-in security guard."

"You can't go home again," Sylvie murmured.

We sipped our drinks in silence for a few minutes. Then she said, "Brady?"

"What, honey?"

"Would your feelings be hurt if we didn't go to Locke-Ober's?"

I shrugged. "No, of course not. I just thought . . ."

"In New York I go to restaurants all the time. Do you understand?"

"Sure. I guess so. I just remembered how you used to love the Men's Bar."

"Oh, I did," she said. "That was when we mostly ate hamburgers that you grilled out on your balcony." She smiled. "That's something I haven't done for a long time."

"I think I've got a steak in the freezer," I said. "And a few bottles of Sam Adams in the refrigerator."

"Perfect," she said.

I called Rocco to cancel. Then we took a taxi over to my apartment, and while I got the grill going, Sylvie went into my bedroom. She came out a few minutes later wearing one of my old T-shirts and a pair of my boxer shorts. She stood just inside the open glass sliders and twirled around. "How's this?" she said.

"My old Sylvie," I said.

She retrieved two bottles of Sam, brought them out to the balcony, handed one to me, then slumped into one of my aluminum patio chairs. She propped her bare feet up on the railing, tilted the chair back on its hind legs, took a big swig of beer, and rested the bottle on her stomach. "I've missed this," she said softly.

I leaned back against the railing and smiled at her. "Have you really?"

She nodded. "Yes. I think about it a lot. Those old times." She closed her eyes and let out a long breath. "It seems like so long ago."

"It's been many years," I said. "I want to know everything that's happened to you. Your books. How are they doing?"

She opened her eyes and shook her head. "I'm not doing books anymore."

"You said you were here on business. I thought . . ."

"Graphic design," she said. "Computer stuff. I work for an advertising agency. We're in town soliciting accounts."

I noticed that Sylvie wore no polish on her toenails. She'd always painted her toenails pink, and sometimes she'd decorated them with stars and butterflies and happy faces.

"Madison Ave, huh?" I said. "The big time. How do you like it?"

She shrugged. "I make a lot of money."

"Nothing wrong with that."

She smiled.

I grilled a steak, cooked some rice on the stove, and tossed a salad, and we ate off our laps on the balcony while the sun set and the air turned cool. We didn't say much. The truth was, I felt awkward and shy, and I sensed that Sylvie felt the same way. I didn't ask about her career in advertising, and she didn't volunteer.

I couldn't picture Sylvie Szabo on Madison Avenue. It didn't fit.

When we finished eating, we took the dishes into the kitchen and loaded everything in the dishwasher. Then Sylvie disappeared in the direction of the bathroom. I put on some coffee and went back out on the balcony.

I was leaning my forearms on the railing, staring out at the dark ocean, when Sylvie came out. I felt her hand on the back of my neck, and then she was leaning against me, hugging me from behind. I could feel her soft breasts against my back. Her hands moved over my chest, and then one of them slipped under my shirt and began to slide down under my belt. Her body was pressing against me, moving in that old slow rhythm.

I didn't move for what felt like several minutes. Finally, I whispered, "Sylvie?"

"Mmm."

"Honey?"

She giggled. "Yes, Brad-ee?"

"Do you really think we can't go home again?"

"I think we could try," she said.


Afterwards, we lay side by side in my bed. I smoked a cigarette and exhaled straight up into the dim light of my bedroom. Sylvie was lying on her side with one arm thrown across my chest. "What's Brady thinking?" she whispered.

"Old times, I guess," I said. "Granny Pond. Mike Fosburg's old Dodge. High school. Oliver's beer."

"Is that all?"

"No," I said. "Truthfully, I was thinking about Alex, too."

"Do you still love her?"

"Sure," I said. "The way I still love Gloria. The way I've always loved you."

"You miss Alex."

"Yes," I said. "I miss her a lot." I hugged Sylvie close to me. "I've missed you, too."

We lay there for a while longer, and I might've dozed off, because the next thing I knew Sylvie had eased away from me and was sliding out of bed. I pretended to still be sleeping.

She came back a few minutes later and sat on the edge of the bed. I opened my eyes and looked at her. She'd changed back into her cocktail dress.

She touched my face, then brushed my hair back off my forehead. "I've got an early meeting tomorrow," she said.

"I thought . . ."

She bent over and kissed me softly. "You better take me back."

"Sure." I nodded. "I've got a busy day, too, actually." I glanced at my watch. It was a little after ten o'clock. "How about some coffee?"

She shook her head. "It'll just keep me awake."

I drove Sylvie back to the Ritz, left my car double-parked out front, and walked her into the lobby.

We stopped by the elevator, and she turned to me and touched my cheek. "Dear Brady," she said. "You're still my best old friend."

"We will be best old friends forever," I said.

She put both hands on my shoulders, tiptoed up, leaned against me, and kissed me softly on the mouth. "Promise?" she whispered.

"Promise," I said.

She wrapped her arms around my neck and hugged me hard. Then she pushed herself away. "I'm here for another week," she said.

"Then back to New York."

"Yes," she said. "Back to New York."

"We should get together again before you leave," I said.

"I'll call you," she said.

"Promise?"

Sylvie smiled. "Of course."


I was munching an English muffin with peanut butter at my kitchen table the next morning, thinking about Sylvie, remembering the silky feel of her skin and the odd sadness that had overwhelmed me afterwards, when the phone rang.

"Brady, it's Lyn," he said when I picked up.

"Oh, sure," I said. "How you doing? What's up?"

"I know it's a Saturday, but I was thinking if you had any time today, maybe you'd like to drop by the house."

"Sure," I said. "Anything wrong?"

"Not really. Erin and Danny are here."

"How are they doing?"

"As well as you might expect, I guess." He paused. "Erin arrived around suppertime. She called from the airport, asking if somebody would give her a ride home. Gretchen had to tell her that she couldn't go to her house, that the place was a crime scene. And Mick's place, too. She hadn't heard about Mick, of course. I guess the poor kid was just bawling on the phone. Ned went in and got her. A few hours later—oh, close to midnight, actually—Danny pulled into our driveway. He borrowed somebody's car down in Rhode Island. He'd already been to his house in Lexington, saw that yellow tape, the big sign on the front door, so he went over to Mick's, saw the same damn thing. Jesus. I mean, what do you say to them?"

"I guess you just love them, Lyn. Tell them the truth as best as you can."

"Sure," he said. "That's what we tried to do." He hesitated. "Erin says she wants to see her mother—her body. Danny doesn't say much of anything. Gretchen's been great with them. She was up half the night talking with them." He blew a long breath into the telephone. "Anyway, I thought it might help if you talked with them, too. Try to give them an idea of what's going on."

"Absolutely," I said. "I want to meet Mick's kids."

# ELEVEN

I wanted to talk to Horowitz's witness, the neighbor who said he'd seen Mick the night Kaye was murdered. So on my way out Route 2 to the Conleys' house in Concord I took the first exit into Lexington and pulled up in front of Mick and Kaye's house a little before noontime.

They'd lived on a narrow shady street that wound through a mature pine-and-oak forest on the east side of town. Their house was set well back from the street, a modern, flat-roofed structure composed of several connected boxlike parts with vertical cedar sheathing and lots of glass, with a paved circular driveway in front. An attached two-car garage of the same design as the house stood to the left. A rock garden featuring big mossy boulders, tall perennials, dark green ground cover, low-growing junipers, and a few bushy red maples shielded the garage and front of the house from the street.

An X of yellow police tape plus a Crime Scene sign were plastered on the front door of the Fallon's house.

According to Horowitz, Mitchell Selvy, the witness who claimed to have seen Mick on the night of Kaye's murder, lived across the street. Selvy's house was a traditional white colonial. It looked like it had been there for many years before the developers came along and built the area up with cedar-and-glass contemporaries on two-acre lots. A pale blue Buick sat beside a large motor home in Selvy's driveway, and I could hear the drone of a lawn mower from the direction of his backyard.

I left my car on the side of the street and wandered around the Fallon property. The side lawn needed mowing, but otherwise the yard was well tended. Clusters of tiny green tomatoes clung to the vines in the little vegetable patch out back, and the azaleas against the foundation were ablaze.

I tried to imagine Mick Fallon as a suburban homeowner, trimming the shrubs, cleaning the gutters, raking the leaves, weeding the gardens, fighting the crabgrass. It was a stretch. But I assumed he'd done all that, just as I had back in the days when I, too, was a suburban homeowner. Before divorce.

I made a complete circuit of the house, and when I got back to the front, I saw a man leaning against the side of my car. He had his arms folded across his chest and a dead cigar butt clenched in his teeth.

I lifted my hand in greeting, and he took the cigar from his mouth and waved. " 'Lo, sir," he called, more loudly than was really necessary.

He was short—five-six or -seven, I guessed—and pear-shaped, with narrow sloping shoulders and wide hips. A red baseball cap a size too big for his head rested directly on his ears, with the visor pulled low over his brow. He wore thick glasses, high-top sneakers, baggy jeans, and a blue cotton shirt with the cuffs and throat buttoned and the tails flapping.

When I got closer to him, I saw that he had the moon face, the uptilted Asian eyes, and the guileless grin of a man with Down's syndrome. A thick stubble of black beard sprouted from his cheeks and chin. I guessed he was somewhere in his mid- to late twenties.

"I'm Darren," he said in a mumbly voice, holding out his hand, still smiling. "Who're you?"

I shook his hand. "I'm Brady."

"I mow the lawn," he said. "That's my job. But Kaye's not home. Kaye's nice, huh? Where's Kaye? Do you think I should mow the lawn?"

"I don't know," I said. "Probably you should wait."

"That's what my mother said," said Darren. "But it's my job. It needs mowing, don't it? Huh?" He was peering intently at me, as if my answer was very important to him.

"Yes, it does need mowing," I said. "Didn't your mother tell you what happened to Kaye?"

He shook his head emphatically. "Nooo," he said, dragging it out. Darren's face suddenly transformed. "She makes me *so* mad." His little eyes blazed, and the corners of his mouth turned down. "She won't tell me nothing. I gotta do my job. It's my 'sponsibility."

"You didn't know that Kaye died?" I said.

He frowned. "Huh?"

"She died, Darren."

I watched his face. It did not change. I still read anger on it.

"She was killed," I said carefully. "Murdered."

He glared at me for a long moment. Then he abruptly turned and started running awkwardly down the street, lumbering pigeon-toed, his elbows flapping at his sides.

"Hey, Darren," I called. "Wait a minute. I need to talk to you."

"Backbug!" he screamed, or something that sounded like "backbug." "Backbug! Backbug!"

I stood there watching until Darren disappeared around the corner. I wondered how his mind worked, what he understood, where that abrupt burst of anger, and then what seemed like fear, had come from. I wondered what he knew. I thought of running after him, but decided against it. I had apparently already frightened him.

After a minute, I crossed the street, where a man was now patrolling his front lawn on a sit-down mower. I stood in his driveway watching him until he turned a corner, spotted me, and waved. I waved back, arched my eyebrows, and lifted one finger.

He putted over to me, switched off the engine, and smiled. "How you doin'?" he said. Close-cut steel gray hair showed beneath his striped engineer's cap. He had sharp blue eyes behind wire-rimmed glasses and a craggy, rather handsome face. He wore a white T-shirt, cut-off jeans, and work boots with white socks. His bare legs were strong and hairy. He looked to be in his early sixties, and he reminded me of Clint Eastwood.

"I see you met Darren," he said.

"I guess I frightened him."

He nodded. "That's Darren, all right. Poor fella."

"Are you Mr. Selvy?" I said.

"That's me. Who're you?"

"My name is Brady Coyne. I'm Mick Fallon's lawyer." I took a business card from my wallet and handed it to him.

He glanced at it, then pursed his lips and shook his head. "How's old Mick doing these days?"

"Not so good, as you might expect. Can you spare me a couple of minutes?"

"Long as you're not from some newspaper, I guess I can. Police told me not to talk to any press. How about a cold beer? Mowing the lawn always makes me thirsty."

"A beer would hit the spot," I said.

"We can sit out here." He waved to the front steps. "I'll be right with you."

He climbed off his mower and went inside. I sat on the steps. His lawn looked like the Fenway Park infield—not a dandelion

**152**

or brown patch anywhere. The foundation plantings were mulched with pine bark and absolutely weedless. All the old iris and peony blossoms had been pinched off, and marigolds and petunias and zinnias grew lush and colorful along the edges of the front walkway and driveway.

From where I sat on the front steps, Mick's house across the street lay deep in shade and shadow.

Selvy returned, handed me a can of Coors, and sat beside me. "You want to talk about Sunday night, I guess."

"Yes, please."

"Well," he said, "it's like I told the police. I came out to turn off the sprinklers. I always water my lawn in the evening, because you get less evaporation that way. I guess it was around ten-thirty, quarter of eleven. Didn't really notice the time, but I did see the eleven o'clock news shortly after I went back inside. Always watch the news before bed. Anyway, Mick's car was parked out front. I figured—"

"You're sure it was Mick's car?" I said.

He shrugged. "Sure looked like it. Maroon Chrysler, just like he drives. If it wasn't, he must've borrowed one just like it, because Mick was leaning against it."

"And you're positive it was Mick?"

"Hard to mistake Mick," he said good-naturedly. "Not many fellows his size around. Hell, I've known old Mick for years. My across-the-street neighbor, eh? So I waved at him. He didn't wave back to me. Guess he didn't see me. Seemed to be deep in thought, if you know what I mean. Just leaning there against his car, staring off into space."

"So did you speak to him?"

"Nope. Figured he had his own problems, probably wasn't in any mood to chat about the weather with old Mitch Selvy."

"Then what happened?"

Selvy shrugged. "I shut off the sprinklers and went back inside." He shook his head. "Next night I heard a ruckus out front, saw all the police cars with their lights flashing. Heard about it on the news the next day."

"But you didn't report seeing Mick for several days."

"No, I didn't. When they finally came around and asked, I told them, of course. But before that, I didn't even make the connection. See, Mr. Coyne—and I realize this sounds pretty naive, but it's what I was thinking—it never occurred to me that Mick might've had anything to do with it. He came around a lot after he moved out, visiting Kaye. Sometimes I'd see him doing some work in the yard. The man loved his family, I can tell you that. Always thought it was a damn shame, them splitting up." He paused. "One thing was odd, though."

"What's that?"

"Him parking out front like that. Usually he'd park in the driveway. Hell, if he'd parked in the driveway, I might not have noticed his car."

"You can't see a car in the driveway from here?"

"Not at night. Not unless I look real hard, and I'm not in the habit of snooping."

I sipped my beer. It was ice cold and felt good going down. "I told you I'm Mick's lawyer," I said.

He nodded.

"Do you think he'd kill his wife?"

"Sure would surprise me if it turns out he did. Known Kaye and Mick for a long time." He clucked his tongue against the roof of his mouth. "Good kids. Just nice, normal folks, if you understand me."

"I wondered if you had any thoughts on who else could've done it?"

He shook his head. "None whatsoever. Been thinking about it, too, I'll tell you that. Not often the lady across the street gets murdered, you know. Makes you wonder if anybody's safe. I'm hoping it was somebody who she knew. Hate to think it might've been some random thing."

154

"Did Kaye have many visitors?"

He cocked his head. "Visitors? Well, sure. Now and again, like anybody else, I guess."

"Anybody you might be able to identify?"

He shrugged. "I mind my own business, Mr. Coyne. They'd generally pull into the driveway where I couldn't see them, even if I did want to snoop. Which I didn't. I'd hear a car door slam shut, some voices, a car pulling away. Usually in the evening. Kaye worked during the day, you know. Like I say, I never paid it much mind. You got your hands plenty full with your own affairs, I always say."

"Any idea whether this was the same visitor every time, or different visitors?"

He shrugged. "Couldn't tell you. Like I said, I don't snoop."

"What about that young man? Darren?"

He smiled. "Darren? Oh, he was like a puppy dog around Kaye. Seems like he was over there mowing her lawn every other day, whether it needed it or not, and I guess she paid him every time. She was like that, Kaye was. Just a nice big-hearted person."

"Darren seems to have a pretty quick temper," I said.

Selvy gazed across the street toward the Fallons' house. "Darren's . . . I don't know what the acceptable word for it is. Retarded?" He waved his hand. "Anyway, he's plenty normal in certain ways. He patrols the neighborhood, always stops to say hello if I'm out in the yard. He's guileless. Like a child, you know? Just says what's on his mind."

"Did he ever talk specifically about Kaye?"

Selvy frowned. "Not that I recall. But it was pretty clear he adored her. Hell, I guess everybody who knew her liked her, Mr. Coyne. Kaye was a very warm, friendly, outgoing person. Not to mention, she was awfully pretty." He looked at me. "I know what you're thinking."

I smiled.

"I liked looking at her," he said quietly. "I might've even thought about how if she and Mick ever ended up properly divorced I might see if she'd like to have dinner with me." He shook his head. "Just the idle daydreams of a lonely old man, Mr. Coyne. Nothing more than that."

"Understandable," I said. "Do you know the Conleys?"

"Oh, sure. Friends of the Fallons. Nice folks. The two families were very close. They came around a lot before Mick left."

"But not afterwards?"

"They might've. Can't say I noticed."

"And how about you, Mr. Selvy? Were you close with the Fallons?"

"Close?" He gazed up at the sky for a moment. "I'm sixty-three years old. Retired from the bank two years ago. Muriel and I, we had it all planned out. Bought ourselves that RV—" he nodded at the big motor home in the driveway "—and we were going to see all of North America. Alaska to Mexico, Hudson Bay to Florida, by God." He shook his head. "Within six months, Muriel was gone. Stroke. Bingo, just like that." He looked at me and smiled softly. "What I'm trying to say is, Mick and Kaye, they had their kids, they worked, they had their own friends. They were like Muriel and I had been when our kids were little. We didn't have much in common. Oh, Kaye was very kind to me when Muriel went. Brought me casseroles, fresh-baked bread, that sort of thing. Neighborly, that's all. Mick and I, we'd stand on our own sides of the street leaning on our rakes talking about flowers or the weather or baseball or politics. Danny and Erin used to come over when they were little. Nice, polite kids. Muriel'd give 'em cookies. Our kids were off to college by then, and Muriel loved kids, you know? Mick and Kaye didn't invite us to their parties, and we didn't expect them to. I guess if we'd had parties, it wouldn't have occurred to us to invite the Fallons, either. We were good neighbors, but not really friends."

"I'm sorry to hear about your wife," I said.

He nodded. "I miss her every day. It doesn't get any better. Always figured I'd go before her. She was two years younger than me, never a health problem. Then she's gone. Just like that. Since then, I've lost my desire to travel or . . . or much of anything. I take care of my yard, watch sports on the TV, and wait for my grandchildren to come visit. That's about my life."

We sat there sipping our beers. Mitchell Selvy was staring out at his lawn. After a few minutes I said, "Where does Darren live?"

"Darren? Down the street that way—" he pointed off to the right "—you'll see a little gray bungalow, green shutters. You can't miss it. Why?"

"I wanted to ask him some questions. When I tried a few minutes ago, he ran away from me. I'm afraid I frightened him."

Selvy smiled. "He's a funny guy, all right. I doubt you'll find him at home."

"That's the direction he was running in," I said.

"Darren'll be at the pond, is my guess. He loves fishing. That's where he is most days. Whenever he's not mowing the Fallons' lawn, that is. When Darren's upset, he goes fishing."

"I'll check the pond, then." I smiled. "I like fishing, too. It'll give us something to talk about. How do I get there?"

"Down the road a ways on the right, just before Darren's house, you'll see some woods and a jogging path leading in. Town conservation land. Just follow that path. It goes around the pond."

I drained my beer can, stood up, and held out my hand. "Well, thanks, Mr. Selvy," I said. "I won't take any more of your time. You've got my card, and if you think of anything, don't hesitate to call me. Okay?"

He nodded and smiled, then stood up and shook my hand. "Sure. I'll do that."

I started down his driveway.

157

"Oh, Mr. Coyne?"

I turned.

"You say hello to old Mick for me, will you? Tell him that Mitch Selvy is in his corner all the way. I hope he isn't upset I told the police about seeing him that night. Figured it was my duty. Tell Mick that, okay?"

I waved to him. "You bet," I said.

If I ever see Mick again, I thought.

I followed a long mulched path through the woods, and after a few minutes I saw the sun glinting off water through the foliage. A narrower path branched off toward the pond. I followed it down a steep slope. And then I saw Darren.

He was sitting back on his heels on the mud bank of the small, round pond holding a spinning rod in both hands and the stump of his cigar in his teeth. A red-and-white plastic bobber floated placidly out on the water alongside a patch of lily pads. Dragonflies and damselflies zipped around in the lazy midday sun, and a few swallows darted and swooped after them. Willows and blueberry bushes overhung the pond's banks, and from the opposite shore came the lazy grump of a bullfrog. It could've been a scene from an old Norman Rockwell *Saturday Evening Post* cover.

Darren squatted there motionless, chewing his cigar, peering at the bobber, infinitely patient. I watched him for a minute, hoping a fish would come along and give his bobber a jiggle. But it didn't. Finally I stepped into the open and called, "Hello."

He turned his head slowly, looked at me from the shadow under the bill of his cap, nodded, then turned his attention back to his bobber.

I went over and squatted down beside him. "How they biting?"

"A few li'l sunnies," he said. "I put 'em back."

"What else do you catch here?"

"Horn pout, crappies, pickerels, perch. Not today." He stood up and cranked in his bobber. He had the hook fixed less than a foot beneath it. There was no bait on it. He reached into a coffee can and plucked out a worm. He frowned and grunted as he awkwardly threaded it onto the hook.

"Have you tried fishing it deeper?" I said.

He looked up at me. "Huh?"

"Lengthen the line under your bobber so the worm will go deeper into the water. On a bright sunny day like this, sometimes the fish like to be deeper in the water."

Darren was shaking his head as if the concept was too complicated to grasp.

"Want me to show you?" I said.

He grinned. "Sure."

He watched as I showed him how to press the little button on the bobber to loosen its grip on the line. I lengthened it to about three feet and gave it back to him.

"Thank you, sir," he said. He cast it out there in front of him and squatted down again. Without looking at me, he said, "Kaye died."

"Yes."

"She was my friend."

"Darren," I said, "do you know anything about it?"

"Not me," he said quickly. "Nope. Not me." He hunched his shoulders and pulled the beak of his cap lower over until it touched the tops of his glasses.

"If you know something," I said, "you should tell me."

"Not me. No, sir." He shook his head violently.

"When I saw you at her house, you yelled something. It sounded like 'backbug.' What did that mean?"

Suddenly he stood up, and I saw his eyes blazing behind his thick glasses. "Leave me alone!" he yelled. "Get outta here!" And then he swung his spinning rod at me.

I ducked away and held up my hands. "I'm sorry I bothered you," I said. "I'll leave you to your fishing. Good luck." I turned and started back up the slope. About halfway up, I stopped to look back. Darren was once more squatting beside the pond, quietly watching his bobber as if nothing had happened. I wished that some kind of fish would come along and jiggle it for him and prove to him that I was his friend.

I watched for several minutes, but his bobber refused to jiggle.

After a while, I turned and walked out of the woods and back to my car where I'd left it in front of Kaye and Mick Fallon's house.

Twenty minutes later I pulled up in front of the Conleys' house in Concord. The Lexus and the Cherokee were parked on the street, and I left mine there, too.

When I approached the house, I saw two shirtless young men in shorts and sneakers playing one-on-one at the hoop on the garage. Ned Conley and Danny Fallon. I remembered Danny from a photo Mick had shown me.

I stopped to watch them. They played intensely, grunting and cursing but not really talking to each other. Danny was a couple of inches taller and considerably beefier than Ned, but Ned was quicker and more deft at handling the ball. Danny's forte was rebounding and bulling his way to the hoop. He was effective, but a bit ungainly. Ned's main strategy was to shoot jump shots, which he hit with good regularity. They both played aggressive defense. In fact, it looked like they fouled each other frequently, but I never saw them stop playing or heard either of them complain.

They ignored me as I walked past them and up to the front door. I rang the bell, and a minute later the Conleys' daughter, Linda, appeared on the other side of the screen. She squinted at me, then smiled. "Well, hi, Mr. Coyne."

"Hello, Linda," I said.

"You came to talk to Danny and Erin, right?"

I nodded.

She pushed open the screen door and held it for me. "Come on in. Boy, this is nice of you."

I stepped into the foyer. Linda clutched my arm and leaned close to me. "Erin just keeps crying, and none of us can think of anything to say to her to make her feel any better. Neddie and Danny, they've been out there all morning going at each other. Bet they haven't said ten words between them."

"I'm not really here to console them," I said. "But I'm happy to talk with them, tell them what I know, answer any questions I can."

"My parents are upstairs. Mom's not feeling well. She was up half the night with Erin. I'll tell them you're here. You want to go sit on the deck?"

"That's fine," I said.

Linda headed up the stairs and I went out onto the deck in back. I lit a cigarette, leaned my elbows on the railing, and gazed out at the marsh. In the distance, the sun glittered off the Sudbury River.

"Thanks a lot for coming, Brady."

I turned. Lyn Conley had come out onto the deck. "Want some coffee or something?" he said.

I shook my head. "I'm fine, thanks."

"Linda's getting the kids." He let out a long sigh. "Any news?"

"On Mick, you mean?"

He shrugged.

"No news on Mick," I said. "I just came from talking with a couple of his neighbors."

"The man across the street who thought he saw him?"

"Yes. And a guy named Darren who mowed their lawn."

"Learn anything?"

I shrugged. "I want to talk to Darren again. I think he might've seen something, and—"

At that moment, Linda stepped out onto the deck. She was holding the hand of a very pretty young woman. Erin Fallon was tall—about five-ten, I guessed—and slender, with long blond hair and her mother's big blue eyes, which were red-rimmed and puffy. She looked younger and more vulnerable than I remembered from Mick's photo. She was wearing cut-off denim shorts and an extra-large gray T-shirt that fell below her hips.

"This is Erin Fallon, Mr. Coyne," said Linda.

I smiled at Erin. "Hi."

She nodded, said, "Hello," and looked down at her feet.

"Danny's on his way," said Linda.

We all sat down.

"Can I get you guys anything?" said Linda.

I shook my head and Erin mumbled something I didn't understand.

A couple of minutes later Danny and Ned came trooping out onto the deck. Ned was toweling his face and chest with his T-shirt. Danny had already put his on. They both were carrying cans of Coke.

"Mr. Coyne, this is Danny," said Linda.

I held out my hand to him. He gripped it firmly, looked me in the eye, and nodded. "How you doin'?" He reminded me of Mick when he played for the Pistons, rangy and rawboned, but he had his mother's delicate face. He wore a goatee and sported a gold stud in his left ear. Mick had told me his son was twenty-one. Danny looked several years older than that.

Lyn stood up. "Well, we'll leave you alone, then." He walked back into the house and Linda followed behind him.

Danny leaned back against the railing. Ned sat beside Erin.

"It might be better if I could talk with Erin and Danny alone," I said to Ned.

He looked up at me, then smiled quickly and slapped the side of his head. "Oh, sure. Dumb me. Sorry." He got up, gave Danny a little punch on the shoulder, and went inside.

I looked from Danny to Erin. "I don't know what Lyn and Gretchen might've told you," I said, "but—"

"They've been great," said Danny. "I guess there isn't much to say." He pulled a chair around and sat down beside Erin. "We know our mother's been killed and we know they think Dad did it. I went to his apartment, and there was police tape there, and then Uncle Lyn tells me Dad's . . . disappeared. He said you might be able to tell us more."

I summarized as objectively as I could how I'd found blood and evidence of a struggle at Mick's apartment. I did not mention the dead blue fish.

Erin stared at me, her eyes brimming.

"You think somebody killed Dad, too?" said Danny.

I shook my head. "There are other ways to interpret it. If I told you I was certain that he was okay, I'd be lying. But I'm trying to be hopeful, keep an open mind, and you should, too."

"You're his lawyer, right?" said Danny.

"Yes."

He glanced at his sister. "We really need to know. They're saying that he . . . ?"

I shook my head. "He has told me repeatedly that he did not harm your mother, and I believe him. They were having their problems, as you know. But your dad loved your mom."

"You have to say that," said Erin.

"If I didn't believe it, I wouldn't say it," I said to her. "I'm not here as your dad's lawyer. I'm here to try to answer your questions."

"He's got a wicked temper," said Danny.

I nodded. "I know. Did he ever . . . hurt your mom?"

He shook his head. "No. Never. He yelled at her sometimes, and I remember a couple times he kicked a door or punched the wall or something. She really knew how to get to him, you

163

know?" He smiled and glanced at Erin, who continued to gaze down into her lap. "Dad never touched her, though," said Danny. "Mostly when he got upset, he'd just walk out and drive around for a while. He always came back pretty soon, and they'd be fine, like they realized they were both wrong and didn't need to talk about it."

"I don't think I can stand this," said Erin softly.

"I understand," I said. "It's not fair. I can't think of anything to tell you that would make it better."

"I want to see my mother," she said. "I mean, her—her body."

"The police have her. You won't be able to see her until they release her."

"When'll that be?"

"I don't know. I'll try to find out for you." I looked from Erin to Danny. "Can either of you think of anyone who'd want to—to harm your mother? Or your dad?"

They looked at each other, then at me. They both were shaking their heads.

"I know this is hard," I said. "But did your mother ever mention another man? Someone she might've been interested in?"

"Mom?" said Erin. "Do you think—?"

"I don't really think anything," I said. "It's just a logical question."

"She never said anything," said Danny slowly, "but . . ."

Erin turned to him. "What? What are you saying?"

He shrugged. "I don't know. Just a feeling. The past year or so she seemed—I don't know—happier. Know what I mean?"

"No," said Erin. "That's nuts. She wasn't, like, dating or anything."

"Yeah," he said, "you're probably right."

"Did she ever mention someone named Will Powers to either of you?"

They both shook their heads.

"Did you know a guy named Darren?"

Erin smiled. "Sure. He lives in our neighborhood. He's kinda sweet." She suddenly frowned. "You're not thinking that Darren . . ."

"I met him today," I said. "He seems to have a quick temper, that's all."

"Darren's harmless," said Danny. "If something happens he doesn't like, he just runs away and goes fishing. He doesn't even kill any of the fish he catches. He talks to them and puts them all back. He's just a gentle guy."

"So what're we supposed to do?" said Erin.

I shrugged. "Nothing, I guess. I'm sorry. Just try to be patient, take care of each other."

"I'm fine," said Danny.

I looked at him. "Are you?"

He nodded. "Sure. I can handle it. I'm . . ." He shook his head. "Shit," he mumbled, and I saw tears well up in his eyes. He wiped at them with the back of his wrist, then turned to Erin. She leaned toward him and put her arms around his neck. He held onto her, and she patted his shoulder and whispered to him, and the two of them cried together.

I sat back in my chair and looked out toward the river. I had to swallow back a lump that was rising in my throat.

After a few minutes, Danny and Erin released each other. "You've been keeping it all bottled up," she said to him.

He gave her a little smile. "And you've been bawling your eyes out."

"We gotta stick together now," she said. She turned to me. "Thanks, Mr. Coyne."

I shrugged. "It was great to meet both of you. Your dad's always bragging on you two, you know."

They smiled.

"I just want you to know that you can call me any time," I said. "I don't expect you've given much thought to questions

**165**

like who might've done this to your mother or what could've happened to your dad. But maybe you'll talk with each other about it, and if you come up with any ideas, I hope you'll share them with me." I gave one of my cards to each of them. "And if I learn anything, I'll tell you, okay?"

They both nodded.

I stood up and held my hand to Danny. "It takes a real man to cry," I told him.

He shook my hand. "I feel like I've gotten rid of a big hole in my stomach."

I turned to Erin. She stood up and hugged me. "Thank you," she whispered.

I smiled and nodded, lifted my hand, turned, and walked off the deck quickly, before they could see the tears in my eyes.

# TWELVE

❯❯—————————————————————————————❮❮

I drove the back roads. I had all the windows rolled down and the Saturday afternoon Red Sox game on the radio and no further obligations for the day. I was in no hurry to get back to the city.

There's still a lot of farmland in Concord—cornfields, pick-your-own strawberry patches, acres of asparagus, celery, squash, pumpkins, tomatoes, and peppers. Old-fashioned farmstands huddle close to the road, with hand-lettered signs on the outside walls advertising the crops that are in season. I stopped at one such farmstand near Nine Acre Corner and bought two pints of organically grown strawberries, prepicked, precleaned, prepackaged, and prewrapped for nonself-pickers such as I.

I zigzagged over more back roads through Concord and Lincoln and out past Walden Pond to Route 2, and I didn't get back to my apartment until around six. I half filled a big bowl with Cheerios, sliced a generous handful of fresh strawberries on top, added a sliced banana, sprinkled it with brown sugar, and took it onto my balcony. No milk. I prefer to crunch my Cheerios, and the sliced fruit gives each mouthful a delicious mixture of contrasting textures.

When I finished eating, I sat there for a long time smoking and watching the sky grow dark.

After a while, I wandered back inside and called the Ritz. The operator let the phone in Sylvie's room ring about a dozen times, but she didn't answer. I declined to leave a message.

Then I tried Horowitz's office. It was a Saturday night, and he wasn't there, of course, so rather than annoy him by calling his cell phone number again, I told his voice mail about meeting Darren and Mitchell Selvy in Lexington and suggested that a cop with any imagination might want to consider them suspects in Kaye Fallon's murder. I did not tell him I'd met Erin and Danny. Knowing Horowitz, he'd probably want to interrogate them. The least I could do was to shield them for as long as possible from Horowitz's evil Jack Nicholson grin.

I thought of calling Alex up in Maine. But I hadn't talked to her in several months, and I realized that hearing her voice would not be likely to cheer me up.

I thought of calling Billy and Joey, my two boys, too. But Billy would be out fishing on some river in Idaho, miles from his telephone, and Joey was in California, three times zones away, and unlikely to be near his phone, either.

I'd run out of people to call. Another wild Saturday night for the bachelor.

So I pawed through my fishing gear and piled what I needed for tomorrow's trip with Charlie beside the door. Then I found an old Robert Mitchum movie on my black-and-white TV. I sprawled on the sofa and watched it all the way through without falling asleep—and without dwelling on the fact that Alex was living in Maine and Sylvie was unavailable and I was alone.

When the movie ended, I decided it was late enough that I could go to bed.

Tomorrow was another day. Tomorrow I'd go fishing.

$M$y eyes popped open at six in the morning. Outside my bed-room window a perfectly cloudless sky was just beginning to grow light. No rain today.

It seems as if more than half of the fishing excursions that Charlie and I plan end up weathered-out by gullywashing rain-storms or tree-rattling winds—and often both—which defies all the odds. Charlie believes that he and I have the power to cure a drought simply by planning to go fishing.

But today the low-angled beams of the just-risen sun streamed in through the sliders that opened onto my balcony. It was im-possible to feel anything except exultant on a morning such as this, especially with a fishing trip to look forward to. I fetched the Sunday *Globe* from outside my door, had a bagel and a hand-ful of strawberries and three cups of coffee and a couple of cig-arettes while I read the sports section, then lugged my gear down to the car. Charlie and I had agreed to meet at nine, and I was going to be early. But I couldn't put it off any longer.

An Italian restaurant called Papa Razzi occupies the struc-ture which had been the Howard Johnson's just east of the traffic circle by the Concord prison. For more than fifty years, the orange-tiled roofs of Howard Johnson restaurants were highway landmarks all over New England. A family couldn't drive past a HoJo's without stopping for one of their fifty-two flavors of ice cream, or a fried clam roll, or a hot dog. Now virtually all of them are defunct, replaced by a new generation of highway food joints—Roy Rogers, Burger King, Popeye's, KFC, Taco Bell. The first thing the new tenants of the old HoJo buildings always do is paint those orange roof tiles a less garish color.

I parked in the Papa Razzi lot a little after eight—an hour before our scheduled rendezvous. Charlie's Cherokee pulled in beside me less than ten minutes later.

I got out and bent down to his open window. "Hey, you're early," I said.

He grinned. "You're always early. I figured for once I'd be the first one here. I should've known better. Pile your stuff in back. Let's get going, before it decides to rain."

It takes a little over two hours to drive from the Concord rotary to the catch-and-release section of the Deerfield River where it flows from the bottom of the Fife Brook Dam a little west of Charlemont, Massachusetts, hard by the Vermont state line. Somewhere around the halfway mark, Route 2 narrows and winds through rural villages, where it becomes scenic as hell and is called the Mohawk Trail.

Charlie and I picked at the strawberries I'd brought and sipped coffee from car mugs. I told him about watching Darren fish with a bobber and worm, how it had reminded me of my youth, how Sylvie and I used to catch perch at Granny Pond, how Alex had nobly tolerated my fishing, how I'd screwed up all my relationships, beginning with my marriage to Gloria and ending, most recently, with Alex, how Sylvie was in town and how seeing her had rekindled a lot of confusing memories and emotions, but how I didn't think I had the courage for another relationship that I'd also surely screw up.

"You and Sarah," I said to Charlie. "Good, solid twenty-year marriage. What's your secret?"

He didn't say anything for a minute or two. Then he said, "Guy's out walking on the beach one morning. California, somewhere. Spots a green bottle on the sand, and when he picks it up, out pops a genie. Before the guy can say a word, the genie says, 'One wish, pal. That's it, and consider yourself lucky. None of this three wish shit.' So the guy shrugs, thinks a minute, and then he says, 'Okay, fine. I've wanted to go to Hawaii all my life, but I'm petrified of flying and I get seasick. So my wish is this: Build me a bridge to Hawaii.'"

Charlie glanced at me. I pretended to be staring out the side window.

"Well," said Charlie, "the genie blows his stack. 'You shitting me?' he says. 'A bridge to fucking Hawaii? You know how far that is? How in hell do you expect me to get supports all the way down to the bottom of the Pacific Ocean? Or,' he says sarcastically, 'did you want me to make you a suspension bridge? What do you think I am, anyways? You better come up with a better wish than that, buddy.'

"The guy shrugs. 'Well, okay,' he says. 'There's something else I've always wanted.' 'Yeah?' says the genie. 'And what might that be? A bridge to the moon?' 'Naw,' says the guy. 'Easier than that. See, genie, all my life I've had terrible luck with women. Three divorces, and that's not counting broken engagements. Even my mother hates me. I just don't get them, you know? Women. They baffle me. So my wish is simple. I just want to understand women.' "

Charlie paused to indicate the punchline was imminent. I nodded. I thought I saw it coming.

"The genie," he said, "looks at the guy, shakes his head, and says, 'So this bridge. Would two lanes be okay?' "

I refused to laugh, and we drove in silence for a few more miles. Then Charlie chuckled. "It's just luck," he said. "We are what we are, and we can't help it. Turns out Sarah loves baseball, and that's made all the difference. There's no way to know if you've married the right woman until you do it."

I didn't believe it, of course, and I don't think Charlie really did, either. But it was very supportive of him to say so.

Charlie did not mention Mick Fallon, and neither did I. That subject qualified as business. We did not talk business on fishing trips.

There were only two other cars in the pull-off by the river. We tugged on our waders, strung our rods, shrugged into our vests, and slipped down the steep bank with all the eagerness of teenagers on a double date with sisters who were reputed to do it.

The water was littered with a smorgasbord of insects—mayfly duns and spinners, midges, terrestrials, caddisflies—and there were enough surface-feeding trout to occupy us all day. Charlie and I fished within shouting distance, which was our agreement on the Deerfield, where sometimes the dam released water suddenly and in great volume and a heedless angler could find himself lifted off his feet and bob-sledded downriver. It had happened to me once. Fortunately, Charlie had been fishing downstream from me, and he'd managed to grab me on the way by and haul me out.

We quit around six. The trout were still rising, and we knew we could continue catching them into darkness. But we hadn't even stopped fishing for lunch, and, anyway, we'd had enough. It had been a perfect day. Anything more would've been too much of a good thing.

We stopped at a roadhouse near Greenfield for burgers and coffee. We listened to Charlie's Miles Davis tapes on the drive home, content to savor our own thoughts, comfortable enough in each other's company that we didn't need to talk.

I transferred my gear from Charlie's truck to my car in the Papa Razzi lot. We agreed it had been a good day and that we should do it again soon. Then I headed back into the city.

It was about ten when I pulled into my slot in the garage under my apartment building. I got out, opened the back door, and leaned in for my stuff. When I straightened up and turned around, a man was standing behind me, not five feet away. He wore an expensive-looking suit and a Dick Tracy hat. In the dim orange light, his face was deeply shadowed, and I didn't recognize him at first.

Then he spoke. "Coyne, right?"

I nodded. "You're Patsy. Or Paulie. I get you two confused."

"Don't worry about it," he said. "Mr. Russo wants to talk to you."

I shut the car door and started for the elevator. "Tell him to call my office for an appointment," I said. "On second thought, don't bother. I'm all booked up."

He moved beside me and touched my arm. "Mr. Russo wants to share some information with you. About a friend of yours. Mick Fallon?"

I squinted at him. "It's Patsy, right?" I said. "You're the one who does the talking."

"Mr. Russo's waiting, Mr. Coyne. He don't like being kept waiting. It shows disrespect."

"He's got information for me?"

Patsy shrugged.

"Where is he?"

"Parked on the street. He came to you. That shows great respect."

"Um," I said. "Flattering. Okay. Let me put my stuff back in the car."

I did, and when I was done Patsy said, "Sorry, I gotta frisk you." He patted me down, then led me out of the garage.

At the end of the block, we turned left, and there, parked next to the curb, sat a big silver Mercedes with tinted windows. The headlights were on and the motor was idling.

Patsy opened the back door, then stood aside.

A gravelly voice from inside said, "Mr. Coyne. Thank you for coming. I assume Patsy treated you courteously, huh?"

I bent down to look in. Vincent Russo was wearing a dark suit and hornrims with yellow lenses. He was a small, dapper man in his sixties—steely hair brushed back tight against his scalp, thin lips, pale skin, dark hooded eyes. His picture appeared in newspapers regularly, but I'd never seen him in person before.

"Patsy was the perfect gentleman, as always," I said. "He mentioned Mick Fallon."

"Please. Sit in here with me so we can talk private."

"To tell you the truth," I said, "I'm not all that eager to get into a car with you, Mr. Russo."

He lifted one hand, then let it fall onto his thigh. "We are not enemies, Mr. Coyne. You have nothing to fear. You got my word on it, huh?"

"You have information on Mick Fallon?"

"You're his attorney. There are some things perhaps you should know." He looked up at me and smiled coldly. "We can help each other, huh?" He patted the seat beside him.

I hesitated, quite certain that I was about to do something foolhardy or worse. I could hear Charlie when I told him about it. "You did *what*?" he'd say.

There were a million reasons why I should not get into the backseat of Vincent Russo's Mercedes on a dark Boston side street on a quiet Sunday night in June.

So I bent down and slid in beside the most notorious mobster in Boston.

Patsy shut the door behind me. It latched with the sound of finality. I wondered if Russo's Mercedes was equipped with disabled rear door latches, making a backseat guest such as me a prisoner. I resisted the impulse to find out, on the grounds that it would betray my discomfort.

A man with a thick neck sat stolidly behind the wheel up front. I looked at Russo, then pointed my chin at the driver.

He nodded. "Paulie, leave us alone, huh?" he said softly.

Paulie immediately switched off the headlights and ignition, got out, and shut the door behind himself. I noticed that the dome light did not go on when the door opened. Paulie went around to the front of the car, leaned against the fender, crossed his arms, and gazed up the street.

I turned to Russo. "You have information about Mick Fallon?"

He shrugged. "Who besides you, I ask myself, might suggest

to Lieutenant Horowitz that Patsy and Paulie could be involved?"

"Oh, I'd give Lieutenant Horowitz more credit than that."

He made a little backhanded brush-off gesture. "No matter, Mr. Coyne. If you mentioned it, you were only doing your job. I respect that. But I want you to understand that Mick's health and happiness is very important to me."

"I'll be sure to tell him when I see him."

"You're mocking me, huh?" he said. "That's okay. Sometimes I beat around the bush. Let me be straight with you, okay?" He reached over, tapped my knee, and held my gaze with those lizard eyes. "We didn't whack him, Mr. Coyne."

"It never occurred to me that you did."

He nodded and smiled. "Of course it did. But let me assure you. *Nobody* whacked him, okay?"

"How do you know?"

"Mick has enemies, Mr. Coyne. But they won't hurt him, because they know it would upset me."

"Do you know where he is?"

Russo shrugged. "We know people who can help us find out, and sooner or later we will."

"The police are looking for him, too," I said.

"Yes," said Russo. "And the way I figure it, Mick is already feeling all those nooses drawing tight around his neck. At some point he'll have to get in touch with somebody he trusts, huh?" He arched his eyebrows.

"If you think I'm going to turn Mick over to you," I said, "you're not as smart as I thought you were."

"It would be best for everybody if you did, Mr. Coyne. You should trust me on this."

"Is this a threat, Mr. Russo?"

He held up both hands, palms out. "I'm a civilized man, sir."

"Good-bye," I said. I tried the back door handle, and it worked. I got out of the car.

"Mr. Coyne," he said.

I bent down and looked in at him.

"A shame, what happened to Mick's beautiful wife." He shook his head. "Terrible, terrible tragedy, huh? Thing like that, I always feel worst for the children. Those two beautiful kids of his. Erin and Danny. College kids, huh?"

I stared at him.

"Well," he said after a minute. "Let's keep in touch, huh?" He held out his hand for me to shake.

I looked at it but did not take it. I shook my head, turned, and headed back to my car in the underground garage. I half expected Patsy and Paulie to follow me and try to teach me a lesson in respect. But they didn't.


When I got to my apartment, I went directly to the cabinet over the refrigerator. I took down my jug of Rebel Yell, poured several fingers over a handful of ice cubes, and carried it out onto my balcony. I noticed that my hand was shaking.

Bad enough that he had threatened me. But that son of a bitch had also threatened Danny and Erin.

I plopped down in my aluminum chair, lit a cigarette, tried to think straight.

Okay. Who stood to gain from Kaye Fallon's death?

Vincent Russo, that's who.

If Mick's divorce had proceeded, he would've been wiped out. I knew that, and I hadn't hidden it from Mick. Kaye would've gotten the house and most of their savings and investments. Mick would've been left with his problems with the IRS, and Russo, who I figured held Mick's gambling debts, would never collect what Mick owed him.

But with Kaye dead, whatever Mick had was all his to dispose of as he chose. Her life insurance was a bonus. Russo's boys could descend upon him and pick him as clean as a murder of crows on yesterday's roadkill.

Vincent Russo knew all this, of course. Men like Vincent Russo knew these things.

A couple of things about this theory didn't really fit. First, Kaye's murder was hardly in the style of the Vincent Russos of the world. It was messy and passionate. Of course, he could've set it up to look that way. But in so doing, he'd have been pointing the finger directly at Mick, and that contradicted his interests. If Mick were convicted of Kaye's murder, Russo wouldn't be able to collect what Mick owed him. If Russo had set it up, he would've made absolutely sure it couldn't be pinned on Mick.

Or maybe I was giving Vincent Russo way too much credit.

I continued smoking, sipping my Rebel Yell, and gazing out over the harbor. But I came up with no new insights. Vincent Russo was looking for Mick. He was willing to hurt anybody— even Danny and Erin—to collect what Mick owed him. Sure. He might've ordered Kaye's murder.

When my glass was empty, I went inside. I loaded the coffee machine, stripped down, took a long hot shower, brushed my teeth, and went into my bedroom. I felt a bit more relaxed. Maybe I'd get some sleep after all.

Then I saw that the answering machine beside my bed was blinking. Wink-wink, pause. Two calls.

Sylvie, maybe. Or maybe even Alex. I wouldn't have minded a message from either of them.

I pressed the button. The tape whirred, beeped, then clicked. I heard the fuzzy buzz of the empty tape playing. There was no message. Just one minute of static before the disconnection.

Another beep, another click. More recorded silence.

---

I was sitting in the backseat of a big car—it might've been a limousine—parked close to the bank of a pretty, slow-moving river. Through the tinted window I was watching Billy, my older son, who stood knee-deep in the water casting dry flies to the huge rainbow trout that were sipping insects off the glassy surface. The slashes along the sides of those trout were crimson, the color of fresh-spilled blood, and when they rose for an insect, they porpoised, their entire bodies arcing out of the water, their eyes big and greedy.

Billy was casting beautiful, graceful loops, and he seemed to raise a trout on every cast, and every time he hooked one, he turned to me with a big grin, raised his fist in the air, and shouted, but I couldn't make out what he was saying.

I rattled and shook the handle on the inside of the car door, trying to get it open so I could leap out and join my son in the river, but the handle broke off in my hand. I tried using it as a hammer, banging and smashing at the window, trying to break the glass so I could get out of that car, and all that banging set off the car's alarm, which kept shrilling—

I groped on my bedside table for the phone, knocked it off its cradle, fumbled it to my ear. "Yeah," I mumbled.

"You sleeping?"

I pushed myself into a sitting position in bed and switched ears. "Mick? Is that you?"

"Sorry to wake you up. We gotta talk."

"Sure," I said. "No problem. Are you okay?"

He chuckled. "Yeah. I'm okay."

"Lousy trick," I said. "Erin and Danny—hell, all of us—we're thinking . . ."

"I know," said Mick.

I rubbed my face. "Have you been trying to reach me?"

"Yeah. I let it ring, but you weren't answering."

"What the hell time is it?"

"Little after three."

"Actually, I appreciate the call. You interrupted a nightmare." I flicked on the light beside my bed, found my cigarettes, got one lit. "Mick, what the hell are you doing? Where are you?"

"I wanted you to know I was okay. I thought you'd be worried."

"Yeah, well, of course I was," I said. "We all are. What's going on?"

"I just had to get away," he said. "I needed some space. Christ, it was worse than being in prison."

"All that blood?"

He chuckled. "Nosebleed. It's what gave me the idea."

"Brilliant," I said. "You had me fooled. It was the goldfish that did it more than the blood."

"Huh? Whaddya mean?"

"Breaking the goldfish bowl, killing the fish. I figured you loved that fish that Erin gave you. When I saw that dead fish, any thought I might've had that you set it up just went right out of my head."

Mick was silent for so long that I said, "Mick? You still there?"

"Yeah, I'm here." He blew out a breath. "Listen, I didn't do that to Neely."

"You didn't? Then who—"

"Fucking Russo," he said. "Who else? See? I got out of there in the nick of time, man."

"Mick, listen to me," I said. "I'm your lawyer, right? Here's what I want you to do. Wherever the hell you are, go to the nearest police station, okay? Do it right now, as soon as we hang up. Tell them who you are, tell them there's a warrant out for your arrest, and tell them to lock you up and call the state police. Tell them to get ahold of Lieutenant Horowitz, and—"

"Wait a minute," he said. "They want to arrest me?"

"Yes, Mick. So go to the police."

179

He was silent for a long minute. Then he said, "I'm not turning myself in, Brady."

"Mick, God damn it, listen to me. I had a sit-down with Russo tonight, and—"

"What? Whose idea was that?"

"His."

"Christ, I'm sorry, man. You okay?"

"Sure. I'm fine." I stubbed out my half-smoked cigarette in the ashtray beside the bed. "Mick, I've got to tell you something."

"What?"

I took a deep breath and blew it out. "You are without question the worst fucking client I've ever had. You keep lying to me, you disobey me, you ignore my advice, you're—you're accused of murdering your wife . . ."

Mick laughed quickly. "I know you can't just fire me, Brady. And listen. I did not murder Kaye, okay? What do you think I'm doing?"

"I think you're panicking. I think you're afraid and confused and—and completely fucked up, and I wish to hell you'd listen to me."

I heard Mick speak to somebody, and then I heard a voice in the background.

"Brady," Mick said into the phone, "I only got a minute. I wanted you to know I was okay, that's all."

"Well, good. That's a relief. I saw your kids yesterday."

He was silent for a moment. Then he said, "How're they doing?"

"They seem like great kids, Mick. They're—they're devastated. Kaye, and now you. You should be with them."

"Yeah, well I'd be in jail now—or maybe dead—if I wasn't here, right?"

"Maybe, but—"

"I couldn't stand it, Brady, having my kids look at me think-

180

ing I killed their mother. I don't want them to see me until they know I didn't do it."

"They don't think you did. But I bet they'd like it if you told them face-to-face. You've got to turn yourself in, let me do my job. As long as you're out there—"

"Yeah, Russo. I know. I can't do it, Brady. Not now. Not yet." He paused. "Hang on," he said. I heard muffled voices. It sounded like Mick had covered the receiver with his hand to engage in an argument. "Listen," he said to me a minute later. "I really gotta go. I just want to know that you're still in my corner."

"Of course I am. Even if you are a crappy client."

He paused. "I was there," he said softly.

"Where?"

"At my house. That night."

"I know that," I said. "And so do the police. The guy across the street, Mitchell Selvy, he saw you leaning against your car. He told the police. I talked to him. I met your neighbor Darren, too."

"Darren, huh? What'd Darren have to say?"

"He acted strange. When I mentioned Kaye, he got very flustered. Tried to hit me with his spinning rod."

"Yeah, that's Darren," he murmured. I heard him take a deep breath. "Brady, I went inside. I—I saw Kaye's body."

"Jesus, Mick."

"Oh, man . . ."

"Mick," I said, "Listen to me."

"I'm not—"

"My job is to protect you, give you good advice, right?"

"I'm not gonna turn myself in, Brady. Fuggedaboutit."

"I've got to tell Horowitz about this conversation, you know."

"Sure. Of course you do. Go ahead."

I sighed. "Be careful, Mick."

"I'm okay." He hesitated. "If you see Danny and Erin . . ."

"I'll tell them you're okay."

"Tell them I love them, willya?"

"I will. Of course."

"Look," he said, "I really gotta go. Hey, Brady?"

"Yes?"

"Keep an eye on your mail."

"What?"

"See ya, bud."

"Mick, wait—"

But he'd disconnected.

# THIRTEEN

I got to the office before Julie, as I usually do on Monday mornings. I turned on Mr. Coffee and the other important office machines, poured a mug for myself, took it to my desk, and tracked down Horowitz at the State Police barracks at Leverett Circle.

"I was actually gonna call you," he said.

"Why?"

"The ME's all done, and Katherine Fallon's body has been released. Figured you should know."

"Have her kids been told?"

"We told them first. They're next of kin. You're just a lawyer."

"What'd the autopsy show?"

"Blow to the head was lethal. All the carving, that was just for fun. She would've died anyway."

"What about physical evidence? Any fingerprints?"

Horowitz sighed. "So far, nothing helpful." He paused. "Listen. You called me. So what did you want?"

"I left you a message yesterday."

"About the two guys in Lexington? The neighbors? Got it. Already thought of it. But thank you. Good to know you're trying to be cooperative. That it? You called to see if I got your message?"

"No," I said. "I called to tell you Mick's alive. He called me last night."

Horowitz was silent for a moment. "Yeah," he said thoughtfully. "Figures."

I told Horowitz that I had no idea where Mick had called from and that I'd tried to convince him to turn himself in, but he'd refused. "There's more," I said. I told Horowitz about my encounter with Vincent Russo. I told him everything, including how Russo had implied threats to Danny and Erin, and how he might've had a pretty good motive to murder Kaye.

"Interesting," mumbled Horowitz.

"You think Russo killed Kaye?"

"Hell, no. That's dumb. Fallon killed his wife, regardless of what he's telling you. Interesting that Russo's using you."

"What do you mean, using me?"

"Look, Coyne," said Horowitz. "You did good, okay? You reported all this to the cops. You're a good citizen. Now you can forget it. Go back to your wills and divorces. We're looking for Fallon. Already got arrest warrants out for him all over the Commonwealth. State cops in contiguous states have been alerted, blah blah. So listen. If you hear from him again, for Christ's sake find out where he is, and the only person you call is me."

"Well, I know that. I'm an officer of the court. Jesus."

"Don't forget it, pal."

"What about that other officer of the court?" I said.

"Which one is that?"

"Cooper. Barbara Cooper. You subpoenaed Mick's deposition from her."

"Yeah, we talked to her."

"Learn anything from her?"

"Not much. Mrs. Fallon did not confide in Attorney Cooper. She seemed to think that the woman was afraid of her husband, but she offered nothing more substantial than her subjective impressions."

"Based on her observations at the deposition?"

"I guess so. And based on things her client said. Mainly, Cooper was just trying to get a good settlement for her client. The way you would've."

"Her way's not my way," I said. I paused. "Look. Can you fill me in a little here? You seem to know things about my client that I don't know."

"Specifically?"

"Specifically Mick's gambling."

"Here's what we know for facts," said Horowitz. "Mick Fallon was in deep with Jimmy Capezza down in East Providence. You know Capezza, right?"

"Heard of him," I said. "Small-timer."

"Not so small anymore. Anyway, Fallon's been a sick gambler for twenty-five years. Rumor has it he shaved a point or two when he was playing college ball for Providence, and Cappy's probably been holding that over his head all this time. Capezza's as dumb as Fallon. Kept bookin' his bets, and Fallon kept losing. Paid Cappy just enough to keep him off his back and taking his bets. Finally, oh a little more than a year ago, Russo bought Fallon's paper off Capezza. Gave him about two bits on the buck for it, from what we hear, then started squeezing Fallon pretty tight." Horowitz let out a long breath. "You didn't know about this, huh?"

"I know Mick had a big gambling debt. I didn't know it was to Russo. Not until last night."

Horowitz was silent for a minute. Then he said, "Listen to me, Coyne. I'm talking to you as a friend here, believe it or not. I know Fallon's your client, and I know you think he's a good guy, just some poor slob who got in too deep and now everything's crashing down on him. You feel sorry for him. That's admirable. But the man whacked his wife, and you gotta come to grips with it."

"Thanks," I said. "I value your friendship."

He chuckled. "Think about it, Coyne."

I thought about it for the rest of the morning. I couldn't square it with the Mick Fallon I knew. But objectively, I could understand Horowitz's thinking. Mick was a desperate man. If Russo would hint to me that he'd hurt Mick's kids, he would've undoubtedly suggested the same possibility to Mick. Get rid of your wife, pal, before she divorces you and cleans you out. Get control of your money so you can pay what you owe, or your kids've had it.

It explained what Patsy and Paulie were doing at Skeeter's back in February, the night Mick threw them out. They had showed up there to get Mick's attention, to remind him that Russo would never leave him alone until he got his money.

I could only hope Horowitz nailed Mick before Russo did.

Julie dumped the morning's mail on my desk a little before noontime. She always kept the bills and checks and most of the legal documents and other business-related stuff for herself and left the junk and the occasional personal letter for me.

Today's delivery contained several fly-fishing catalogs and the office copy of the new *American Angler*, all of which I set aside for careful study later.

There was just one piece of first-class mail—a plain business-sized envelope with my name and address scrawled on it with a black felt-tip pen. The word *Personal* was printed across the bottom and underlined twice. It was postmarked Boston. There was no return address.

I stuck my finger under the flap and tore it open.

It contained a single sheet of paper, a computer-generated statement from Blue Cross/Blue Shield. Across the top was printed the legend: "Explanation of Benefits. This is not a bill."

Subscriber's name: Michael S. Fallon
Date of claim: February 14–18, 1998
Patient's name: Katherine M. Fallon
Hospital: Emerson Hospital, Concord, Massachusetts

A long list of services—surgery, anesthesia, medical and surgical care, interpretation of laboratory tests, diagnostic X rays, medication—were itemized, adding up to $15,746.72. The patient balance was zero.

There were numerous codes and acronyms which I couldn't decipher, so I could not figure out by whom Kaye had been treated, or for what complaint.

But the statement did tell me where and when. I checked my desk calendar. February 14–18 were the Saturday through Wednesday that included the Washington's birthday holiday—now known as President's Day and always celebrated on a Monday. Vacation week for public schoolchildren—and teachers—in Massachusetts.

Gretchen Conley had told me that Kaye Fallon went cross-country skiing in Vermont that week. Kaye had given Gretchen a key so she could feed the cat and water the plants.

But Kaye had actually spent most of that week in the hospital. Either Gretchen had lied to me, or Kaye had lied to Gretchen.

Mick had mailed it to me, of course. When he called, he'd told me to watch my mail. As the health insurance "subscriber," this statement would've been mailed to him. I figured he'd just received it. It was typical that it would take about four months to get to him.

I looked over the explanation of benefits again. It told me nothing.

I thought about it for a couple of minutes. Then I picked up the phone and pecked out the Conleys' number in Concord. After three or four rings, Gretchen answered.

"It's Brady Coyne," I said.

"Oh," she said brightly. "Brady. How are you?"

"Just fine. How about you?"

She sighed. "Oh, better, I guess. It's been hard, and having Danny and Erin here . . . well, I'm certainly not complaining . . . I mean, I'm really happy that we can be of some help to the poor kids . . . but it's been, you know, stressful. And now . . . I don't know if you heard, but Kaye's body has been released."

"Yes," I said. "I heard this morning."

"It looks like Lyn and I are the, um, surrogate parents here." She blew out a breath. "Don't get me wrong. We really love those kids, and I'm glad we can be here for them. And I guess it's helped me get some perspective, if you know what I mean. I did spend a lot of time feeling sorry for myself."

"Sure," I said. "Are the Fallon kids there now?"

"No. They're off with Lyn. He's helping them make funeral arrangements for Kaye."

"How are they handling it?"

"Well, of course, this business with the funeral isn't easy for them. But they've seemed a little better since you talked with them the other day. Erin isn't crying all the time, and the two of them are spending a lot of time together. Whatever you said to them helped."

"I'm glad." I hesitated. "Gretchen, I have some business out your way, and I wondered if I stopped by, might I possibly prevail upon you for a glass of iced tea?"

"Iced tea? Well, gee. Sure. That would be nice. I'm here. It's just me and this big empty house and nothing but a pile of laundry. I'd love the company."

"I'll be there sometime this afternoon. Will that be all right?"

"I'm not going anywhere, that's for sure. I don't even have a

**188**

car." She hesitated. "What is it, Brady? Has something happened?"

"Nothing new," I said.

It was a little after two o'clock when I pulled into the lot at Emerson Hospital in Concord.

Hospital bureaucracies, in my experience, rival those of governments in evasiveness, unapproachability, and high-handedness. On the other hand, I knew that what medical people fear above all things are lawsuits.

Hey, I was a lawyer.

I entered the emergency area. From behind drawn curtains off to my right, in the subsonic electric hush of the place, I heard a soft moan. A matter-of-fact female intercom voice summoned Dr. Paulsen. The faint smell of Lysol mingled with rubbing alcohol and something sweet—cherry-flavored cough syrup, maybe—and something sour, like vomit.

I could've closed my eyes and I would've known I was in a hospital.

Behind a counter straight ahead of me a thirtyish man in a white jacket stood talking to a fortyish woman, also in a white jacket. Another woman, this one wearing a blue cardigan sweater over a white blouse, was seated behind the counter peering at a computer monitor.

As I approached them, the white-coated pair wandered away. I stood in front of the seated woman. She was Asian and quite attractive, with straight black hair cut very short, black eyes, and beautiful smooth skin. The plaque pinned to her sweater read "B. Liu."

"Excuse me?" I said.

She looked up. "May I help you, sir?"

"I don't know if you're the one to help me or not," I said. I removed the Blue Cross/Blue Shield form from my jacket pocket, unfolded it, and laid it on the counter in front of her. "I'm investigating this admission."

She glanced at the form, then cocked her head at me. A smile played around the corners of her mouth. "Investigating?"

"I'm an attorney."

"Yes?"

"I need to know the name of the doctor who handled this case."

"I'm sorry, sir, but all hospital records are strictly confidential. I can't give you that information."

"Who can?"

She looked down at the form. "Is there a problem with the billing or something?"

I leaned my elbows on the counter and bent close to her. "The patient died," I whispered.

She leaned back in her chair and looked up at me. "Oh, dear," she said.

"And I am the family lawyer." I took a business card from my wallet and handed it to her. She glanced at it, then tucked it under the corner of her desk blotter.

I pointed to Kaye's name on the Blue Cross form. "Ring a bell?"

She looked at it. "Fallon." She frowned.

"You might've read about her," I said. "She died about a week ago."

"Did she die here? In the hospital?"

"No. Suddenly. At home."

"Locally?"

"In Lexington."

She shrugged. "You know," she said, "most people who die around here were patients at this hospital at one time or another. You should probably talk to Banyon."

"Who's Banyon?" I said.

190

"Assistant director," she said. "Her job is to worry about things like lawsuits."

"I didn't say anything about a lawsuit."

B. Liu smiled and leaned across her desk toward me. "You want information out of Banyon," she whispered, "you might want to try it."

"So how do I get to see this Banyon?"

"I'll page her for you. You can sit over there." She waved to a row of plastic chairs against the wall.

"Well, okay," I said. "But just so you know, I hate hospitals, and I hate waiting."

"Who doesn't?" she said.

"If you can impress upon Ms. Banyon the, um, urgency of this situation . . ."

"Everything in the emergency room is urgent, Mr. Coyne." She smiled. "I will tell her you're a lawyer. That should expedite things."

The molded plastic seats were bolted to the floor so that you had no choice but to stare at the television screen mounted on the opposite wall. It was playing some afternoon talk show.

A television talk show, with the sound muted. That's entertainment.

I flipped through a couple of month-old *Newsweek* magazines, and when I glanced at my watch, I saw that I'd been sitting there for half an hour. I got up and went to the counter. B. Liu looked up at me and shrugged. "She knows you're here," she said, "and she knows you're a lawyer."

"Perhaps you'll tell her that I'm growing impatient," I said.

"I can do that. For what it might be worth."

"I'm stepping outside. I have not given up. I'm not going to give up."

She smiled. "Of course you're not."

I went out into the afternoon sunshine, found a bench to sit on, and lit a cigarette. I felt vaguely criminal, sitting under the hospital Emergency sign, sucking carcinogens into my lungs. Dozens of smashed cigarette butts lay scattered under the bench. This was a popular place for worrying, I guessed.

When I went back inside, I saw a tall slender woman in a blue business suit leaning both elbows on the counter talking with B. Liu. She had reddish brown hair that fell below her shoulders. Her skirt was very short. She had extraordinarily long legs. Long and quite shapely legs, one of which she had cocked up behind her. Her shoe was dangling from her toes.

B. Liu glanced at me, then spoke to the woman, who turned, squinted at me, then smiled. She slipped her shoe back onto her foot, then came toward me with her hand extended. "Mr. Coyne," she said. "I'm Evelyn Banyon. Assistant director of the hospital." She smiled. "Public relations, community liaison, press secretary, all-round helpful person."

I took her hand. She had pale blue eyes, almost silver, and a fine dusting of freckles across the bridge of her nose. In her heels, she was nearly as tall as I.

"Thanks for seeing me," I said. "Can we talk?"

"Sure," she said. "We can go back to my office, which is up two floors and down several corridors, or we can go outside so I can have a smoke."

"A no-brainer," I said.

We went outside and sat on the same bench I'd occupied a few minutes earlier. Evelyn Banyon took a pack of Merit Lites from a pocket and lit one with a slim gold lighter.

"So," she said, blowing out a long plume of smoke. "You planning to sue us?"

"I don't know," I blustered. "My client's next of kin was not properly notified when she was admitted, and—"

She put her hand on my arm. "Mr. Coyne," she said, "I have a suggestion."

"What's that?"

"Don't bullshit me, okay?"

"What makes you think—?"

"I checked out this case," she said. "I know who Katherine Fallon is—was—and when she was here and how she died. You're not here because of anything the hospital did wrong. You're investigating her murder. Now, I talked with the director, and he said if that were in fact the case, there is no reason why I shouldn't cooperate with you. So I'm willing to cooperate with you. So why don't you just tell me how I can do that?"

"Oh," I said. "Good idea. See—"

"Or," she said quickly, "if you'd rather try to bullshit me, okay, that's fine, too. Then I could use my training and experience, deflect and cut through your bullshit, because that's mostly what I do. Deal with bullshit. Give it and take it."

"No," I said. "Let's just—"

"In fact," she interrupted, "bullshit is my best thing, Mr. Coyne." She grinned wickedly. She was obviously enjoying herself. "But the truth is, it would be refreshing not to do bullshit with someone for a change. So it's up to you. It's a pleasant day, nice to be outside, we can't smoke in my office, and if you think it would be fun to bullshit for a while, okay by me."

I smiled. "No, that's all right."

"Up to you."

"All I'm really after," I said, "is a chance to talk to the doctor who treated her."

"Not that it matters," she said, "but can I ask why?"

"Kaye Fallon came in with an emergency, ended up staying in the hospital for five days, and I need to know what the problem was."

"And this is, um, relevant to your investigation, huh?"

"It might be."

"So you can catch whoever murdered Mrs. Fallon."

I smiled. "Not really. I'm a lawyer, not a detective."

"Both of us deal with secrets and client privilege, huh? We're both into the bullshit game."

"I really can't tell you much more than that, Ms. Banyon," I said.

"Evie, please," she said. "Okay?"

I nodded. "Sure. Evie. I'm Brady."

She smiled quickly, dropped her cigarette butt onto the ground, and ground it out with the toe of her shoe. "Dr. Allison," she said. "That's the surgeon who was on call that night."

"How do I get a hold of him?"

"Her," she said. "Dr. Allison's a woman. And there are several ways to get ahold of her. One is to call her office and make an appointment. She'd probably be able to squeeze you in toward the middle of September. Two, get a subpoena and deal with our team of crackerjack lawyers. Three, follow her when she leaves and waylay her in the parking lot. Four, ask me to expedite it for you."

"You'd do that?"

"It's my job."

"Gee," I said. "I thought it was because I was charming and persuasive."

"No," she said. "It's my job."

"I can live with that. So what do we do?"

"We head over to the next wing, the John Cummings Building, where Dr. Allison's office is located. We enter her office, and I confer briefly with the receptionist, who will then usher us into Dr. Allison's sanctum, where, I happen to know, she is seeing, as we speak, her last patient of the afternoon. The receptionist expects us, and by the time we get there, Dr. Allison should be ready to see us. I will introduce you to her, shake your hand, and depart, quite happy to have made your acquaintance and to have served the hospital's public in a useful and constructive manner."

"She's already expecting us?"

"I'm pretty good at my job, Brady."

"Wow," I said.

"Disappointed you didn't get to threaten me with lawsuits?"

"A bit," I said. "I'll just have to deal with it."

"Shall we go?"

"Let's have another cigarette first."

She grinned. "Good plan."


Dr. Allison was a tiny, fortyish African American woman. She was Jeff to Evie Banyon's Mutt.

When Evie introduced us, Dr. Allison stood up from behind her desk and cocked her head at me. Her intelligent brown eyes regarded me solemnly. "Evie assures me that your intent is not litigious, Mr. Coyne."

"It's not," I said.

Dr. Allison glanced at her watch, then sat down. "Okay. Let's get to it. I've got rounds in fifteen minutes."

"I'll be heading along, then," said Evie. She handed me a business card. "Anything else comes up, give me a call."

"Thanks." I tucked her card into my wallet.

After Evie Banyon left, Dr. Allison said, "Katherine Fallon, right? So what do you want to know?"

"She was admitted to the emergency room early on the morning of February 14. You treated her." I shrugged. "Can you just tell me about it?"

She picked up a manila folder from her desk. "I refreshed my memory," she said, tapping the folder. "Sometimes things get crazy in the E.R. But actually, I remember the Fallon case very clearly. We saved her life."

I nodded.

"She presented symptoms of acute appendicitis," she continued. "Abdominal pain, shortness of breath, faintness. I was afraid that it had ruptured. I talked with the woman who brought her in, and she mentioned that Mrs. Fallon had complained of pain in her shoulder. That was the key."

"Key to what?"

"That was the key to my diagnosis. I proceeded with a laparotomy—that's an incision directly into the abdomen—and I found that she'd begun to hemorrhage. It was a close thing."

"It *was* a ruptured appendix, then?"

Dr. Allison shook her head. "No, Mr. Coyne. It was a ruptured fallopian tube."

I frowned. "How—?"

"Another hour, maybe less, and she might well have died from the hemorrhaging," she said. "Or after a few days from peritonitis. Mrs. Fallon had an ectopic pregnancy."

As I headed out to the parking lot, I thought about what Dr. Allison had told me. An ectopic pregnancy occurs when a fertilized egg lodges somewhere other than in the uterus, most commonly in the fallopian tube, which was the case with Kaye Fallon. If it's diagnosed early, it can be terminated by a simple outpatient procedure. But if it's left untreated, the egg grows until it causes a rupture, massive hemorrhaging, peritonitis. Without emergency surgery, this would almost surely be fatal.

Well, it didn't kill Kaye, thanks to Gretchen's help and Dr. Allison's skill. At least not directly.

But as far as I was concerned, the key word was *pregnancy.*

I pulled into the Conleys' driveway a little before four. I parked alongside the red Honda, got out, and went to the front porch.

Before I could touch the doorbell, Gretchen pushed open the screen door. "Hi, there," she said. "I heard your car. Come on in."

I went in. She was wearing sneakers and a shapeless, ankle-length dress that could only be described as frumpy. Her face was damp and pink, as if she'd been working outdoors.

She gripped my arm and led me out to the deck. "Iced tea's all fixed," she said. "Make yourself comfortable. I'll fetch it."

I slumped into one of the big wooden deck chairs, and a minute later Gretchen was back with two tall glasses and a cut-glass pitcher tinkling with ice cubes. She poured the glasses full, handed one to me, put the pitcher on the table, then leaned back against the deck rail.

I took a sip. "Mm," I said. "Perfect."

She pressed her glass against her forehead. "The heat gets to me," she said. "Lyn says it wouldn't be so bad if I lost a few pounds, and I suppose he's right." She shrugged. "I try. I really do."

This was one of those no-win topics that I'd learned long ago to avoid. "I noticed your car in the driveway," I said. "I thought you said you didn't have a car."

She waved her hand. "Oh, that's Neddie's. It hasn't run for a month. Broken alternator, I think it is. Lyn insists that Neddie save his money to get it fixed. It'll cost something like six hundred dollars." Gretchen smiled wryly. "Well, he's right, I suppose. Kids have to be responsible. But meanwhile, Neddie just borrows our cars. Takes mine to school most of the time. I'm not exactly clear on what lesson he's learning by this."

I nodded and sipped my tea. Child-rearing theory was another one of those lose-lose topics.

Gretchen smiled. "I know this is not just a social call, Brady."

I nodded. "I just came from Emerson Hospital."

She nodded with no expression.

"Kaye was there back in February. When you told me she'd been skiing in Vermont."

Gretchen looked down into her lap.

"You lied," I said.

197

"Yes," she said softly.

"Tell me about it," I said. "Tell me what happened."

She let out a deep breath, then looked up at me. "Kaye called me at around two A.M. A Friday night, it was. Saturday morning. She was crying. She was in terrible pain, she said, having trouble catching her breath. Said she hadn't been feeling well for a few days. She thought she might have appendicitis or something. I told her to call 911, but she said no, she wanted me to drive her. I tried to argue with her, but she said she didn't feel like it was an emergency, didn't want to overreact. By the time I got to her, she was doubled over, crying. Dizzy, her pulse racing, cold sweat. Terrible, terrible pain. It was very scary. I raced her to Emerson. They admitted her and operated right away. They said it was a close call." She shrugged. "They kept her for four or five days. Then I brought her home. She missed a couple days of school, then she was back on her feet and none the worse for wear."

I looked at her. "So why'd you lie about it?"

Gretchen closed her eyes, rubbed her forehead, then shrugged. "She asked me to. Made me promise." She bowed her head. "I'm sorry," she mumbled.

At that moment a car door slammed out front, and an instant later the screen door slapped shut. Then Ned appeared on the deck.

He went to Gretchen, bent over, and kissed her cheek. "Where's Danny and Erin?"

"They're with your father. Planning the funeral."

"Oh, jeez," he said. Then he looked at me. "Why're you here again?"

"Neddie," said Gretchen. "Don't be rude."

"Look," he said to her, "I'm sorry, but why can't everybody just leave us alone? Haven't we all been through enough?"

"We want to help, don't we, honey?" She reached up and touched his face.

Ned shrugged. "Yeah, I guess." He looked at me. "Sorry about that. Haven't they caught up with Uncle Mick yet?"

"No," I said.

"Mr. Coyne and I need to talk," said Gretchen.

"What about?"

"Privately," she said.

"Oh, right." Ned shrugged. "I just stopped in to get some stuff. I might not be home for dinner, okay?"

"Where are you going?"

"Oh, Mom." He kissed her cheek. "Places to go, people to see, you know?"

She smiled and shook her head. "Where's your sister?"

"I dunno."

"You know you're supposed to bring her home. That's part of the deal. You use my car, you drive Linda."

"Oh, she said she had a ride. I checked with her."

"So you're taking my car?"

"Well, yeah."

"Aren't you forgetting something?"

"Huh?" He frowned. "Oh, right." He grinned. "Um, hey, Mom? Can I borrow your car this afternoon?"

"Well, sure. Of course you can. You might put some gas in it. And drive carefully."

"Sure, sure. I always do." He leaned down and kissed her again, said, "Take it easy" to me, and left. I heard him clomp up, then down, the inside stairs, and a minute later he roared away.

Gretchen looked at me and shook her head. "Will I survive this?"

I smiled.

"What difference does it make?" she said softly.

"What?"

"Whether Kaye was in Vermont or in the hospital."

"Do you know why she was in the hospital?" I said.

She stared at me for a moment, then nodded.

"You knew she was pregnant?"

"Not until then. Not until that night I took her to the hospital. She never would've told me."

"Gretchen," I said, "don't you see—"

"What?" she said. "That Kaye having an affair was important information?" She shook her head. "Of course I see that."

"Then why did you lie?"

"Kaye was horrified and embarrassed. She made me vow to keep her secret. So when—when this happened, when she was killed, my first thought was to honor my friend's wish. Nobody but me knew she'd been in the hospital and not in Vermont. I was the only one who knew she'd been pregnant." She smiled quickly. "I've been wrestling with it for a week, Brady. My promise to Kaye, her reputation. And the possibility that somebody who loved her, someone other than Mick . . ." She tilted her head back and gazed up at the sky.

"That somebody she was having an affair with," I said, "might have killed her."

She nodded. "Yes. That it might not be Mick. Although Mick still makes the most sense, don't you think? I mean, if he found out about it . . ."

"So who was it?" I said.

"Kaye's lover?" Gretchen smiled. "You didn't really know her, did you?"

"No."

"I asked her, of course. I told her I was happy for her, that she'd found somebody. I teased her. I tried every way I knew. I was dying of curiosity. But when Kaye made up her mind about something, that was it. She'd just smile and get that twinkle in her eye and say he looked like a famous movie star."

"A movie star." I smiled. "Did she indicate whether he was, say, John Wayne? Or Brad Pitt? Or maybe Woody Allen?"

"Of course not," said Gretchen. "She was just being evasive. I understood, and didn't press it."

"Not even a hint?"

She shook her head. "None."

"So was she planning to marry this—this movie star? Is that why she was proceeding with her divorce?"

Gretchen shrugged. "She wouldn't talk about that. She was very coy about the whole thing."

"The man," I said. "Did he visit her in the hospital? Send flowers? Call her?"

She shrugged. "If he did, it certainly wasn't when I was there. The only flowers in her room were ones I brought. As far as I know, I was the only one who knew she was there."

I stood up, propped my elbows on the deck rail and my chin on my fists, and gazed off toward the river.

Gretchen came over beside me. She put her hand on my shoulder. "I am sorry," she said.

"You should've told somebody right away. The police, me."

"I know," she said. "You're right. I've been . . . not exactly thinking straight, since I—I saw her body. I guess I've been more concerned about protecting Kaye's reputation than . . ." She shook her head. "What can I say? I'm sorry."

I shrugged. "What about Lyn? Does he know?"

She nodded. "We always talked about Kaye and Mick. He kept me up-to-date on Mick, and I told him about Kaye. We used to be a foursome, you know. We all liked each other. Even when Lyn . . . well, he used to drink. Thank God, that's passed. We had some rough times, but Mick and Kaye were always there for us. Anyway, we never stopped being close with Kaye and Mick. So, sure. I told Lyn that Kaye was involved with somebody. He thought that was nice for her. I made him promise to keep Kaye's secret." She smiled. "We both wished Mick would meet somebody, too, but as far as I know, he just kept on loving Kaye."

"Yes," I said. "He still does."

She nodded. "So now what happens?"

201

"I'll have to tell Lieutenant Horowitz," I said. "He'll probably want to talk with you."

"Yes, okay. I understand."

"If you think of anything else . . ."

"I know. I'll tell you. I promise. I feel so stupid."

"You were just trying to be a friend," I said.

"I know, but . . ."

"You're right, of course," I said. "It was wrong and stupid not to tell us."

She smiled. "Thank you for your support."

She followed me out to the driveway. I opened my car door, started to climb in, then stopped. "Gretchen," I said, "do me a favor."

She nodded. "Of course."

"When you see Danny and Erin, tell them that their father loves them."

She frowned. "Well, okay, but . . ."

"I talked to him on the phone last night. He's okay."

She smiled. "Oh, gee. That's wonderful."

"For now, anyway."

She nodded. "I'll tell the kids. Of course I will."

# FOURTEEN

$\mathbf{I}$t was nearly five-thirty by the time I pulled out of the Conleys' driveway. I headed back into the city. Rush-hour traffic was solid in both directions all the way from Crosby's Corner on Route 2 in Concord, to the bottleneck by the Alewife MBTA station, to the Fresh Pond traffic circle in Cambridge, to Storrow Drive along the Charles, to the upramp onto the expressway by the science museum, to the exit to the New England Aquarium, to Atlantic Avenue, to my apartment building at Lewis Wharf on Boston's inner harbor.

I smoked cigarettes and played Stevie Ray Vaughn CDs very loud while I inched along with the traffic, which helped. But it was still harrowing as hell, and it took about an hour and a half to travel those twenty-odd miles.

In the old days—the Alexandria Shaw days—she would've been waiting for me when I lurched into my apartment, dropped my briefcase inside the doorway, and shucked off my jacket and tie. She'd be sitting on the sofa wearing one of my Yale University Property of the Department of Athletics T-shirts and a pair of my boxer shorts, with her bare legs tucked up under her, sipping from a Sam Adams bottle and shouting out answers as *Jeopardy* played on my old black-and-white Hitachi TV. Her big round glasses would've slipped down to the tip of her nose, and when I came in, she'd peer myopically up at me, poke her glasses up with her forefinger, then give me that beautiful smile and say, "Hi, sweetie."

And she'd tilt up her face and purse her lips for a kiss, which I would deliver, and if I held it too long, she'd let her mouth slide away so she could shout, "Ayn Rand" or "the Battle of Fallen Timbers" or "the Canary Islands" at the television. Alex could've been a *Jeopardy* champion, except she kept forgetting to say "What is . . . ?"

Some spicy aroma would be wafting in from my kitchen, and I'd go to check it out, and it would be lentil soup or twice-baked potatoes or vegetarian chili, something full of vitamins and minerals and low in fat and cholesterol, something delicious even though it was good for me.

Well, Alex wasn't there on this Monday evening in June, and she hadn't been since she'd moved to Garrison, Maine, two years earlier, and now it had been nearly ten months since I'd seen her—Labor Day, to be precise, which was when I'd driven out of her driveway for the last time.

Ten months, and I still hadn't figured out exactly what happened.

I climbed out of my suit and into a pair of jeans, found a bottle of Blue Moon in the refrigerator, and took it out onto my balcony. I flopped into an aluminum chair, tilted back with my heels up on the railing, balanced the bottle on my stomach, and closed my eyes.

All the way home from Concord, while part of my mind rode the rhythms of Stevie Ray's guitar, the other part had flipped randomly through the facts of Kaye Fallon's ectopic pregnancy, looking for insight and connection to her murder.

It still kept coming back to Mick.

He was my client, innocent or guilty. All the objective evidence pointed to guilty. But he'd told me he didn't do it, and I wanted to believe him.

I sipped my Blue Moon and watched the gulls cruise on the thermals and the ferry inch across the harbor, and when the bottle was empty, I set it on the concrete floor of the balcony and let my eyes fall shut.

When I woke up, darkness had seeped in over the harbor. Blinking airplane lights were circling over Logan, and the pinpricks of other lights showed out on the islands.

I pushed myself out of my chair, went into the kitchen, heated a can of Hormel beef stew, and ate it from the saucepan at the table.

Then I called Horowitz at his secret number.

"You in the middle of dinner or something?" I said.

"Oh, hell, no," he said. "This is a perfect time for you to interrupt me, Coyne. I was sitting here watching TV with my wife, and we were just saying, Wouldn't it be great if Coyne'd call again, because, hell, we haven't talked to him since this morning, and here we are, just the two of us, and when was the last time we had any time together, and it's really just too fucking weird, being relaxed, having actual time to ourselves here without somebody like Coyne buggin' me."

"Okay," I said. "Catch you later."

I hung up and lit a cigarette.

The phone rang thirty seconds later. "This better be good," said Horowitz.

"Kaye Fallon was pregnant."

"The hell she was. I saw the ME's report."

"She had an ectopic pregnancy. Emergency surgery at Emerson Hospital in February."

"Ectopic—"

"That's a fertilized egg in the fallopian tube."

"Christ, Coyne," he growled. "I know what an ectopic preg-

205

nancy is. I mean, I didn't go to a fancy Ivy League college, but that doesn't mean I don't know anything." He was silent for a moment. "She was pregnant, huh?"

"It means she was having an affair."

"No shit, Sam Spade. So, okay. Tell me what you know."

I told him how Mick had mailed me the Blue Cross/Blue Shield form and about my conversations with Gretchen Conley and Dr. Allison.

"So Mick found out," said Horowitz. "Went to her house to confront her, blew his stack, and whacked her with that statue."

"*The Thinker,*" I said. "That was the statue. I don't think he found out about the pregnancy until after Kaye was already dead."

"How so?"

"Why else would he send me that form when he did?"

"Hmm," said Horowitz. "Go on."

"He mailed it to me the day before he disappeared. He got it in the mail, figured out what it was all about, and that's probably when he blew his stack. Maybe he wanted to kill Kaye when he saw it. But he couldn't even if he wanted to, because someone else had already done it. Anyway, I think he's got an idea who her lover was. I think that's what Mick's doing now. Tracking down the guy who was having this affair with Kaye. That's who probably killed her, not Mick."

"Save it for the courtroom, Coyne. You gotta have your head up your ass way past your shoulders not to see that this is just one more finger pointing at your client."

"Maybe it is," I said. "Still, it'd be good to know who this lover is, wouldn't it?"

"Sure. So you gonna tell me? That why you called? You got an actual piece of useful information for me?"

"No," I said. "I don't know who it is. I've already told you about Will Powers, that kid who used to be her student, who might've been stalking her, and I also mentioned Ronald Moyle, the principal of the school where she taught. But Kaye Fallon probably knew a hundred guys who thought she looked pretty good. Hell, any guy would think Kaye Fallon looked good. Your witness there, Mitchell Selvy, he told me he liked looking at her. And there's that Down's syndrome guy, Darren."

I heard Horowitz sigh. "Yeah, okay, so I guess I better talk to Mrs. Conley again. And that doctor—what was his name?"

"Allison. It's a woman. Her office is in the John Cummings Building at Emerson Hospital."

"Got it." He paused, then said, "Uh, Coyne?"

"Yes?"

"I just want you to know. I'm gonna get my cell phone number changed, okay? And when I do, I'm counting on you to help me remember not to give it to you."

Then the phone went dead.

When I stepped out of the shower the next morning, my door buzzer was ringing steadily. I wrapped a towel around my waist and went to the intercom, leaving wet footprints on the carpet.

I pressed the button. "I'm here. Who is it?"

"Sergeant Benetti. The lieutenant wants you to come down."

"Christ, I just got out of the shower. What's the—"

"Get dressed," she said. "Make it quick."

The last time Horowitz had come for me, Mick was holding Skeeter hostage. I guessed this had something to do with Mick, too.

I slipped into a pair of jeans and a cotton shirt, grabbed my cigarettes and a car mug full of coffee, and took the stairs down to the lobby. Horowitz's Taurus was parked directly in front of the door with the back door hanging open for me. I slid in, and before I could settle back, Benetti had peeled away from the curb.

Without preamble, and without even turning in his seat, Horowitz said, "Guy name of Watts."

"I don't know any Watts," I said.

"Darren Watts. Ring a bell?"

"Darren? Oh, the Down's syndrome guy in Lexington. What about him?"

"Why the fuck do you think I came for you?" said Horowitz. "You think I wanna buy you breakfast? He's dead, that's what."

I blew out a breath. "Darren? Homicide?"

"Don't know. Unattended death. Lexington cops called it in. I mean, one day you mention this guy's name, the next day he's dead, and I figured, friend of Coyne's, another God damn dead body in the same neighborhood, maybe he'd like to join me, help shed a little light on the subject."

"You didn't give me much choice," I said.

Benetti had the flasher blinking and the siren wailing, and she weaved and darted expertly among the early-morning traffic. Morning rush hour was coming into the city, not going out the way we were, and she made good time.

A jogger had spotted Darren's body facedown in the pond where he liked to fish. That's all Horowitz would tell me. Then he turned to the side window, and neither he nor Benetti said anything all the way to Lexington.

There were three Lexington cruisers and a medical examiner's van parked at awkward angles alongside the road just around the corner from the Fallons' house when we got there. A small cluster of gawkers had gathered where the jogging path led into the woods. They were being held at bay by three or four uniformed officers. I noticed a gray-haired woman sitting on the ground crying into her hands. She was wearing a flowered housedress and bedroom slippers. A younger woman was kneeling beside her with her arm around her shoulder.

I followed Horowitz and Benetti along the path and down to the pond, where a couple of uniformed cops stood with their backs to the water. About ten feet from shore, two men in shirt-sleeves stood thigh-deep in the water. They were bent over Darren's body.

Horowitz spoke to the cops, then went to the water's edge. "Hey," he said.

One of the two men straightened up, shielded his eyes, nodded, and waded to shore. He was tall, bald, big-beaked, and stoop-shouldered. "Drowned," he said.

"Accident?" said Horowitz.

The tall man shook his head. "Not unless you can figure how he might smash in the back of his own head and then fall facedown in three feet of water, not to mention explaining where the finger bruises on his neck and throat came from."

Horowitz turned to Marcia Benetti. "Take Mr. Coyne back to the car and keep him humored till I get there."

"Wait a minute—" I began.

But Benetti grabbed my elbow and led me away.

I sat in the backseat. She sat behind the wheel, looking out the window.

"You don't say much," I said to her.

"No," she said.

"What's your partner thinking?"

"I don't know."

Fifteen minutes later, Horowitz strolled back. Instead of coming over to where I was waiting, he went to the woman in the housedress, who was still sitting on the ground. He squatted down directly in front of her, and I saw her head lift up to look at him. I heard the rumble of his voice, but couldn't make out what he was saying. The woman was shaking her head. Tears were streaming down her cheeks, and she made no effort to wipe them away.

After a few minutes, Horowitz patted her arm, stood up, and came to the cruiser. He slid in beside me. "Mrs. Watts," he said. "Divorced lady. Darren was her only child."

I blew out a breath. "What happened?"

"Looks like someone whacked him from behind, then held his head under water."

"When?"

"ME figures he's been dead around twelve hours."

"So it happened early last night."

Horowitz nodded.

"She didn't report him missing?" I said.

"She says he stays out late most nights, doesn't come in till after she's gone to sleep. He's a big boy, she says. Twenty-six years old. She tries to treat him like an adult. Doesn't ask where he's been or what he's been doing, and he doesn't tell her. He likes fishing. That's about all she could say."

"If he stays out at night," I said, "he might've seen who killed Kaye." I thought for a moment. "Or—"

"I know what you're thinking," said Horowitz.

"Or Darren might've done it," I finished.

Horowitz tapped my knee. "Got a question for you."

I nodded.

"You were out here the other day."

"Yes. Saturday."

"You talked with Darren Watts."

"Yes. I told you. He acted strange. Angry, afraid, or something. Got very agitated when I mentioned Kaye Fallon. He ran away from me, and when I followed him to the pond, he swung his fishing rod at me, chased me away."

"My question is this," said Horowitz. "Who'd you tell about this?"

I thought for a minute. "Well, you. And I think I mentioned it to Gretchen and Lyn Conley, and—" I stopped and looked at Horowitz.

"Fallon," he said. "You talked to Fallon on the phone."

"Yes. I mentioned it to Mick, too."

Horowitz nodded and proceeded to question me about every

detail of my two encounters with Darren, first at the Fallons' house and then at the pond. He made me remember everyone I'd told about seeing Darren. Then I had to go back all over it again for him.

When we finished, he gave me his quick, cynical grin. "Why not do everybody a favor, Coyne. Hereafter, mind your own fucking business. Okay?"

"You think I—?"

"I hope you got a good look at young Mr. Watts's body, pal, because this one's on your head."


Horowitz stayed at the crime scene in Lexington, and Marcia Benetti drove me back to my apartment. I didn't try to make conversation with her. I was trying to get my mind around the possibility that Mick Fallon had murdered his former neighbor, Darren Watts. I knew what Horowitz was thinking: either Darren had killed Kaye, and Mick had figured it out and taken his revenge, or Darren had seen Mick kill his wife and Mick had killed the witness.

Either way, Mick was a helluva suspect. And I was the one who'd put Darren Watts into his mind.

Horowitz was probably right. Everyone would be better off if I'd just stick to wills and divorces.


Around noontime, Lyn Conley called me at my office. "Just thought you'd want to know," he said. "Kaye's going to be waked Wednesday at the Douglas Funeral Home in Lexington. Visiting hours'll be three to five and seven to nine. Funeral's Thursday at ten A.M. at the Immaculate Conception Church. It's in today's paper."

"Gretchen told me you were helping Danny and Erin with the arrangements," I said.

"The least I could do, I guess."

"So how are they handling it?"

"I was with them when they saw her. That was pretty rough. But I think it got them over a hump. Made it real, you know? They're good, solid kids. They'll be okay." He hesitated. "It'd sure help if Mick was around, though."

"It sure would," I said. I saw no purpose in mentioning Darren Watts to Lyn. "Did Gretchen tell the kids that I talked with Mick?"

"Yeah. Hard to tell how they felt about that."

"Knowing he's alive . . ."

"I don't think they ever allowed themselves to think he wasn't. Or Kaye, either, for that matter, until they saw her body."

"Right," I said. "Well, I appreciate your calling. I guess I'll see you at the funeral. I'm not much for wakes."

He laughed humorlessly. "Me neither. Who the hell likes wakes? Oh, we're having a kind of reception at the house afterwards. After the interment, I mean. I think it would mean a lot to the kids if you dropped in."

"Sure," I said. "I'll be there."

# FIFTEEN

⟝————————————————————⟞

The Immaculate Conception Church was an imposing old brick structure—well, I guess all Catholic churches are imposing, at least to non-Catholics. This one had wide front steps that descended directly to the sidewalk, as if to lure in all passersby. Rhododendrons and azaleas in spectacular bloom grew against its granite foundation, and it was flanked by a pair of towering elms which had somehow been spared from the Dutch elm epidemic.

I parked across the street and sat there in my car with all the windows rolled down and the sunroof open. It was around twenty to ten, one of those intoxicating New England June mornings when birdsong and flower scent saturate the air. As good a day as any for the funeral of a murdered young wife and mother and teacher.

I could watch the front entrance of the church from where I sat. The double doors were wide open, and already people had begun to cluster on the sidewalk and front steps. Some of them were already drifting inside. They came in singles and pairs and groups and whole families. The teenagers—Kaye's former students along with friends of Danny and Erin, I guessed—clung to each other in bunches. The girls wore pastel dresses and straw hats. The boys, awkward in their suits and ties, were tugging at their shirt collars and rolling their shoulders inside their jackets.

After about ten minutes, I climbed out of my car. The funeral cortege had not yet arrived, and I wanted to be already seated inside when it did. I crossed the street and weaved among the crowd gathered outside the church, nodding to the strangers who nodded to me, then climbed the steps.

Mounted on the outside wall beside the church doors was a brass plaque like the scores of brass plaques scattered around the history-rich town. Lexington calls itself "The Birthplace of American Liberty." On its village green the American Revolution began when a British soldier fired "the shot heard 'round the world." The Minutemen got clobbered, but history records the event as "a glorious morning for America."

This plaque read: "Constructed in 1768, this is the oldest continually active Roman Catholic church in Massachusetts. Here on April 19, 1775, a wounded British soldier found sanctuary during the retreat from the Battle of Concord. This church was an important way station on the Underground Railroad. When a fire set by antiabolitionists gutted its insides in 1856, it was rebuilt with donations from townspeople of all denominations."

I went inside. A cranberry-colored carpet covered the wide central aisle down to the altar. Tall stained-glass windows on both side walls filtered in rosy sunlight. It was airy and bright and altogether cheerful in there, although the faint, sweet scent of incense brought back old feelings of awe. An organ was playing Mozart's "Ave Verum Corpus," itself not an uncheerful tune.

The old wooden pews were nearly half-filled already. Many folks were kneeling with their forearms braced on the pew back in front of them, heads bowed, hands clasped together. A few of the older women fingered rosaries and wore veils over their faces.

I paused at the rear corner of the church, scanning the faces, looking for any that I might recognize. I spotted Barbara Cooper, Kaye's lawyer, and Ron Moyle, her principal. The rest were strangers to me.

I moved around to the side aisle and slid into a pew near the back. I didn't kneel and I didn't pray, because I had never been taught how to do those things.

But I tried to think about Kaye Fallon, and to mourn her in my own inept, pagan way. I realized that I barely knew her—had, in fact, only met her once, at Mick's deposition. I had probably not seen her at her best that day.

I tried to conjure up her face in my mind, but the image that kept appearing was that of Meg Ryan, the actress. Close, but I knew that wasn't quite right. Kaye was actually prettier, though not quite as cute as Meg.

But even though I couldn't picture Kaye, I felt that I knew her. I knew that people liked her. Many of them loved her. She'd done nothing wrong. She'd just wanted to carve out some happiness for herself in the eyeblink of time that was her life.

And I thought of poor Darren Watts, and wished I had the powers to pray for him.

I became aware of someone standing in the aisle beside me, and when I looked up, I saw that it was Mitchell Selvy, the guy who lived across the street from the Fallons. He was wearing a gray suit and a plaid tie, and his Clint Eastwood face looked even craggier than I'd remembered.

"Oh, hey," he said when he saw who I was. "How you doing, Mr. Coyne?"

I smiled and nodded. Selvy dropped quickly to one knee in the aisle and crossed himself, then stood and slid in past me. He sat in the pew beside me, pulled out the kneeler, knelt on it, and dropped his forehead onto his clasped hands.

After a minute or two, he sat back, gripping his thighs. "We buried my wife from this church," he whispered to me.

The people were arriving in a steady procession now, and I watched all of them. Many were young people. Kaye had had a lot of friends. I thought it would please Danny and Erin to see the church filled.

Then the organ stopped playing. The sudden silence was filled with the creaking of the pews, an occasional cough, and the soft buzz of whispered voices. A priest had appeared down front. He knelt with his back to us and crossed himself perfunctorily, then stood up, climbed the two or three steps up to the altar, and began moving around, as if he were double-checking that everything was in place. He had thinning white hair and a gap-toothed smile that reminded me of Ernest Borgnine.

The organ started a different tune, something slower and more somber that I recognized but couldn't quite place. Bach, maybe.

Two men in black suits marched very slowly down the aisle, each bearing a spray of flowers. They placed them on the altar, then retreated.

Then the priest, with his hands folded in front of his belly, started up the aisle. Everyone stood and turned to face the back of the church.

Gretchen and Lyn Conley entered first. They were followed by four men and two women I didn't recognize flanking the bronze casket on its rolling casters. Behind them came Danny and Erin Fallon, with their heads bowed and their arms around each other's waists. Ned and Linda Conley followed Danny and Erin.

The priest met the little contingent of mourners halfway down the aisle. He touched hands and whispered to each of them, then turned back to the altar. The organ stopped, and then a soprano, without accompaniment, began singing "Amazing Grace." Her voice was so clear and sweet that it brought tears to my eyes.

As she sang, the casket and its bearers moved to the front of the church. I became aware of Mitch Selvy beside me, craning his neck. Then he poked me with his elbow and pointed with his thumb.

It was Mick.

He had not been in the church before Kaye's casket arrived. He'd waited until everybody's eyes had turned to the rear. Then he'd materialized near the front, close to the altar, and slipped into a pew along the side aisle six or eight rows from the front, a couple dozen rows directly in front of me. I noticed a curtained entryway on the side wall. He must have slipped in from there.

The priest was reading Scripture. I kept my eyes on Mick. His head was bowed and he had his face in his hands.

I wondered if Danny and Erin had spotted him.

The funeral mass proceeded exactly like all the others I'd ever been to. I hoped the believers who were there were more comforted than I was by the familiarity of the words and rituals and prayers and songs.

The priest delivered a short homily on the subject of life everlasting, the sacrifice of Jesus, and the blessing of faith. His singsong voice was gravelly and hesitant, as if he were trying to find the right balance between grief and celebration. He spoke of Kaye's important roles as mother, wife, friend, and teacher, and I got the impression that he hadn't known her all that well.

He concluded with a quote from Scripture, said "Amen," nodded toward one of the front pews, and Gretchen Conley stood up. She hesitated, and I saw Lyn reach up and give her hand a squeeze. Then she moved to the dais and laid a piece of paper on the lectern.

She cleared her throat, looked at us, tried to smile. "Kaye . . ." she began. She stopped, looked down to where Danny and Erin were sitting, and gave her head a little shake. "I'm sorry," she mumbled.

She dabbed at her eyes with a handkerchief, coughed, cleared her throat again.

"Kaye Fallon," she began, and this time her voice was clear and firm, "was my friend." And then she spoke lovingly of Kaye's goodness and generosity and loyalty, the special friendship they'd shared for so long, Kaye's love for her children, all that she'd contributed to her students, the lives she'd touched. She told stories about their college days and the times when they'd both had young children, and in a couple of places soft laughter rose up from the mourners.

It wasn't until she said, "Good-bye, my dearest friend," that she shook her head, covered her face with her hands, and began sobbing. The priest moved to her side, put his arm around her shoulder, and guided her back to her front-row pew, where Lyn stood up, hugged her, and helped her to sit down.

The priest returned to the altar, mumbled a benediction, and then the organ began to play. Everyone stood, and the pallbearers and Danny and Erin and Gretchen and Lyn began moving back up the aisle with Kaye's casket.

I looked down front for Mick.

But he had disappeared—slipped out the side entrance when everyone was looking in the other direction, I assumed.

The church emptied from the front to the back, and I had to wait my turn. By the time I got outside, Kaye's casket had already been loaded into the hearse, and the funeral cars were lined up behind it with their engines running, ready to begin their procession to the cemetery.

A crowd was milling on the steps and the sidewalk in front of the church, shaking hands with the priest and murmuring their sympathies to Danny and Erin, who were standing on the top step.

I scanned the crowd. I wondered if Mick had managed to slip into one of the funeral cars.

Then I saw Patsy. Or maybe it was Paulie. In his dark silk suit, he could have been mistaken for a pallbearer or a funeral director. He was moving among the people. Now and then he

218

stopped and went up on tiptoes. As I watched, he paused at the sedan that was waiting in the line directly behind the hearse, shielded his eyes, and looked inside.

He was looking for Mick. I figured he wasn't the only one.

I went over to the priest, who was bending to an elderly woman and holding her hand in both of his. I grabbed his arm. "Excuse me, Father," I said. "I've got to talk to you."

He turned and frowned at me. "Not now, my son."

I pulled him to the side. "I'm sorry, but this can't wait."

"Can't you see—"

"Where's Mick?" I said.

He shook his head and turned away from me.

I yanked at his arm. "Listen," I said in an urgent whisper, "there are men here who want to kill him. I'm Mick's lawyer. I've got to get to him before they do."

"This is God's sanctuary," said the priest. "He is safe here."

"Like hell he is. I don't know what he's told you, but—"

"I heard Michael's confession this morning."

"Well, good," I said. "If he told you the truth, then you know I'm telling the truth, too. Vincent Russo's men are here, and if they get to him before I do . . ."

The priest jerked his head back. "Russo? Here?"

I nodded.

He fingered the cross that hung around his neck, narrowed his eyes, and scanned the crowd. Without looking at me, he said, "I gave Michael my word. God's word."

"The only sanctuary for Mick is with the police," I said.

He closed his eyes for a moment, then turned to me. "How do I know you are who you say you are?"

I hastily fumbled a business card from my wallet and slipped it to him. He glanced at it, mumbled something that sounded like a prayer, then whispered, "The rectory."

"Where?"

"I don't want to point," he said. "Those men might be watching us. If you look off to my right across the lawn, you'll see a white house. Michael is waiting in my office, in the rear, on the first floor."

I glanced over and saw a big old white colonial set well back from the street and surrounded by ancient maple trees. "How'd he get there without being seen?"

"There's a tunnel. From the Underground Railroad days. You should take it, too. So they won't follow you."

He told me how to find it, said, "God speed," crossed himself, and turned away from me.

I slipped back into the church, went down to the front, and ducked through the curtained archway at the side. A narrow stairway led down to a big meeting room in the church basement. Folding metal chairs were arranged in rows facing a podium, and tacked to the walls were childish crayon drawings of animals.

I crossed the room, followed a long corridor, and found the furnace room. I slipped inside, pulled the door shut, latched it from the inside, and stood there, trying to control my breathing while my eyes adjusted to the dim light.

The metal sliding door that the priest had described was directly behind the big oil burner. It had no knob, and except for the fist-sized hole that served as a handle, it blended in with the wall.

As I began to slide the door open, I heard the rumble of a voice from outside the furnace room. I froze. There were two male voices. Then the door rattled.

I wasn't going to wait. I slipped through the doorway, slid the metal door shut behind me, and found myself in a cool, musty, absolutely dark place. The priest had said the dirt-floored tunnel went under the lawn for about a hundred yards and ended at stone stairs that led up into the rectory.

I moved as fast as I dared in the darkness, trailing my right hand along the damp granite wall and holding my left arm up in front of my face to fend off cobwebs. I kept listening for footsteps behind me. But aside from the echo of my own shuffling feet, I heard nothing.

The sliding wooden door at the top of the stairs opened into an empty closet, and the closet door opened into a bathroom. I stood there for a moment, blinking at the light, waiting for my eyes to adjust.

Then I went directly to the priest's office.

I tried the knob. It wouldn't turn. I tapped softly on the door.

A minute later I heard a soft voice. "Who is it?"

"Mick, it's me. Brady. Let me in."

"Go away. Stay out of this."

"Russo's boys are looking for you. They might have followed me. For Christ's sake, open the door."

He waited so long that I thought he might've slipped away. Then the door pulled open a crack. I pushed my way inside, and Mick shut the door behind me. He stood there leaning back against it, frowning at me. "How'd you find me?"

"The priest."

"Sonofabitch," he mumbled.

"I convinced him that your life was in danger."

"Yeah, so what else is new?" He shook his head. "I had to come today, Brady. I had to say good-bye to Kaye."

"Sure," I said, "and now that you have, it's time to do the right thing."

"The cops?" He smiled. "No way, man. Not yet."

"Look," I said, "I don't know what you're up to, but I for one would like to avoid having Danny and Erin end up orphans." There was a telephone on the priest's desk. I reached for it, but Mick grabbed my wrist.

"Don't do it, Brady," he said.

"I'm calling Horowitz," I said.

Mick kept his powerful grip on my wrist.

"Come on, Mick," I said. "Let go."

He smiled and shook his head. "I'm sorry, man," he said

221

softly, just before his fist smashed against my cheekbone and everything went utterly black.

When you've been knocked unconscious, it's impossible to tell whether it's for a second or an hour. So when I opened my eyes and saw Patsy kneeling beside me, my first thought was that Mick had slugged me just an instant earlier and that Patsy had nailed him.

Then Patsy said, "Where the fuck is he?" and I knew Mick had made it.

"Huh? Who?" I mumbled, feigning more confusion than I felt.

"Fallon, God damn it. What'd you do with him?"

"Dunno what you're talkin' 'bout."

"He was here, right?" said Patsy. He grabbed my shirt and shook me. "Did you see him?"

So he didn't know. He was guessing.

"I was waiting for the priest," I said. "I wanted to talk to the priest."

"Why?"

"I'm looking for Mick," I said. "We're both looking for Mick, right?"

Patsy narrowed his eyes. "Then who slugged you?"

"Huh?" I touched my cheek. "Tripped on the rug. Must've banged my face on the desk. Hurts like hell." I shook my head slowly. "Kinda dizzy. I think I'm gonna puke. Get me a glass of water, will you?"

Patsy frowned, then let go of my shirt and pulled away from me. I figured he didn't believe me. On the other hand, Mick wasn't here. And Patsy wouldn't want anybody to vomit on his pretty suit. He stood up and brushed his hands over the front of his jacket. He looked down at me, frowning uncertainly. Then he said, "We'll take care of you later, pal." He turned for the door.

"Wait a minute," I said. "How about that glass of water?"

"Fuck you," said Patsy. Then he was gone.

Mick's fist had caught me flush on my left cheekbone, but in the bathroom mirror it was just a little red lump. Barely noticeable. I touched it gingerly with my fingertip. It hurt right through the bone and into the middle of my brain.

But my head was clear and the dizziness had passed.

I splashed cold water on my face, combed my wet fingers through my hair, straightened my necktie, and declared myself presentable.

I thought of calling Horowitz. But I saw no purpose to it. Mick was gone.

I walked out of the rectory, stood on the front steps, and looked over toward the church. The funeral cars had left, and so had most of those that had been parked along the street.

I glanced at my watch. Eleven-thirty. I knew the ceremony at the cemetery would be brief. After that, the mourners would gather at the Conleys' house in Concord. I didn't intend to miss that.

To be on the safe side, I'd wait a couple of hours before I showed up at Lyn and Gretchen's. I figured I'd find a takeout somewhere in Lexington center, buy myself a sandwich and a Coke, and then head for Walden Pond in Lincoln. I'd have myself a picnic with Thoreau's ghost, see if any trout were rising, think Transcendental thoughts, ponder life and death and Nature's ways—my version of a religious observation in a sacred place.

I lit a cigarette, crossed the rectory lawn, and started up the sidewalk to where my car was parked.

Then I stopped.

A young man wearing a checked sports jacket and blue jeans was leaning against my front bumper. I didn't recognize him until he turned and lifted his chin to me.

It was Will Powers. And parked directly in front of my BMW was an old black Volkswagen Beetle.

A black bug.

Darren Watts had called it a "backbug."

# SIXTEEN

———————————————————

I walked up to Will Powers and held out my hand. "I didn't see you in there," I said, nodding toward the church.

He shook my hand. "I was sitting in the back row. I saw you." He grinned and touched his cheek. "What happened?"

"Bumped into something," I said. "Nice you could make it here today."

He shrugged. "She was a good lady. Those were her kids, huh?"

I nodded.

"They're like my age." He shook his head. "Their mother got murdered. God, that really sucks."

"It sure does." I cleared my throat. "Were you waiting for me, Will?"

"Yeah," he said. He patted the fender of my BMW. "Remembered your car," he added with a quick smile. Then the smile disappeared. "I need to talk to you."

"Yes," I said. "I know you do. I was just going to get a sandwich and a Coke and take it over to Walden Pond. Why don't you join me?"

He nodded. "Okay. Sure. Sounds good. Walden Pond. I never been there. Heard about it." He smiled. "Believe it or not, Mrs. Fallon used to talk about that book. She knew I like nature and stuff, told me she thought I'd like it. Never tried it, though. I'm not much of a reader."

"Well," I said, "Walden is a good book and a pretty place. Maybe it'll inspire you." I got into my car. "Follow me."

I found a parking slot in front of a deli in the center of town. Will pulled his black VW alongside of me. I got out and went to his window. "Why don't you just double-park here. I'll pick up something for you. What would you like?"

He shrugged. "I dunno. A sandwich, I guess."

"Corned beef? Pastrami? Ham-and-cheese?"

"That sounds good. Ham-and-cheese. And a root beer, if they have it."

I bought a Reuben sandwich for me, a ham-and-cheese for Will, two little bags of potato chips, a Coke, and a root beer. Fat kosher dills came with the sandwiches, wrapped separately in their own waxed paper.

I kept my eye on Will in my rearview mirror as he followed me out of Lexington, through the Minuteman National Park on what they were now calling Battle Road, which was actually Route 2A, and onto Route 2. We turned left on Walden Street and pulled into the parking area across from the pond. Will parked beside me.

I got out, threw my jacket and tie in the backseat, and retrieved the bag that held our lunches. Then Will and I headed down to the pond.

Walden is a kettle pond, formed by the giant hunks of ice that broke off and stayed behind when the glaciers retreated northward from this part of the world more than ten thousand years ago. Icemelt from the glacier flowed south, carrying with it millions of tons of sediment, which built up around the left-behind hunks of ice, and when the ice melted, a kettle-shaped pond was formed, roundish and deep, with no islands, inlet, or outlet, and surrounded by high banks.

Thoreau dropped a codline through the ice to map Walden's bottom and found that it was over 100 feet deep in places. He speculated that its name derived from the phrase *walled-in,* a reference to the steep wooded banks that surrounded it, although "Walden" might've been the corruption of an Indian word. Most likely, Thoreau had concluded, it had just been named after some Englishman named Walden.

On this June noontime, crowds had gathered on blankets on the sand beach near the road, and more folks plodded along the mulched path that encircled the pond. There were clusters of young mothers with toddlers in bathing suits splashing in the water and digging in the sand, male and female executive types in business attire—like me—with their bag lunches, and hippies and pilgrims of all ages who'd come to pay homage to Thoreau's shrine.

Will and I followed the path almost halfway around the pond, and down near the cove where Thoreau had built his cabin, we found a couple of private boulders to sit on.

We unwrapped our sandwiches and pickles, ripped open our potato chip bags, popped the tops of our sodas, and looked out at the rippled water.

Walden was a pretty good trout pond. If it had been calm, I might've been able to spot a rising fish or two.

But a freshening easterly breeze had blown up. It felt ten degrees cooler than it had in the morning, and dark clouds had begun to skid across the sky.

I munched my sandwich and didn't say anything. Will knew he had to talk to me. I figured I'd give him the chance do it in his own way.

He waited until we'd finished eating and had lit cigarettes. "I told you a lot of lies," he said softly.

I nodded. "I know you did."

His face jerked up. "How'd you know?"

"When I saw your car. Darren saw it, too."

He frowned. "Who's Darren?"

I shook my head. "Why don't you just tell me what you want to tell me."

"Yeah, okay," he said. He looked out at the water. "I lied to you about Mrs. Fallon. I didn't really feel bad about it until—until I had a chance to think about it." He laughed quickly. "I lied about me, too. I was scared. The fact is, Mr. Coyne, I, um, I did kinda follow her. They said I was stalking her. I didn't think of it that way. I just thought she was so damn pretty and nice and—and sexy, you know? Anyway—well, I guess I did try to kiss her. But see, it wasn't anything she did. I told you she flirted with me? Well, it wasn't like that. She never came on to me. Or anybody, as far as I could see. It was me. She was just being nice, and I . . ." He shook his head. "Anyway, Moyle kicked me out of her class, and that made me mad. I never meant to hurt or scare her or nothing. But I know he was right. I never should've tried to kiss her."

I turned to look at him. His head was bowed, and it looked as if he might start crying.

"Did you kill her, Will?"

His head jerked up. "What? Oh, Jesus, no. Honest to God. Kill her? No way, man." He blew out a breath. "I was there, though. That night, I mean."

"The night she was murdered?"

"Yeah. I was there."

"Did you see her? Was she alive when you—"

He was shaking his head. "I never saw her. Look, lemme try to just tell you what happened, okay?"

"Please," I said.

He took a sip from his can of root beer, then wiped his mouth on his sleeve. "I used to think about her all the time. How she looked, how she smelled, the sound of her voice . . ." He shook

228

his head. "Mrs. Fallon was the only reason I went to school."
He laughed quickly. "Dumb, I know. I used to make up stories
in my head about her. About her and me, you know? Even after
they kicked me out, I still couldn't get her out of my head. It
got worse, actually." He turned and frowned at me. "You know
what I mean?"

I nodded. I understood the power of fantasy.

"Anyway," he said, "I used to drive out to her house all the
time. After dark. I didn't want anyone to see me. And that's what
I did that night. The night she got killed. I left Frank's, got into
my car, and drove out to Lexington. I drove real slow past her
house and saw that she had company, so—"

"Company?" I said.

"There was a car in her driveway. That wasn't the first time.
It drove me nuts, thinking she—she had somebody, some guy
who—"

"What kind of car was it?"

He shrugged. "I don't know. Like I said, I saw the car so I
kept going. I didn't really look at it, you know?"

"This is important," I said. "Come on. You work on cars all
day long. You must've noticed something."

"Yeah, well it was nighttime and the car was pulled into the
driveway, parked behind a lot of bushes and stuff, and there was
only one little outside light on. I mean, I saw there was a car,
and I knew it wasn't Mrs. Fallon's, so I kept driving."

"Was it light colored or dark?"

He squeezed his eyes shut. "Light."

"White?"

"Light blue, maybe, or green. One of those off colors."

"Big or small?"

"Medium-sized." He opened his eyes and looked at me. "I
mean, it wasn't a little sports car, and it wasn't a truck. Some
kind of sedan."

"What else, Will? Come on, son."

He shook his head. "That's about it. I think I'd seen that car in her driveway other times, but I never really studied it. I'm sorry. Like I said, it was dark, and when I saw she had company, I kept driving."

"Okay," I said. "So what else happened?"

"Well, I drove around for a while, found a McDonald's, had a cup of coffee, and then I went back."

"To her house?"

He nodded. "That car was gone. I pulled up in front and I shut off the ignition and . . . and I just sat there."

He showed no inclination to continue, so I said, "You didn't go up to the house."

"No."

"Did you see anybody?"

He shrugged. "No. I just sat there."

"You didn't see Darren?"

"I told you," he said. "I don't know any Darren."

"Okay. Then what?"

He shrugged. "Then nothing. I did what I did every damn time I drove out to her house at night. I sat there in the dark maybe ten or fifteen minutes, trying to get my courage up to go knock on the door. But I didn't. I never did. I kept trying to figure out what I was gonna say to her, and everything I thought of sounded stupid. I mean, first I thought, Okay, I'll just give her my big old smile and say, 'Hi, Mrs. Fallon. Remember me?' Dumb, dumb. So then I said to myself, Grow up, Will. Apologize to the lady. That's what you should do. Just say, 'Mrs. Fallon, I'm sorry I tried to kiss you.' But, see, I knew I didn't have the guts to do that. Hell, I didn't have the guts to do anything. So I didn't. I just sat there smoking cigarettes the way I always did, feeling stupider and stupider, and after a while I drove home."

"You sure you didn't see anyone else?"

He shook his head. "That's a quiet street. Maybe a couple cars drove by." He shrugged.

"And you never saw who belonged to that car in her driveway?"

"No."

"Or a young man on foot who might've seen you?"

He shook his head.

"What about Mick Fallon?"

"Her husband?" He shook his head. "I told you. I didn't see anybody."

I let out a long breath. "Will, how come you didn't tell me this the first time I talked to you?"

"I was scared. Scared and embarrassed. I mean, think about it. Suddenly you show up, this lawyer from Boston, asking questions? I didn't want to deal with it, man. I knew I didn't do anything wrong. I mean, I was there that night, and I figured I could be in trouble. But I didn't kill her. And I didn't know anything. It was easier."

"To lie."

He nodded.

I smiled at him. "Do you feel better now?"

"Well, yeah, actually I do."

"Are you prepared to tell this to the police?"

He frowned. "I figured, you're a lawyer, and—"

"You're not my client, Will, and I'm an officer of the court. That means I'll have to tell them what you've told me, and then they'll interrogate you."

He shrugged. "I guess I got no choice, right?"

"No, not really."

Will was staring out at the pond, where miniature whitecaps rolled across the surface. The wind had picked up, and now the sky was dark with ominous clouds.

I thought of Darren Watts, dying in a pond considerably

smaller than Walden. "Will," I said, "Where were you Monday night?"

"Monday? Why?"

"Somebody was murdered Monday night."

"Oh, jeez. Murdered?"

"Yes. Darren Watts. He saw your car at the Fallons' house that night."

"I didn't kill anybody," he said. "I told you, I—"

"I hope you didn't," I said. "So where were you?"

"Monday?" he said. "That's easy. I have the afternoon shift on Mondays. I'm in the pit until we close at nine. Stay another hour helping Frank clean up, get home around ten-thirty. My mother always keeps dinner waiting for me. I take a shower, and me and my parents watch TV together while I eat."

"Every Monday?"

"Yes."

"Including this past one?"

"Right."

"I hope this isn't a lie," I said.

"Don't you believe me?"

"It doesn't matter whether I do. The police will check. If you're lying, they'll know it."

"Well, I'm not lying this time."

I nodded, stood up, and brushed the sand off the seat of my pants. "Okay. Come on. We'll talk to the police. But first, we're going to a party."

"Party? What kind of party?"

"The sad kind, Will. The kind of party they have after a funeral, where people who knew the deceased tell her loved ones how much they appreciated her."

He shook his head. "Oh, man . . ."

"I want you to meet Kaye Fallon's two children. You can tell them she was a good teacher. They'd appreciate that."

He nodded. "She *was* a good teacher. She cared about kids, you know?"

"Danny and Erin would like to hear that," I said.

"Sure," he said. "I can tell them that. But what about . . . ?"

"What you told me?"

He nodded.

"You'll have to tell the police, of course. I'll be with you if you want. As your friend, not as a lawyer. But as long as you're telling the truth, you won't need a lawyer."


Will Powers followed me in his black Volkswagen bug over the back roads of Concord to Gretchen and Lyn's house. I kept my eye on the rearview mirror. I half expected Will to chicken out, but he stayed with me.

The Conleys' winding street was lined with cars on both sides. Will and I parked about fifty yards from the house and began to walk back.

"You okay?" I said to him.

He glanced sideways at me and laughed shortly. "I was thinking," he said. "What if somebody sees my car and knows I used to drive by her house all the time? Or what if she told her kids about me? You know, the dumb pervert who tried to kiss her in the parking lot? If I was her son, I think I'd punch me out."

"Just tell them you were one of her students," I said. "They've got other things on their mind. Anyway, I doubt if she would've told them about that."

He nodded skeptically.

The breeze was cold and moist, and the black clouds hung low in the sky. Rain was coming.

I heard mingled voices and an occasional burst of laughter as we rounded the corner to the Conleys' house. A few people were standing on the front lawn, and others were sitting on the steps, holding plastic glasses and paper plates. The women were pressing their dresses against their legs in the swirling wind, and they were all talking in groups of twos and threes.

Will and I turned up the driveway. Suddenly he stopped and grabbed my arm.

I turned to him. "What's the matter?"

His fingers dug into my forearm. "That's it," he whispered.

"What are you talking about?"

He pointed at Lyn Conley's gunmetal gray Lexus. "That car. That's the one that was in her driveway that night."

# SEVENTEEN

⟫————————————————————⟪

"Are you sure?" I said to Will.

He nodded emphatically. "Damn right. It was a ninety-seven Lexus. Definitely. Don't know why I didn't recognize it, except maybe because it was so dark, plus we don't get many Lexuses coming in to Jiffy Lube. Lexus people probably get their oil changed at the dealer. And that's the color. That's it, all right. That's the one."

"I doubt if this is the only gray 'ninety-seven Lexus on the road," I said.

He looked at me. "Oh, yeah. I see what you mean." He shrugged.

"Any way you could distinguish this car from another one of the same make, model, and color?"

"No, I guess not." He looked at me and smiled. "It's pretty obvious you're a lawyer, you know? I sorta jumped to a conclusion, I guess. I'm sorry."

"Don't worry about it," I said. In fact, I had no doubt that Lyn Conley's Lexus was the car Will had seen in Kaye's driveway that night. But I didn't want him to know it. Not yet. I slapped his shoulder. "Don't worry about it. Come on. Let's go inside."

We started for the front door.

"I guess I shouldn't say anything about that car to anybody, huh?" said Will.

"Not a good idea."

He looked at me and grinned. "Must be hundreds of cars like that around here."

"Will," I said, "for Christ's sake—"

"I'm not stupid," he said. "What do you want me to do?"

"Nothing. Just don't say anything."

He nodded. "You can trust me."

The folks on the front lawn were filtering back into the house. The breeze seemed to be softening, but the air had become downright chilly.

Will and I followed a pair of middle-aged couples inside, then paused in the foyer. I tiptoed up to look over the heads of the people who were milling around, and I spotted Danny Fallon. I grabbed Will's elbow. "Come on. I'm going to introduce you to Kaye Fallon's son. His name is Danny. He's about your age."

We shouldered our way over to Danny. He was standing there with Erin and Ned and Linda Conley and four or five other young people. They were all holding cans of Coke or Sprite.

Erin spotted me, smiled, and came over. "Mr. Coyne. Thanks a lot for coming." She hugged me.

I returned her hug, then stepped away from her. "How're you doing, Erin?"

She bobbed her head from side to side. "It's so—so weird. But, gee, everybody's been really supportive and nice, you know?"

"Your mom had a lot of friends." I put my arm on Will's shoulder. "This is a friend of mine. Will Powers. He was one of your mother's students."

Erin smiled at him and held out her hand. "It's really nice of you to come." She turned her head. "Hey, Danny. C'mere a minute."

Danny came over. He saw me and held out his hand. "Hey, Mr. Coyne."

I shook hands with him. "You doing okay?"

"Pretty good," he said. "Aunt Gretchen and Uncle Lyn have been great, and so've Ned and Linda. And all these people . . ." He waved his hand around.

Erin touched Danny's shoulder. "This is one of Mom's students," she said. She was holding Will's hand.

"Hey, man," said Danny.

The two of them banged fists, and Erin tugged Will over to the group of young people they'd been talking with.

Will looked back at me with a smile. "Catch you later," he said.

Danny was frowning at me. "Did you see him?"

"Who?"

"My dad. At the church."

I nodded.

"I didn't tell Erin. She didn't see him." He shook his head. "He—he never came over, or caught up with us afterward, or . . ."

"Danny—"

"No, man. Listen. He didn't come to the cemetery, and he's not here, and I'm trying to figure it out, but the only thing that makes any sense—"

"Don't do this," I said. "I'm not sure exactly what you're thinking, but trust me on this. You must not think bad things about your father. Have faith in him, okay?"

He shook his head. "I'm trying, man, but . . ."

"Please. Trust me."

He narrowed his eyes at me. "You know something, huh?"

Just then Gretchen grabbed my arm and gave me a hug. "Thanks for coming, Brady," she said. "It means a lot to all of us." She turned and smiled at Danny. "Right?"

He nodded. "Right. Definitely." He jerked his chin at me. "Later, okay?"

"Later," I said.

Danny turned and joined Erin and Will and the others, who were all talking and smiling like old friends.

Gretchen still had her arm hooked through mine. "That was a very fine eulogy you gave," I said to her.

"Boy, it was hard," she said. "I felt ridiculous, breaking down like that."

"We were all moved."

She smiled quickly. "Want to meet some people?"

I smiled. "Not especially, to tell you the truth. In fact, I dread the prospect. I just wanted to pay my respects to Danny and Erin. And you and Lyn, too, of course." I looked around. "Where is Lyn?"

"Last I saw him, he was out in the kitchen helping with the food. Lyn's not such a great mingler. He likes it better when he has something to do. Makes him feel useful."

"I'm the same way," I said. "I'll go find him."

She tiptoed up and kissed my cheek. "Thanks for everything," she said softly. "Get yourself a drink, something to eat." Then she turned and wandered away.

I made my way to the kitchen, where a good-sized crowd had gathered, the way party crowds usually gather in kitchens. I stood in the archway and watched. Lyn and three or four women were peeling the plastic wrap off platters of hors d'oeuvres, sliding casseroles into and out of the oven, popping other things into the microwave. Lyn was wearing a flowered apron over a white button-down dress shirt. Somewhere along the way he'd taken off his necktie and rolled up his sleeves. He seemed to be taking orders from one of the women.

When he spotted me, he rolled his eyes, grinned, and held up a finger.

A minute later he came over. He held out his hand. "Brady," he said. "Boy, am I glad to see you. Give me an excuse to escape that." He jerked his head back toward the kitchen.

I shook his hand. "This is terrific, what you're doing for those kids," I said. "Why don't you ditch that apron, take a break, come get some fresh air with me?"

"You don't have to ask twice." He took off his apron and tossed it onto a chair. "Let me get you something to drink. There's wine and beer."

"Just a Coke, please."

"Be right with you. Meet you out back."

I opened the screened slider and went out onto the deck. Nobody else was outside. They'd all been driven in by the cool mist that had begun to sift down from the gray sky. The breeze had died completely now, as if the clouds had decided to settle right where they were for a while so they could proceed with some serious raining.

The mist felt refreshing on my face after the closed-in stickiness of the house. I lit a cigarette and leaned my forearms on the rail. The misty air blurred and muted the colors of the meadow as it sloped off toward the marsh and the river beyond. It looked like a watercolor painted mostly with ochres and umbers on wet paper.

A minute later Lyn appeared at my side. He put a can of Coke on the rail beside my elbow. He was holding a plastic glass.

"Thanks," I said. "What're you drinking?"

"Oh, the usual." He grinned. "Tonic water with a twist. Today makes one more day, you know?" He laughed shortly. "Can't say I haven't been tempted lately, though."

I nodded. "You can't drink anything at all, huh?"

"The whiff of it's poison to me," he said. "A party like this—it tests me. That's why I hang out in the kitchen wearing an apron and taking orders from women. It keeps me occupied." He cocked his head and smiled. "I still go to meetings. I'll always have to, they tell me."

"Not even a beer, huh?"

"Hell, no." He frowned at me. "What happened to your face?"

I touched my tender cheekbone. It felt swollen and very tender. "Nothing," I said. "Little accident. Kind of embarrassing, to tell you the truth."

"Looks like someone hit you."

"I know," I said. "It does look like that."

We were both leaning on our forearms, gazing off into the distance.

"I told Gretchen how much I admire what you folks are doing," I said after a minute.

"We all loved Kaye." He hesitated. "And Mick, of course. Danny and Erin are family."

"So what's the plan?"

"Oh, the kids know they're welcome to stay as long as they like. They're starting to talk about getting on with their lives. I think Danny's going to head back to Block Island tomorrow or the next day. I'm not sure what Erin's plans are. I have the feeling she might want to hang around for a while. She and Linda get along well, and Erin doesn't really have anyplace to go." Lyn glanced sideways at me. "I think they both feel like they have unfinished business, though."

"Mick, you mean?"

He nodded.

"He was there this morning, you know. At the church."

"Yes," said Lyn. "I saw him. I'm glad he's okay, but I can't understand what he's thinking."

I nodded and took a sip of Coke. "So how are *you* doing with all this?"

"Me?"

240

I nodded. "Gretchen got a lot of sympathy, and Danny and Erin, of course. You were close to Kaye, too."

"Yes," he said. "I was."

"People sometimes assume we guys don't feel things the way women and kids do. It must've devastated you."

"Boy, you've got that right." He let out a long breath. "Gretch was hysterical. I had to take care of her. I really couldn't . . ." He shook his head, smiled quickly, then brushed the back of his hand across his face and blinked a couple of times.

"Never having the chance to say good-bye to her," I said. "Until it was too late. That had to be tough."

"Oh, I think about that, believe me. She was . . ."

"Special," I said. "I know."

"But you *don't* know, Brady." He was shaking his head. "You don't know the half of it."

"You're wrong," I said quietly. "I *do* know."

I felt him stiffen momentarily beside me. Then he tried to laugh. It came out strangled, like a sob.

I touched his arm. "I *know*, Lyn."

"What? What do you know?"

"About you and Kaye."

He straightened up and frowned at me. "There's nothing to know," he said. "Kaye and I . . ."

I shook my head.

He stared at me for a minute. "You couldn't know," he whispered. "Nobody knew."

"You're wrong about that. I know."

He gazed off toward the meadow. Then he blinked, and the tears welled up in his eyes. "Shit," he muttered. He fumbled a handkerchief from his pocket, wiped his eyes, and stuffed it back. "We really loved each other, Brady. I hope you can understand that. This wasn't some—some *affair*. We—we loved each other for years. I mean, since we were young together, before we had kids, even. We never—I mean, *never*—did anything. Didn't speak of it, even to each other. But we both knew. We each knew how the other one felt. That's how it was, and we lived with it. It was like it would always be that way. I never expected it would be any different. But I knew I'd never stop loving her." He put his hand to his mouth for a moment, as if he wanted to stop his words from coming out. Then he shook his head. "When she split with Mick, I thought I knew why. And I—I had to—to see her, to make sure I was right." He shook his head. "And I was. One night I went to her house. She—"

"When?" I said. "When was this?"

"A year ago last winter. January or February. A few weeks after Mick moved out. She said she never would've called me. But she wanted me to come to her. We talked for hours. And then we made love. And we made promises to each other."

"That you'd both get divorced?" I said.

He nodded. "I was going to, too. But I kept putting it off. I mean, I didn't think Gretchen deserved that. Me and Kaye? Her best friend?" He shook his head. "I just couldn't figure out how to say it right. And my kids? I didn't see how I could face them. I wasn't sure I had the courage for that. Kaye never really pressured me. She understood, or at least she said she did. But *she* didn't put it off. That was the difference between us. When Kaye made up her mind about something, she just did it. She split with Mick and she got a lawyer, and I knew that sooner or later I'd have to . . ." He waved his hand as if he couldn't bear to say the words.

"Tell Gretchen," I said.

"Yes."

"So Kaye became more insistent?"

He shook his head. "Not really. But—" He stopped. His mouth opened and closed. Then he said. "You think I—?"

"No," I said. "You didn't kill her."

"Hell," he said. "I couldn't've. I was with Gretchen that night.

242

We had dinner at the Claymans'." He shook his head. "God, for a minute there I thought you—"

"What car did you take?"

"Huh? You mean to the Claymans'?" He frowned. "The Cherokee. Ned had the Lexus."

"Right," I said, "And—"

Lyn was staring at me. "Oh, God," he whispered. Then he lifted his head and looked past my shoulder. I saw his eyes widen.

I turned in time to see Ned staring at us through the screen slider. Then he turned away. "Hey!" I yelled. "Hey, Ned. Wait."

Ned shoved aside some people, and darted back into the house. A moment later I heard the front door slam.

I turned and started to run off the deck so I could intercept him out front. I'd almost made it to the steps when Lyn grabbed my leg. I lost my balance, spun sideways, and fell hard on my shoulder. Then Lyn was on top of me. He was pounding my back and shoulders with his fists, saying things I didn't understand, his voice a kind of wail, oozing grief and pain.

I arched my back, bucked and heaved, managed to throw him off me, and scrambled to my feet. He reached out and hooked my ankle, tripping me again. This time my head bounced off the flooring of the deck, and my cheekbone—the one where Mick had slugged me—grazed something. An arrow of pain shot into the pit of my stomach, and for a moment the world went spinning around me. I got to my knees, shook my head, then heaved myself onto my feet. Lyn grabbed my shoulder and aimed a fist at my face. I ducked away and punched him as hard as I could. My fist caught him on the point of his chin, and his head snapped back. I hit him again, this time on the jaw, and he staggered, stumbled, and slammed onto his back.

People had begun to gather on the deck. A couple of them reached out to me. I shook them off and hurried down the steps, and about the time I hit the lawn I heard a car engine roar to a start from out front. I sprinted around the side of the house—just in time to see Lyn Conley's Lexus swerving and fishtailing backwards down the driveway. The engine was racing and the driver's door hung open, and Mick Fallon was holding onto the handle. Ned was behind the wheel, dragging Mick along, and Mick's feet were running and skidding on the driveway as he tried to get them underneath himself.

At the foot of the driveway Ned suddenly jammed on the brakes, and the door swung against the car. Mick's legs lifted off the ground, but he somehow kept his grip on the door handle. Ned shifted into first gear and slammed into the street. The door flapped open, then crashed back and latched itself. Mick was still hanging on with one hand, and I saw him reach in through the open window, trying, I thought, to grab the wheel, or maybe to grab Ned.

I stood there and watched the Lexus peel up the narrow car-lined residential road. Suddenly, Ned swerved. The Lexus ricocheted off a parked car with the screech of speeding metal scraping against metal, and then Mick's big body flew into the air. It seem to hand there for a moment before it crashed down on the hood of a parked car, bounced, and flopped onto the ground.

The Lexus screamed up the narrow street and skidded around the corner on squealing tires.

I was halfway across the street to where Mick had been thrown when in the distance I heard the desperate screech of rubber on wet asphalt, followed by the unmistakable thudding crash of two tons of hurtling steel and glass exploding against some large, hard, immovable object.

That awful sound echoed, then died, and the absolute silence that followed was awesome and terrifying and seemed to last several minutes.

A moment later, a cloud of black smoke billowed up over the tops of the trees from where Ned Conley had crashed his father's gunmetal gray Lexus.

# EIGHTEEN

I realized I'd been standing there at the end of the driveway, holding my breath. I shook myself and dashed across the street.

I found Mick sprawled on the grass behind the line of parked cars alongside the street. He was curled fetally on his left side with one leg twisted awkwardly under him. Dark blood soaked his hair and had trickled down the side of his face. His eyes were closed. He lay very still.

I knelt beside him and bent my ear to his mouth. It took me a panicky moment to detect his breathing. It was shallow and rapid.

"Mick," I said. "Hey, Mick."

His eyes blinked open, darted around, then focused on me. "Hey," he whispered. "You don't have to yell, man."

A choking sob came from behind me. I turned. Erin Fallon was standing there hugging herself. Tears were streaming down her cheeks.

"I think he's okay," I said to her.

She came and knelt beside me, then reached down and touched Mick's face. "Daddy?"

"Hi, baby," he mumbled. "I'm sorry."

She touched his blood-soaked hair, then bent and kissed his cheek. "Shh," she said. "It's okay."

A murmur of voices made me turn. A crowd had gathered around us—people from the party and maybe some neighbors and passersby. "Anybody call an ambulance?" I said.

"They're coming," somebody answered.

Then Danny pushed his way through. He stood there, clenching and unclenching his fists, looking down at Mick. "Pop?" he said.

Mick turned his head. He grimaced, closed his eyes for a moment, then looked up at his son and tried to smile. He lifted his hand an inch or two, then let it fall back. "How's it goin', bud?" Then he sighed and his eyes closed.

Erin bent close to him for a minute, then looked up at me and nodded. Mick was still alive.

I knelt there beside him, feeling helpless, waiting for the ambulance to arrive. Then I felt a hand on my shoulder. I turned. Horowitz was standing behind me. "Is he conscious?" he said.

"Where'd you come from?" I said.

Horowitz crouched beside Mick, ignoring me. "Hey, Fallon," he said. "Can you hear me? It's Lieutenant Horowitz."

Mick's eyes fluttered open. "Guess you got me, man," he mumbled. "Took you long enough."

Horowitz cleared his throat. "Michael Fallon," he said, "you are under arrest for the murder of Katherine Fallon. You have the right—"

I grabbed Horowitz's arm. "Hold on," I said.

He whirled to face me. "Don't interrupt, Coyne."

I shook my head. "Mick didn't do it."

"Don't tell me my job."

"Ned Conley killed her," I said.

Horowitz frowned. "Who?"

"The driver of that Lexus that crashed up the street."

"Huh?" Horowitz narrowed his eyes. "What the hell are you talking about?"

"I'll tell you the whole story. Then if you still feel you've got to arrest Mick, you'll probably be able to find him. These—" I waved my hand, indicating Danny and Erin "—are his kids. Have some consideration for a change."

He glanced from Erin to Danny, nodded, then turned back to me. "Can you prove this?"

"You shouldn't have a problem getting a confession out of Ned," I said.

Horowitz gave me his sardonic Jack Nicholson grin. "Might not be that easy," he said. "That Lexus was going about seventy when it flipped. Smashed into a big oak tree. Impact flush on the driver's side."

A few minutes later came the wail of sirens, and then two EMTs shouldered their way through the crowd. Erin and Danny and Horowitz and I stepped back while they examined Mick. After a few minutes, they got him strapped onto a board and lugged him to the ambulance.

I followed behind them. One of the EMTs climbed in back with Mick. The other slammed the door and started around to the front. I touched his arm. "How is he?" I said.

"Broken femur, coupla cracked ribs, lacerated scalp, for starters. Don't know about internal injuries. Looks like his spine and skull are okay."

"He's going to be all right, then?"

He shrugged. "If you say so."

"Taking him to Emerson?"

He nodded, climbed behind the wheel, squawked the siren a couple of times, then started up the street.

I found Danny and Erin, and we got into my car and followed the ambulance to the hospital.

247

We sat in the emergency waiting room for four or five hours. Neither of Mick's kids seemed inclined to talk, and I didn't push it. We watched the muted television, thumbed through old magazines, drank Cokes from the machine, and every half hour or so I went outside for a cigarette. I used the same bench I'd sat on with Evie Banyon a few days earlier.

Sometime after seven that evening a doctor came into the waiting room. He said Mick was going to be okay, and we could see him if we wanted. They let us in one at a time. Erin went first, then Danny, and they both came back red-eyed but smiling.

Mick's eyes were closed. Wires ran from under the sheet to a ticking and humming machine on a table beside the bed, and he was getting oxygen through a tube under his nostrils. A bandage covered his head like a turban, and his left leg, which wore a cast from foot to hip, was cranked up on a traction device.

I sat on the chair that was pulled close to his side and touched his arm. "You awake, Mick?"

I saw his eyes roll under his eyelids, but he didn't open them. His lips moved. I leaned close.

"That you, Brady?"

"It's me," I said.

He gave me a week, lopsided grin. "You got yourself a mouse there, bud."

I touched my cheek. "Yes," I said. "Thank you."

"Hurt?"

"I'm fine," I said. "How about you?"

"Thirsty," he rasped.

I found a glass of water on the table. I held it for him, and steered the straw to his lips. He took a couple of sips, then turned his head away.

He licked his lips. "C'mere," he whispered.

I bent closer to him.

"It was Ned," he murmured.

"I know."

"They get him?"

"They got him, Mick. It's all over."

"Danny and Erin," he said. "They know it wasn't me, huh?"

"They know."

"Tell 'em I love 'em," he mumbled.

"They know that, too," I said.


When I went back out to the waiting room, Horowitz was sitting there talking with Erin and Danny. He looked up at me, nodded, and said, "Got a minute?"

We went outside and sat on the smokers' bench.

I lit a cigarette. "What about Ned Conley?"

He nodded. "I talked to him before they wheeled him into surgery. He admitted both of 'em."

"Kaye and Darren?"

He nodded.

"Why Darren?"

Horowitz shrugged. "Ned thought Darren could finger him."

"What else did he say?"

Horowitz shrugged. "His old man told him he was gonna ask his mother for a divorce. Kid freaked. Went over, tried to talk Mrs. Fallon out of it, and . . ." He shook his head.

"She refused and he hit her."

"Yeah," he said. "Something like that."

"So it's all cleared up," I said. "Except for the trial."

"No trial, Coyne. They lost him in surgery."

"Ned died?"

He nodded.

"Jesus." I shook my head. "What a mess. The whole thing."

"Ah, it's a fucking tragedy, Coyne. Bunch of people who all love each other?" He waved his hand dismissively. "I see it every day. What a job."

"So what happens now?"

"I still gotta question your client. Doctors tell me he'll be able to talk tomorrow."

"Why?"

Horowitz shrugged. "I gotta interrogate Mr. and Mrs. Conley and a few other people, too. Loose ends, that's all." He cocked his head and peered at me. "Did you figure it out?"

"Not until today. Will Powers told me he saw that Lexus in front of Kaye's house the night of the murder. I thought of Lyn, and when I did, it occurred to me that he might've been Kaye's lover, the one who got her pregnant. That would fit with how Kaye handled it with Gretchen. But Lyn couldn't have done it."

"Why not?"

"The beer bottle. Lyn was on the wagon. Kaye wouldn't have given him a beer. So then I thought Ned. He'd been borrowing his parents' cars."

"How old was Ned?"

"Just seventeen," I said.

"What a world, huh?"


Danny and Erin decided to spend the night at the hospital. I hung around with them for a while, and finally they told me they'd be fine and I looked tired and why didn't I go home and get some sleep.

I didn't argue with them.

I got back to my empty apartment around nine-thirty, shucked off my funeral suit, and climbed into sweatpants and a T-shirt. Then I scrambled some eggs and toasted an English muffin and ate an evening breakfast out on my balcony.

The storm had passed, leaving the air clean and sweet. A nearly full moon was playing peek-a-boo with some skidding clouds. Tomorrow, if I wasn't mistaken, would be humid and hot with afternoon thunder showers, the first truly summery day of the season, even if the calendar insisted it was still spring.

I tried to make sense out of what had happened. But I couldn't. There was no lesson in it, no moral, nothing to be learned. Three people were dead and two nice families had been wrecked, all because a man and a woman loved each other, and because a boy loved his family. It was just a damn tragedy, and that was the only way to understand it.

I'm all for love. But sometimes I think we'd be better off without it.

After I finished eating, I went inside, stacked the dishes in the sink, retrieved the phone, and dialed the Ritz. I asked to be connected to Sylvie's room.

Instead of ringing me through, the receptionist said, "One moment, sir."

A minute later, she said, "I'm sorry, sir. Ms. Szabo checked out this morning."

"Are you sure?" I said. "She was supposed to be there until Sunday."

"Yes, sir. I'm sure."

"Did she leave a forwarding address? Did she switch hotels or something?"

"Who is this, please?"

"Me? I'm Brady Coyne. A friend of Ms. Szabo's."

"Yes, sir. One moment, please." A moment later, she said, "Mr. Coyne?"

"Yes. I'm here."

"I have a message here for you from Ms. Szabo."

"Why don't you read it to me."

"Are you sure?"

"Yes, please."

The receptionist cleared her throat. "All right, sir. It says:

'Dear, dear Brady. I am so sorry. I have finished my business in Boston, and I cannot continue to deceive you. I have decided to return to New York, to my husband. I do not know if I will remain with him or not, but I know I must decide. Until then, it is better for us both if we do not see each other. I have more fun with you, my dearest oldest friend, than anybody. You are tempting for me. You make it hard for me to make good decisions. So it is better this way.' " The receptionist paused and gave a little cough. "She signs it, 'Your Sylvie, who will love you forever.' "

I sat there with the phone pressed against my ear, and after a minute, the receptionist said, "Mr. Coyne? Are you still there?"

"Yes," I said. "I'm here. Did she say 'husband'?"

"Um, yes sir. I'm afraid so."

"Thank you," I said. "I didn't know she was married, you see."

"I'm sorry, sir," she said.


I beat Julie to the office the next morning, and by the time she arrived I had the coffee brewed. I delivered a mugful to her, hitched my butt up on the corner of her desk, and recounted the events of the previous day. "I'm heading out to Emerson Hospital this afternoon," I concluded. "I've got to clear up some loose ends with Mick."

Julie nodded. "He isn't out of the woods yet, right?"

"Right." I wrote the words *Vincent Russo* on a piece of paper and put it in front of her. "I need to talk to him."

Julie's eyes widened. "You want to talk to him directly?"

"Yes. No flunkies, no intermediaries, no lawyers or account-ants or—or right-hand men, or whatever they call them. Who-ever you get ahold of, tell them that."

"Consigliere," said Julie.

"Huh?"

"The right-hand man. That's what they call him."

"Right," I said. "Robert Duvall."

"Okay," she said. "You want Marlon Brando. The godfather himself. Not Robert Duvall."

I went into my office, found Mick Fallon's divorce file, and spent half an hour refreshing my memory. Then I put it aside and started to work my way through the stack of papers Julie had left for me. It was the price I always paid for being away from my desk for a day.

Sometime in the middle of the morning my phone rang. I picked it up, and Julie said, "It took some doing, but I have Mr. Russo on line two."

"Good work, kid."

"It was actually rather disappointing," she said.

"How so?"

"When I gave that consigliere your name, he didn't even say no."

I pressed the button for line two and said, "Mr. Russo?"

"Mr. Coyne," he said. "So maybe we oughta talk, huh?"


I got to Emerson Hospital in the middle of the afternoon.

The receptionist told me Mick had been transferred out of intensive care, and I tracked him down to a private room on the second floor of the orthopedic wing. Danny and Erin had pulled up chairs beside his bed. When I stepped into the room, Erin was holding Mick's hand in both of hers. All three of them were crying.

I shook hands with Danny and hugged Erin, who turned to her brother and said, "Come on. Let's get something to eat. They've got stuff to talk about."

After the kids left, I took the chair beside Mick's bed.

"How're you feeling?"

"Like I just spent forty-eight minutes trying to keep Kareem away from the boards. Doctor says that's a good sign."

"Doctors are noted for their wit," I said.

"We were talking about Kaye," he said. "Me and the kids."

I nodded.

"This is gonna be hard, man."

"It'll take time, Mick."

His eyes welled up. "I can't tell you how great it feels, having my kids around, knowing they don't think . . ." He wiped his wrist across his eyes and tried to smile.

I squeezed his shoulder. "Has Horowitz been here yet?"

He nodded. "Him and that pretty partner of his. Brought their trusty tape recorder. I told the truth, the whole truth, and nothin' but the fucking truth."

"For a change," I said.

"I told a bunch of lies before, I know," he said. "To you, to everybody. Myself, even. Been doing that for years, I guess. It got to be a habit, lying. Like a reflex." He grinned quickly. "Muscle memory, you know?"

"Mick," I said, "when did you know about Kaye and Lyn?"

Mick frowned at me. "What are you saying?"

"Didn't Horowitz tell you?"

Mick stared up at the ceiling. Finally he said softly, "He didn't tell me anything. But some of his questions . . ." He looked at me. "Lyn? My best friend? Sonofabitch."

"It was Kaye, too," I said. "Don't forget that."

"Yeah. Right." He let out a long breath. "Do Danny and Erin know?"

"I don't know," I said. "I don't think so."

"I don't want them to know."

"They've got to know, Mick. They know Ned killed her, and sooner or later they're going to want to know why."

Mick stared at me for a minute, then nodded. "Sure. You're right. I gotta tell them."

"So why'd you go to the the Conleys' house yesterday," I said, "if it wasn't to confront Lyn?"

Mick looked at me and smiled. "I just wanted to see my kids, Brady. Simple as that. Hell, I called the state police from my car phone, told them to tell Horowitz I'd be there. That's why I slugged you, man. I had to see my kids before they locked me up."

"But you didn't do anything wrong," I said. "They weren't going to lock you up."

"They had a warrant out for me," he said. "That Horowitz, he would've arrested me, all right. Anyway, I—"

"Wait a minute," I said. "If you didn't know anything, how did you glom onto Ned?"

Mick shook his head. "I'm just walking up their driveway when Ned comes barreling out from the house. He sees me and he stops short like he's seen his worst nightmare. I started to smile at him. Hell, I had no idea what was going on. And then Ned looks me right in the eye and he says, 'It was me. I did it. I killed her. I'm sorry, Uncle Mick. I loved her. I'm really sorry.' And I see that he's crying, tears streaming down his face, Brady, and I just wanted to give the kid a hug. I took a step toward him, and suddenly he gives me a little fake-left-go-right and zips around me. He jumps into the car and starts it up, so I grab onto the door, and . . ." Mick shrugged.

"I know the rest," I said.

He tried to smile. "What a mess, huh?"

"It's all over now."

He shook his head. "It won't be over for a long time. It'll never be over, far as I'm concerned."

I nodded. We sat in silence for a minute, then I said, "I had a conversation with Vincent Russo this morning."

Mick closed his eyes. "Shit," he mumbled. "I been trying to forget him."

"That's just another form of lying to yourself, Mick. Russo's not going to disappear just because you got a broken leg, you know."

He opened his eyes and looked at me. "So what'm I gonna do about him?"

"Pay him off."

"Huh? I can't—"

"Russo bought your debt from your pal in East Providence. Jimmy Capezza. He paid eighty thousand dollars for it."

"Christ, I owed Cappy over three-hundred grand."

"Right. Three-hundred-and-twenty, to be exact. Russo'll accept eighty thousand now and another eighty a year from now and call it even."

"How the hell did you—?"

"Russo fancies himself a businessman, Mick. He made an investment, and he understands about cutting his losses. He and I talked this morning, came to an agreement. I looked over all the stuff you prepared for your divorce. You can do it. Sell that rental property, maybe. The way I figure it, you can get Russo off your back and still have enough to keep food on your table and Erin and Danny in school."

Mick's hand snaked out from under the sheet and grabbed my wrist. "Thanks, bud."

"This'll only work if you quit gambling."

"I learned my lesson, man."

"I sure hope so," I said. "Have you—?"

"I know. Already decided. I've gotta get help."

I sat there talking with Mick until Danny and Erin returned. Erin told me she planned to stick around, help Mick get back on his feet. Mick had convinced Danny to return to his job at the hotel on Block Island. He was leaving in a couple of days.

After a few minutes, I glanced at my watch, stood up, said good-bye to what was left of the Fallon family, and left.

I found a directory out in the reception area, and five minutes later I was knocking on the door marked Administrative Services—Assistant Director.

A voice called, "It's open. Come on in."

I went in.

Evie Banyon had risen from behind her desk. When she saw me, she smiled and came around, holding out her hand. I'd forgotten how tall she was.

I took her hand. "I happened to be in the neighborhood."

"I know," she said. Her silvery eyes crinkled, and she continued to hold onto my hand. "How's Mr. Fallon doing today?"

"Do you know everything?"

"It's my job," she said. She showed no inclination to let go of my hand. In fact, she gave it a little squeeze when she smiled at me.

"And you're very good at your job."

"Yes, I am."

"Well, anyway," I said, "since I was in the neighborhood, I was wondering . . ."

"Dinner?" she said.

"You *do* know everything," I said. "That's exactly what I was thinking." I glanced down at the floor for a moment, then looked up at her. I held out my other hand, and she took it, too. "Actually," I said, "I was wondering how you felt about beer out of bottles, cheeseburgers on the charcoal grill, catsup dribbling down your chin. T-shirts, shorts, and bare feet, salt air on your face, seagulls perching on the balcony rail, a view of the harbor towards sunset, Miles Davis on the stereo inside, the gong of my old bell buoy echoing out there in the fog . . ."

Evie Banyon was smiling. "Absolutely perfect," she said.

PIERRE MORAN BRANCH

WITHDRAWN

**ELKHART PUBLIC
LIBRARY**
**Elkhart, Indiana**

DEMCO